MIRACLE OR MONSTER

They were in the laboratory huddled around the oxygen tent staring at the tiny thing wrapped in a blanket. Its face was hidden by a mask.

"Is it living?"

"Yes," answered Professor Dawnay. "It's a baby."

"A human baby?"

"I would say so, though I doubt if Dr. Fleming would."

The creature in the tent seemed to thrive on intravenous feeding. It grew half an inch a day and it was clear it was not going to go through the usual childhood. It would, in fact, reach full adult stature within a few months.

"Kill it!" cried Fleming.

They glared at him icily.

"Listen to me," said Fleming. "It may look like a human being, but it isn't one. It's an extension of the machine, like the other creature, only more sophisticated. The other was just a first shot at an attempt to produce an organism like us, acceptable to us. But this is a better shot, based on more information. I've worked on that information. I know how deliberate it is."

"Are you suggesting," asked Dr. Geers, "that having achieved this miracle of life, we kill it?"

"If you don't do it now," warned Fleming, "you'll never be able to. People will come to think of it as human. They'll say we're murdering it. And then it will have us . . . the machine will have us—where it wants us!"

A
FOR ANDROMEDA

by
Fred Hoyle
and
John Elliot

CREST BOOK

A CREST REPRINT

Fawcett Publications, Inc., Greenwich, Conn.
Member of American Book Publishers Council, Inc.

A Crest Book published by arrangement with Harper & Row, Publishers

PRINTING HISTORY

Harper & Row edition published July 5, 1962
Second printing, September 1962

A Science Fiction Book Club selection, Fall 1962

This book is based on the BBC television serial of the same name and is published by arrangement with the British Broadcasting Corporation.

First Crest printing, December 1964

Crest Books are published by Fawcett World Library,
67 West 44th Street, New York, N. Y. 10036.
Printed in the United States of America.

contents

A
FOR ANDROMEDA

one

ARRIVAL

LIGHT WAS soaking out of the sky when they drove up to Bouldershaw Fell. Judy sat beside Professor Reinhart in the back of the staff car as it slid up the road from Bouldershaw town to the open moor; she peered hopefully out of the windows, but they were nearly at the crest of the hill before they could see the radio-telescope.

Suddenly it stood in front of them: three huge pillars curving together at the top to form a triangular arch, dark and stark against the ebbing sky. Hollowed out of the ground between the uprights lay a concrete bowl the size of a sports arena, and above, suspended from the top of the arch, a smaller metal bowl looked downwards and pointed a long antenna at the ground. The size of the whole thing did not strike the eye at first; it simply looked out of proportion to the landscape. Only when the car had drawn up and parked beneath it did Judy begin to realize how big it was. It was quite unlike anything else she had seen—as completely and intensely itself as a piece of sculpture.

Yet, for all its strangeness, there was nothing particularly sinister about the tall, looming structure to warn them of the extraordinary and disastrous future that was to emerge from it.

Out of the car, they stood for a moment with the soft, sweet air filling their heads and lungs, and gazed up at the three huge pylons, at the metal reflector that glistened high above them, and at the pale sky beyond. Around them a few low buildings and smaller arrays of aerials were

9

scattered about on the empty moor-top, enclosed by a wire-link fence. There was no sound but the wind in the pylons and the curlews calling, and they could almost feel the great concrete-and-metal ear beside them straining to listen to the stars.

Then the Professor led the way to the main building—a low stone-faced affair with a half-finished entrance and a newly-laid approach. Men were putting in gateposts and direction notices and painting it all: it all looked very new and sharp against the soft, dark hilltop.

"There's all sorts of subsidiary gubbins," said the Professor, with a small delicate wave of his hand. "This houses the main control room."

He was a man in his sixties, small, neat and cozy, like a family doctor.

"It's quite a baby," said Judy.

"Baby? It's the biggest baby I've ever given birth to. A ten years' labor."

He twinkled at her and his small black shoes pattered up the steps into the control building.

The entrance hall had an unfinished but at the same time familiar look: inevitable pegboard ceiling, inevitable composition floor, plain color-washed brick walls and fluorescent lighting. There was a wall telephone and a drinking fountain; there were two small doors in the side walls, and there were double doors facing the entrance; and that was about all. A faint hissing noise came from behind the double doors. When the Professor opened them the hissing became louder. It sounded like atmospherics from a radio.

As they went through the double doors a man in a cleaner's brown coat came out. His eye met Judy's for a moment, but when she parted her lips he looked away.

"Good evening, Harries," said the Professor.

The room they entered was the control room, the center of the observatory. At the far end an observation window gave a view of the gigantic sculpture outside, and facing the window was a massive metal desk, like an organ console, fitted with panels of buttons, lights and switches. Several young men were working at the desk, referring from time to time to the two computers which stood in tall metal cases on each side of it. One side wall was covered with enlargements of optical-telescope photographs of stars, and the other was two-thirds glass partition behind which more young men could be seen working at equipment in an inner room.

"The opening ceremony will be in here," said Reinhart.

"Where does the Minister break the champagne bottle, or cut the ribbon, or whatever he does?"

"At the desk. He presses a button on the control desk to start it."

"It isn't working yet?"

"Not yet. We're running acceptance tests."

Judy stood by the doorway taking it in. She was the sort of good-looking young woman who is more often called handsome than pretty, with a fresh complexion and alert, intelligent face and a very positive, slightly ungainly, way of standing. She might have been a nurse, or an officer in the Services, or simply the product of a good hockey-playing school. She had rather large hands and deep blue eyes. Under one arm she held a bundle of papers and pamphlets which she pulled out and looked at, as if they might explain what she saw.

"It's the biggest radio-telescope, well—anywhere." The Professor smiled happily round the room. "It's not as big as an interferometer, of course, but you can *steer* it. You can shift your focus by the small reflector up top, and by that means you can track a source across the sky."

"I gathered from these," Judy tapped her papers, "that there are other radio-telescopes operating in the same way."

"There are. There were in nineteen-sixty, when we started this—and that's several years ago. But they haven't our sensitivity."

"Because this is bigger?"

"Not entirely. Also because we've better receiving equipment. That should give us a higher signal-to-noise ratio. It's all housed in there."

He pointed a small, delicate finger to the room behind the glass panel.

"You see, all you pick up from most astronomical sources—radio stars for instance—is a very faint electrical signal, and it's mixed up with all kinds of noise, from the atmosphere, from interstellar gas, from heaven knows what —well, heaven indeed."

He spoke in a precise, matter-of-fact tenor voice; he might

have been a doctor discussing a cold. The sense of achievement, of imagination, was all hidden.

"You can hear sources other people can't?" asked Judy.

"Hope to. That's the idea. But don't ask me how. There's a team evolved it." He looked modestly down at his little feet. "Doctors Fleming and Bridger."

"Bridger?" Judy looked up sharply.

"Fleming's the real brains. John Fleming." He called politely across the room. "John!"

One of the young men detached himself from the group at the control desk and wandered towards them.

He said, "Hi!" to the Professor and ignored Judy.

"If you have a moment, John. Dr. Fleming, Miss Adamson."

The young man glanced at Judy, then called across to the control desk.

"Turn that flaming noise down!"

"What is it?" Judy asked. The atmospherics reduced themselves to a faint hissing. The young man shrugged.

"Interstellar hiss, mainly. The universe is full of electrically charged matter. What we pick up is an electrical emission from these charges, which we get as noise."

"The background music of the universe," Reinhart added.

"You can keep that, Prof," said the young man, with a sort of friendly contempt. "Keep it for Jacko's press handouts."

"Jacko's not coming back."

Fleming looked faintly surprised, and Judy frowned as if she had mislaid some piece of information.

"Who?" she asked the Professor.

"Jackson, your predecessor." He turned to Fleming. "Miss Adamson's our new press officer."

Fleming regarded her without relish. "Well, they come and go, don't they? Inheriting Jacko's spheres?"

"What are they?"

"Dear young lady, you'll soon find out."

"I'm showing her the layout for Thursday," the Professor said. "The official opening. She'll be looking after the press."

Fleming had a dark, thoughtful face which was less surly than preoccupied; but he seemed tired and bitter. He grumbled away in a thick Midland accent.

"Oh yes—the Official Opening! All the colored lights will

be working. The stars will sing 'Rule Britannia' in heavenly chorus, and I'll be round at the pub."

"You'll be here, John, I hope." The Professor sounded slightly irritated. "Meanwhile, perhaps you'd show Miss Adamson round."

"Not if you're busy," said Judy in a small, hostile voice. Fleming looked at her with interest for the first time.

"How much do you know about it?"

"Very little yet." She tapped her papers. "I'm relying on these."

Fleming turned wearily to the room and spread an arm wide.

"This, ladies and gentlemen, is the largest and newest radio-telescope in the world—not to say the most expensive. It has a resolution of fifteen to twenty times greater than any existing equipment and is, of course, a miracle of British science. Not to say engineering. The pick-up elements"—he pointed out of the window—"are steerable so as to be capable of tracking the course of a celestial body across the heavens. Now you can tell them everything, can't you?"

"Thank you," said Judy icily. She looked at the Professor, but he seemed only a little embarrassed.

"I'm sorry we worried you, John," he said.

"Don't mention it. It's a pleasure. Any time."

The Professor turned his kindly general-practitioner's attention to Judy.

"I'll show you myself."

"You do want it operating by Thursday, don't you?" said Fleming. "For His Ministership."

"Yes, John. It'll be all right?"

"It'll look all right. The brass won't know if it's working. Nor the news touts."

"I should like it to be working."

"Yeh."

Fleming turned away and walked back to the control desk. Judy waited for an explosion, or at least some sign of affront, from the Professor, but he only nodded his head as if over a diagnosis.

"You can't push a boy like John. You may wait months for an idea. Years. It's worth it if it's a good one, and it generally is with him." He looked wistfully at Fleming's receding back: sloppy, casual, with untidy hair and clothes. "We depend on the young, you know. He's done all the low-temperature design, he and Bridger. The receivers are based on low-temperature equipment and that's not my subject. There's a hand-out on it somewhere." He nodded vaguely at her bundle of papers. "We've run him a bit ragged, I'm afraid."

He sighed, and took her off on a conducted tour of the building. He showed her the wall photographs of the night sky, telling her the names and identity of the great radio stars, the main sources of the sounds we hear from the universe. "This," he explained, pointing to the photographs, "is not a star at all, but two whole galaxies colliding; and this, a star exploding."

"And this?"

"The Great Nebula in Andromeda. M.31 we call it, just to confuse it with the motorway."

"It's in the Andromeda constellation?"

"No. It's way, way out beyond that. It's a whole galaxy in itself. Nothing's simple, is it?"

She looked at the white spiral of stars and agreed.

"You get a signal from it?"

"A hiss. Like you heard."

Near the wall was a large perspex sphere with a small dark ball at its center and other white ones set around it like the electrons in a physicist's model of the atom.

"Jacko's spheres!" The Professor twinkled. "Or Jacko's folly, they call it. It's a display of things in orbit near the earth. All these white units represent satellites, ballistic missiles and so on. Ironmongery. That's the earth, in the middle."

The Professor waved it daintily aside.

"A gimmick, I think you'd call it. Jacko thought it would interest our government visitors. We have to keep tabs, of course, on what's happening near the earth, but it's a waste of a machine like this. Still, the military ask us to, and we don't get the sort of money we need unless we can tap the defense budget." He sounded as though he was being naughty and enjoyed it. He made one of his small, manicured gestures to take in the room and the huge thing outside. "Twenty-five millions or more, this has cost."

"So there's a military interest?"

"Yes. But it's my establishment—or rather, the Ministry of Science's. Not your Ministry's."

"I'm on your staff now."

"Not at my request." His manner stiffened, as it had not done when Fleming was rude to him; Fleming, after all, was one of his own.

"Does anyone else know why I'm here?" Judy asked him.

"I've told no one."

He steered her away from the subject and into the other room, where he went carefully over the receiving apparatus and the communications equipment.

"We're simply a link in a chain of observatories all round the world, though not the weakest link." He looked around with a kind of pure pleasure at the switchboards and wires and racks of equipment. "I didn't feel an old man when we started to put all this together, but I do now. You have an idea and you think: 'That's what we must do', and it just seems the next step. Quite a small step, possibly. Then you start: design, research, committees, building, politics. An hour of your life here, a month there. Let's hope it'll work. Ah, here's Whelan! He understands all about this part of it."

Judy was introduced to a pasty-faced young man with an Australian voice who held on to her hand as though it was something he had lost.

"Haven't we met before somewhere?"

"I don't think so." She stared at him candidly with large blue eyes, but he would not be put off.

"I'm sure of it."

She wavered and looked around for help. Harries, the cleaner, was standing across the room, and when she looked at him he shook his head very slightly. She turned back to Whelan.

"I'm afraid I don't remember."

"Maybe at Woomera. . . ."

The Professor piloted her back into the main control room.

"What was his name?"

"Whelan."

She made a note on her pad. The party at the control desk had split up, leaving only one young man who was sitting in the duty engineer's seat checking the panels. The Professor led her across to him.

"Hallo, Harvey."

The young man looked up and half rose from his seat. "Good evening, Professor Reinhart." At least he was polite. Judy looked out of the window to the great piece of gadgetry beyond and the empty moorland and the sky, now growing dark purple.

"You know the principle of the thing?" Harvey asked her. "Any radio emission from the sky strikes the bowl and is reflected to the aerial, and received and recorded on the equipment in there." He pointed through the glass partition. Judy did not look for fear of seeing Whelan, but Harvey—keen, dogged and toneless—was soon directing her attention to something else. "This bank of computers works out the azimuth and elevation of whatever source you want to focus on to it and keeps it following. There's a servo link arrangement. . . ."

Eventually Judy managed to escape to the hall and have a moment alone with Harries.

"Get Whelan moved," she said.

She had left her suitcase at the hotel in the town and driven on up the hill with very little idea of what to expect. She had visited a good many service establishments and served as security officer in a number of them, from Fylingdales to Christmas Island. Whelan, she knew, had met her on a rocket range in Australia. She had worked with Harries on a tour of duty at Malvern. She did not think of herself as a spy, and the idea of informing on her own colleagues struck her as an unpleasant business; but the Home Office had asked for her, or at least for someone, to be transferred from the Ministry of Defense security section to the Ministry of Science, and an assignment was an assignment. Before, the people she worked with had always known what she was, and she had thought of her duty as protecting them. This time they themselves were suspect and she was to be palmed off on them as a public relations stooge who could nose around and ask questions without putting them on their guard. Reinhart knew, and disliked it. She disliked it herself. But a job was a job and this—she was told—was important.

She could act the part without difficulty: she looked so honest, so forthright, so much a team member. She had only to sit back and listen and learn. It was the people she met who discomforted her; they had their own world and their own values. Who was she to judge them or be party to their judging? When Harries nodded and sauntered away to do what was needed, she despised both him and herself.

The Professor left soon afterwards and handed her over to John Fleming.

"Perhaps you'd drop her at the Lion when you go back to Bouldershaw. She's staying there."

They went out on to the steps to see the old man off.

"He is rather sweet," said Judy.

Fleming grunted. "Tough as old nails."

He took a hip-flask from his pocket and drank out of it. Then he handed it to her. When she refused he took another swig himself, and she watched him standing in the light of the porch, his head thrown back, his Adam's apple working up and down as he gulped. There was something desperately keyed-up about him; perhaps, as Reinhart had said, they had run him ragged. But there was something else beside—a feeling of a dynamo permanently charging inside him.

"Play bowls?" He seemed to have forgotten his earlier indifference to her. Perhaps the drink. "There's an alley down at Bouldershaw. Come and join our rustic sports."

She hesitated.

"Oh come along now! I'm not going to leave you at the mercy of these mad astronomers."

"Aren't you an astronomer?"

"Do you mind? Cryogenics, computers, that's really my stuff. Not this airy-fairy nonsense."

They walked across to the small concrete apron where his car was parked. A red beacon light shone on top of the telescope, and in the dark sky behind it stars began to show. Some could be seen through the tall arches of the pylons, as though they had already been netted by man. When they reached the car, Fleming looked back and up.

"I've an idea," he said, and his voice was quieter, quite gentle and no longer aggressive. "I've an idea we've got to the breakaway stage in the physical sciences."

He started to unclip the tonneau cover from his car, a small open sports, while she moved round to the other side.

"Let me help you."

He hardly seemed to notice.

"Some moment, somewhere along the perimeter of our knowledge, we're going to go—*wham!*—clean through. Right out into new territory. And it might be here, on this stuff." He bundled the tonneau cover in behind the seat. "'Philosophy is written in that vast book which stands forever open before our eyes, I mean the universe.' Who wrote that?"

"Churchill?"

"Churchill!" He laughed. "Galileo! 'It is written in mathematical language.' That's what Galileo said. Any good for a press hand-out?"

She looked at him, uncertain how to take it. He opened the door for her.

"Let's go."

The road dropped down to Lancashire on one side and into Yorkshire on the other. On the Yorkshire side it ran down a long valley, where every few miles a tall old brick mill stood over the river, until they came to the town of Bouldershaw. Fleming drove too fast, and grumbled.

"They get on my wick ... Flogging Ministers' opening! ... The old Prof sweating on the Honors List; the Ministry bunch all needling and nagging. All it is, really, is a piece of lab equipment. Because it's big and costs the earth, it becomes public property. I don't blame the old man. He's caught up in it. He's stuck his neck out and he's got to show results."

"Well, won't it?"

"I dunno."

"I thought it was your equipment."

"Mine and Dennis Bridger's."

"Where is Dr. Bridger?"

"Down at the alley. Waiting for us with a lane booked, I hope. And a flask."

"You've got one flask."

"What good's one? They're dry, these places."

As they swung down the dark winding road, he started telling her about Bridger and himself. Both had been students at Birmingham University, and research fellows at the Cavendish. Fleming was a theorist, Bridger a practical man, a development mathematician and engineer. Bridger was a career scientist; he was set to make the most he could out of his particular line. Fleming was a pure research man who did not give a damn about anything except the facts. But they both despised the academic system into which they

grew up, and they stuck together. Reinhart had picked them
out, several years ago, to work on his new telescope. As
he was, perhaps, the most distinguished and respected
astro-physicist in the western world, and a born leader of
teams and picker of talents, they had gone along with him
without hesitation, and he had backed and encouraged and
generally fathered them throughout the long and tortuous
business of development.

It was easy to see, when Fleming talked, the mutual trust
that tied him to the older man, behind his surliness. Bridger,
on the other hand, was bored and restless. He had done
his part. And they had, as Fleming said without modesty
or conceit, given the old boy the most fabulous piece of
equipment on earth.

He did not ask about Judy, and she kept quiet. He waited
in the bar of the Lion while she went to her room. By
the time they reached the bowling alley he was pretty much
the worse for wear.

The bowling alley was a converted cinema which stood
out in a wash of neon and floodlighting against the dark
old mill town. Its clientele seemed to have come from
somewhere other than the cobbled streets. They were mostly
young. They wore jeans and soda-jerks' jackets, crew-cuts,
and blouses with slogans on them. It was difficult to imagine
them at home in the old terraced houses, the grimy Yorkshire
valleys. Their native voices were drowned under a flood of
music and the rumble and clatter of bowls and skittles on
the wooden planking of the lanes. There were half-a-dozen
lanes with ten pins at one end of each and, at the other,
a rack of bowls, a scoring table, a bench and a quartet
of players. When a bowl pitched down and scored a strike,
an automatic gate picked up the skittles again and returned
the bowl to the rack at the players' end. Except in the
concentrated, athletic moment of bowling, the players seemed
uninterested in the game, lounging around and talking and
drinking Coca-Cola out of bottles. It was more transatlantic
than the cinema had been: as though the American way
of life had burst out through the screen and possessed the
auditorium. But that, Fleming remarked, was just bloody
typical of the way things are generally.

They found Bridger, a narrow, pointed man about Fleming's
age, bowling on a lane with a curvy girl in a vermilion
blouse and tight, bright yellow slacks. Her bosom and hair

were swept up as high as they would go, her face was made
up like a ballet dancer's, and she moved like something in
a Hollywood chorus; but when she opened her mouth all
Yorkshire came out of it. She bowled with a good deal of
muscular skill, and came back and leaned on Bridger, sucking
a finger.

"Ee, I got a bit o' skin off."

"This is Grace." Bridger seemed slightly ashamed of her.
He was prematurely lined and nervous, mousily dressed in
dull sports clothes like a post office assistant on Saturday
morning. He shook hands tentatively with Judy, and when
she said "I've heard of you," he gave her a quick, anxious
look.

"Miss Adamson," said Fleming, pouring some whisky into
Bridger's Coke, "Miss Adamson is our new eager-beaver—
lady-beaver—P.R.O."

"What's your other name, love?" inquired the girl.

"Judy."

"You haven't got a bit of sticking-plaster?"

"Oh, ask at the desk!" said Bridger impatiently.

"One of your team?" Judy asked Fleming.

"Local talent. Dennis's. I've no time."

"Pity," she said. But he appeared not to hear. Taking another
swig from the flask, he addressed himself unsteadily to the
bowling. Bridger turned confidentially to her.

"What have you heard about me?"

"Only that you'd been working with Dr. Fleming."

"It isn't my cup." He looked aggrieved; the point of his
nose twitched like a rabbit's. "I could get five times my
salary in industry."

"Is that what you want?"

"As soon as that lot on the hill's working, I'm away."
He glanced across at Fleming, conspiratorially, then back
at her. "Old John will stay, looking for the millennium. And
before he's found anything, he'll be old. Old and respected.
And poor."

"And possibly happy."

"John'll never be happy. He thinks too much."

"Who drinks too much?" Fleming lurched back to them
and marked up his score.

"You do."

"All right—I drink too much. Brother, you've got to have
something to hold on to."

"What's wrong with the railings?" asked Bridger, twitching his nose.

"Look—" Fleming slumped down on to the bench beside them. "You're going to walk along those railings, and then you'll take another pace and they won't be there. We were talking about Galileo—why? Because he was the Renaissance. He and Copernicus and Leonardo da Vinci. That was when they said 'Wham!' and knocked down all the railings and had to stand on their own feet in the middle of a great big open universe."

He heaved himself up and took another of the heavy bowls from the rack. His voice rose above the din of the music and bowling.

"People have put up new fences, further out. But this is another Renaissance! One day, when nobody's noticing, when everybody's talking about politics and football, and money—" he loomed over Bridger, "then suddenly every fence we know is going to get knocked down—*wham!*—like that!"

He made a great sweep with the bowl and knocked the bottles of Coke off the scoring table.

"Oi! Careful, you great clot!" Bridger leapt to his feet and started picking up the bottles and mopping at the spilt drink with his handkerchief. "I'm sorry, Miss Adamson."

Fleming threw back his head and laughed.

"Judy—her name is Judy."

Bridger, down on his knees, rubbed away at the stain on Judy's skirt.

"I'm afraid it's gone on you."

"It doesn't matter." Judy was not looking at him. She was gazing up at Fleming, puzzled and entranced. Then the Tannoy went.

"Doctor Fleming—telephone call, please."

Fleming came back after a minute, shaking his head to clear it. He pulled Bridger up from the bench.

"Come on, Dennis boy. We're wanted."

Harvey was alone in the control room, sitting at the desk adjusting the receiver tune. The window in front of him was dark as a blackboard, and the room was quiet except for a constant low crackle of sound from the loudspeaker. From outside—nothing, until the noise of Fleming's car.

Fleming and Bridger came pushing in through the swing

doors and stood, blinking, in the light. Fleming focused blear-
ily on Harvey.

"What is it?"

"Listen." Harvey held up a hand, and they stood listening.
In among the crackle and whistles and hiss from the speaker
came a faint single note, broken but always continuing.

"Morse code," said Bridger.

"It's not in groups."

They listened again.

"Short and long," said Bridger. "That's what it is."

"Where's it coming from?" Fleming asked.

"Somewhere in Andromeda. We were sweeping through—"

"How long's it been going on?"

"About an hour. We're over the peak now."

"Can you move the reflector?"

"I expect so."

"We're not supposed to," said Bridger. "We're not supposed
to start tracking tests yet."

Fleming ignored him.

"Is the servo equipment manned?" he asked.

"Yes, Dr. Fleming."

"Well, try to track it."

"No, listen, John." Bridger put an ineffectual hand on
Fleming's sleeve.

"It may be a sputnik or something," said Harvey.

"Is there anything new up?" Fleming disengaged himself
from Bridger.

"Not that we know of."

"Someone could have put something fresh into orbit—"
Bridger started, but Fleming cut him off.

"Dennis—" He tried to think clearly. "Go and get this
on to a recorder, will you? There's a good chap. Get it
on a printer too."

"Hadn't we better check?"

"Check after."

Fleming walked carefully out into the hall, bent his face
over the drinking fountain and sluiced it with water. When
he returned, fresh and shining and remarkably sober, he
found Bridger already setting up in the equipment room and
Harvey phoning the duty engineer. There was a dip in the
lights as the electric motors started. The metal reflector high
up outside swung silently and invisibly, its movement compen-

sating for the motion of the earth. The sound from the speaker grew a little louder.

"That the best you can get?"

"It's not a very strong signal."

"Hm." Fleming opened a drawer in the control desk and fished out a catalogue. "Have its galactic co-ordinates shifted at all?"

"Hard to say. I wasn't tracking. But they couldn't have shifted very much."

"So it's not in orbit?"

"I'd say not." Harvey bent anxiously over the faders on his desk. "Could it be some ham bouncing Morse code off the moon?"

"Doesn't really sound like Morse code, and the moon isn't up."

"Or off Mars, or Venus. I hope I haven't brought you out on a wild goose chase."

"Andromeda, you said?"

Harvey nodded. Fleming turned the pages of the catalogue, reading and listening. He became quiet and gentle again as he had been earlier with Judy at the car. He looked like a studious small boy.

"You're holding it?"

"Yes, Dr. Fleming."

Fleming walked across to the desk and flicked on the intercom.

"Getting it, Dennis?"

"Yes." Bridger's voice came tinnily back. "But it doesn't make sense."

"It may by morning. I'm going to try to get some idea of the distance."

Fleming flicked back the key and crossed, book in hand, to the astronomical charts on the back wall.

They worked for a while with the sounds from space the only noise in the room, Fleming checking the source and Harvey holding it with the great silent telescope outside.

"What do you think?" Harvey asked at last.

"I think it's coming from a long way out."

After that they simply worked and listened, and the signal went on and on and on, endlessly.

two

ANNOUNCEMENT

IN THE LATE nineteen-sixties, when these things happened, the Ministry of Science was moved into a new glass-walled building near Whitehall. It was elegantly furnished and staffed, as if to prove that technology was on a par with the arts, and the Permanent Under-Secretary of State, Michael Osborne, was one of the most cultivated of its many cultivated servants. Although he wore tweeds in the office, they were the smoothest and most formal of tweeds. He seldom sat at his huge desk—more often in one of the low easy chairs by the low marble-topped coffee table.

He sprawled there, decoratively, the morning after the message had started to come through at Bouldershaw Fell, talking with General Charles G. Vandenberg of the U.S. Air Force. The light from the venetian blinds fell across him in neat lines.

England by that time was something like the advance headquarters of a besieged land: an area consisting of Western Europe and North America. Pressure from the East, and from Africa and Asia, had pushed western civilization up into one corner of the globe, with America north of Panama a fairly secure center and Western Europe an embattled salient. Not that anyone was officially at war with anyone else; but economic sanctions and the threat of bombs and missiles gripped the remains of the old world in a fairly acute state of siege. The lifeline across the Atlantic was maintained almost entirely by the Americans, and American garrisons in Britain, France and Western Germany held on

24

with the same desperate tenuousness as the Roman legions in the third and fourth centuries.

Protocol insisted that Britain and her neighbors were still sovereign states, but in fact initiative was fast slipping out of their hands. Although General Vandenberg was modestly styled representative of the Defense Co-ordination Committee, he was, in effect, air commander of a friendly but dominant occupying power to whom this country was one square on a large chessboard.

An ex-bomber-boy, bull-necked and square-headed, he still looked brash and youthful in middle age; but there was nothing brash about his manner. He was a New Englander, quietly spoken and civilized, and he talked with authority, as if he knew more about the world than most of the people in it.

They were speaking about Whelan. A note about him hung limply from Osborne's hand.

"I can't do anything now."

"There is a kind of priority—"

Osborne heaved himself up out of his chair and called his secretary through the intercom on his desk.

"The Defense Co-ordination Committee have a low boiling-point," Vandenberg observed.

"You can tell them we'll cope."

Osborne gave the note to the secretary as she came in.

"Get someone to look after that, will you?"

She took it and put a folder of papers on his desk. She was young and pretty and wore what looked like a cocktail dress: the civil service had moved on.

"Your papers for Bouldershaw."

"Thanks. Is my car here?"

"Yes, Mr. Osborne."

He opened the folder and read:

"The Minister's party will arrive at Bouldershaw Fell at 3:15 p.m. and will be received by Professor Reinhart."

"That's tomorrow," remarked Vandenberg. "Are you walking up?"

"I'm going a day early to meet Reinhart." He stuffed the folder into his brief case. "Can I give you a lift to the top of Whitehall?"

"That would be a Christian deed."

They were wary of each other, but polite—almost old-fashioned. As he rose, Vandenberg asked casually:

"Do you have an operational date for it?"

"Not yet."

"This grows a little serious."

"The stars can wait. They've waited for a long time."

"So have the Defense Co-ordination Committee."

Osborne gave a shrug of sophisticated impatience. He might have been a Greek arguing with a Roman.

"Reinhart will undertake military programs as and when he can. That's the arrangement."

"If there's an emergency . . ."

"*If* there's an emergency."

"You read the newspapers?"

"I can never get beyond the magazine section these days."

"You should try the news pages. If there's an emergency we'll need all the ears we can grow this side of the Atlantic." Vandenberg nodded to an artist's impression of the radio-telescope on the wall of the office. "It's not a kid's toy to us."

"It's not a kid's toy to them, either," said Osborne.

After they had gone, Fleming phoned through from Bouldershaw Fell; but it was too late.

Judy arrived at the radio-telescope just before Osborne and Reinhart, and had a quiet chat with Harries in the hall.

"What about Bridger?"

Harries tried to look as though he were polishing a door handle.

"Two or three visits to a back-street bookie in Bradford. Apart from that, nothing."

"We'd better watch him."

"I'm watching him."

When Osborne and Reinhart arrived, they took her into the control room with them. The place was quiet and almost empty; only Harvey sat tinkering at the desk, surrounded by a litter of papers and cigarette ends and empty drinking cups. Reinhart clucked at it like a disturbed hen.

"You'll have to keep this place clean."

"Will they be able to swing the focus for the Minister?" Osborne asked.

"I hope so. We haven't tested the tracking apparatus."

Reinhart puttered round busily while Harvey tried to attract his attention.

"You look as if you've been up all night, Harvey."

"I have, sir. So have Dr. Fleming and Dr. Bridger."

"Struck a snag?"

"Not exactly, sir. We've been tracking."

"On whose instruction?"

"Dr. Fleming's." Harvey was quite casual about it. "We're lining up again now."

"Why wasn't I told?" Reinhart turned to Osborne and Judy. "Did you know about this?"

Judy shook her head.

"Fleming appears to make his own rules," observed Osborne.

"Where is he?" Reinhart demanded.

"In through there." Harvey pointed to the equipment room. "With Dr. Bridger."

"Then ask him to spare me a minute."

While Harvey spoke into a microphone on the desk, Reinhart paced to and fro on his small feet.

"What were you tracking?" he asked.

"A source in Andromeda."

"M.31?"

"Not M.31, sir."

"What then?"

"Another signal near there. An interrupted signal."

"Have you heard it before?"

"No, sir."

When Fleming came in he was tired and unshaven, sober but very excited in a subdued way. He held in his hand a bunch of papers from a line-printer. This time Reinhart made no allowances.

"I gather you've taken over the telescope."

Fleming stopped and blinked at them.

"I beg your pardon, gentlemen. I didn't have time to fill in the proper forms in triplicate." He turned to Osborne. "I did telephone your office, but you'd gone."

"What have you been doing?" asked Reinhart.

Fleming told them, throwing the papers down on the desk in front of them.

"—And that's the message."

Reinhart looked at him curiously.

"You mean signal."

"I said message. Dots and dashes—wasn't it, Harvey?"

"It did sound like that."

"It went on all night," said Fleming. "It's below the horizon now, but we can try again this evening."

Judy looked at Osborne, but got no help from him.

"What about the opening?" she asked diffidently.

"Oh, to hell with the opening!" Fleming turned on her. "This is something! This is a voice from a thousand million, million miles away."

"A voice?" Her own voice sounded weak and unreal.

"It's taken two hundred light-years to reach us. The Minister can wait a day, can't he?"

Reinhart seemed to have recovered himself. He looked up at Fleming with amusement.

"Unless it's a satellite."

"It's not a satellite!"

Reinhart wandered over to Jacko's folly.

"Before you get too excited, John, let's check on the ironmongery in orbit."

"We have."

Reinhart turned to Osborne.

"You haven't heard of anything new going up?"

"No."

"Look," said Fleming, "if it were a satellite it wouldn't have stayed put all night, in the middle of the Andromeda constellation."

"You're sure it wasn't the Great Nebula?"

"We located that separately, didn't we, Harvey?"

Harvey nodded, but Reinhart still looked unconvinced.

"It could have been pattern interference—anything."

"I know a message when I meet one!" Fleming said. "Besides, there's something about this message I've never seen before. Between the groups of dots and dashes there's a fantastic amount of fast, detailed stuff. We'll have to lash up special receiving gear to record that."

He keyed down the intercom and called Bridger to come from the other room, then he picked up the papers and pushed them into Reinhart's hand. "Have a look! Ten years or more people have been waiting for this. Ten centuries for that matter."

"Is it intelligible?" asked Osborne in his detached civil-servant's voice, high and whinnying.

"Yes!"

"You can decipher it?"

"For heaven's sake! Do you think the cosmos is populated by Boy Scouts sending Morse code?"

Bridger came in looking pale and twitchy, but his presence seemed to calm Fleming and he confirmed Fleming's reports.

"It could be from a very distant probe," Osborne suggested.

Fleming ignored him. Judy plucked up her courage.

"Or another planet?"

"Yes!"

"Mars or somewhere?"

Fleming shrugged: "Probably a planet going round some star in Andromeda."

"Signalling to us?"

Reinhart handed the papers to Osborne.

"It's certainly a coherent form of dots and dashes."

"Then why has no one else picked it up?"

"Because no one else has got equipment like this. If we hadn't given you a thundering good piece of circuitry, you wouldn't be getting it now."

Osborne sat down on a corner of the control desk, looking at the papers in a dazed sort of way.

"If some sentient being is trying to communicate . . . No, it doesn't make sense."

"It's possible." Reinhart glanced down at his small delicate fingers, as if this were something he would prefer not to talk about. "If there are other creatures—"

Fleming interrupted him: "Not creatures—another intelligence. It doesn't have to be little green men. It doesn't have to be organic at all; just an intelligence."

Judy shuddered, then pulled herself together.

"Why do I shiver?"

"For the same reason I do," said Fleming.

Osborne came out of his daze.

"For the same reason everyone will, if it *is* an astronomical source."

They decided in the end to listen for it again that night. The message had not stopped, merely faded as the rotation of the earth had swung the telescope away from it. The chances were that it would still be going on. Once he had accepted the possibility, Reinhart became calm and business-like. He and Fleming and Bridger spread out the papers and examined them.

"You know what it might be?" Fleming said. "Binary arithmetic."

"What's that?" asked Judy.

"It's arithmetic expressed entirely by the figures 0 and 1, instead of the figures 1 to 10, which we normally use and which we call denary. 0 and 1, you see, could be dot and dash. Or dash could equal 0 and dot 1. The system we use is

arbitrary, but the binary system is basic; it's based on positive and negative, yes and no, dot and dash—it's universal.
Strewth." He turned on her with his eyes bloodshot and
feverish with strain and excitement. " 'Philosophy is written
in mathematical language!' Remember? We're going—
Wham!—clean through on this!"

"We'd better put off the opening," said Osborne. "We don't
want this in the *Social Gazette*."

"Why not?"

Osborne looked pained. Nothing in his world was as simple
as that; nothing could be said or done without permission.
On his files, what happened at Bouldershaw Fell was one
small part of an intricately complex pattern of arrangements,
and behind them loomed everything that Vandenberg stood
for. Everything had to be weighed and considered with caution.

"What do I tell the press?" Judy asked him.

"Nothing."

"Nothing?"

"Are we a secret society or something?" Fleming regarded
him with contempt, but Osborne managed to sound at the
same time official and reasonable.

"You can't throw this kind of undigested information about.
There are other people to consult, and besides there might
be a panic: space-ships, saucers, bug-eyed monsters. Every
idiot in the country will be seeing them. Or it may be
someone up to something. Nothing must appear in the press,
Miss Adamson."

They left Fleming seething, went to the Professor's office
to telephone the Ministry, and drove away.

At the Lion at Bouldershaw the press had already begun
to arrive to cover the opening ceremony. Judy piloted Reinhart
and Osborne round by the back door to a small room where
they were given dinner rather late and were able to dodge
the growing phalanx of scientific correspondents living it up
in the lounge. Osborne made covert dashes to the phone
box between each course and came back each time looking
more harassed and depressed.

"What did the Minister say?"

"He said—ask Vandenberg."

They ate through some tepid meat and he went off again.

"What did Vandenberg say?"

"What did you imagine he'd say? 'Keep quiet about it.' "

Judy was to tell the press, the next morning, that the

opening had been cancelled because of a technical hitch, nothing more. Any other statement would be made from London to the Fleet Street desks. They contrived to slip out again, unnoticed, by the back door.

Half an hour later, Fleming's car pulled up outside and Fleming, tired and thirsty, disappeared into the lounge.

The message was picked up again that evening. It went on all through the night and was recorded by Fleming and Bridger in turns, not only the audible dots and dashes, but the high speed part of the message as well. The next morning Dennis Bridger went down by himself to Bouldershaw and Harries followed him. After leaving his car in the Town Hall car park Bridger walked down a cobbled side-street to the lower part of the town. Harries followed him on foot at a distance of one street corner. With a raincoat in place of his overall, Harries looked more like an Irish gunman than a lab cleaner and he was careful not to let Bridger see him. Harries himself did not notice a couple of men standing on the pavement on the opposite side of the road to a small doorway marked JAS. OLDROYD, TURF ACCOUNTANT. There were a number of people around; two men talking were not conspicuous.

Bridger turned in at the doorway and entered a narrow dark passage with stairs and linoleum treads running up to the floor above and a door with a frosted glass panel near the foot of the staircase. When he closed the outer door, the noise of the street was sealed off, leaving the passage as solitary as a crypt. The door with the frosted glass bore the same lettering for Jas. Oldroyd. It also said *Knock and Enter;* Bridger did so.

Inside, Jas. Oldroyd was having a late breakfast at his desk. An elderly man in rolled-up sleeves and a dim colorless cardigan, he was sopping up fried egg with a piece of bread on the end of a fork when Bridger walked in. There was no one else in the office, yet the small room seemed full, with a litter of papers, telephones, an adding machine, a ticker-tape and a teleprinter. Several tradesmen's calendars hung on the walls, torn off at different months, but there was a prominent, very accurate clock. Mr. Oldroyd looked up from his web of old litter and new equipment and eyed Bridger for a moment.

"Oh, it's you."

Bridger nodded towards the teleprinter machine.
"O.K.?"

Mr. Oldroyd put the piece of egg-soaked bread in his mouth by way of answer and Bridger set to work on the telex.

"How's business?" he asked as he switched it on and dialled a number. It sounded like a stock greeting between old acquaintances.

"Chancy," said Mr. Oldroyd. "Horses 'ave no sense of responsibility. If they're not bunchin' they're crawlin', like t'ruddy buses."

Bridger typed: KAUFMAN TELEX 21303 GENEVA. Then he became aware of a scuffling in the passage outside. A single head was silhouetted for a moment against the glazed panel of the door. Then there was a grunt and a groan, and the head was pulled away by other less distinct figures. Bridger glanced at Oldroyd, who appeared to have noticed nothing and was cutting the rind off a piece of curled up bacon. He went back to the printer. When he had finished typing, he stepped cautiously out into the passage. It was empty. The street door was swinging open, but in the street outside there was no sign of anything unusual. There was no one standing opposite, no one watching from the corner. A car driving away might or might not have had something to do with it.

Dennis Bridger set off towards the car park, his legs shaking.

News of the message came out through one of the wire agencies in time for the evening papers. By the time General Vandenberg called on the Minister of Science to protest, a government statement was being broadcast on television. The Minister was out. Osborne stood with Vandenberg in his senior's office watching the newsreader mouthing earnestly out of the screen in the corner of the room.

The government of the time was a well-sounding but purposeless coalition of talents, nicknamed the Meritocrats, a closing of ranks in time of crisis. They were able men and women with no common principle except survival. The Prime Minister was a liberal Tory, the Minister of Labor a renegade trade-unionist; key posts were held by active and ambitious younger men like the Minister of Defense, others by less capable but publicly impressive figures with a good turn of phrase, such as the Minister of Science. Party

differences had been not so much sunk as mislaid: possibly
it was the end of party government in this country. Nobody
cared much, the whole nation was apparently sunk in hopeless
apathy in the face of a world that had got beyond its control.
Some remaining left-wing anti-Establishment movements
caused *Vichy* to be chalked up occasionally on Whitehall walls,
but that was the only visible sign of spirit. People went
quietly about their lives and an odd silence fell over public
affairs. Someone said it was so quiet you could hear a bomb
drop.

Into this vacuum fell the news of a message from space.
The newspapers inevitably got it hopelessly wrong. SPACE-
MEN SCARE: IS THIS AN ATTACK? they asked. The young
man on the screen earnestly read out the official statement:

"The government this evening forcibly denied rumors of
a possible invasion from space. A Ministry of Science
spokesman told reporters that, while it was true that what
appeared to be a message had been picked up by the new
giant radio-telescope at Bouldershaw Fell, there was no reason
to believe that it originated from either a space-ship or a
nearby planet. If indeed the signal received was a message,
it came from a very distant source."

There was no satisfactory explanation for the leak. Reinhart
knew nothing about it and the Ministry of Defense's security
man on the spot—Harries—was unaccountably missing. The
military, however, were after heads. Vandenberg produced
two dossiers which he opened on the Minister's table.

" 'Fleming, Dr. John—1960 onwards: anti-N.A.T.O., pro-
African, Aldermaston marcher, civil disobedience, nuclear
disarmament.' Do you call that reliable?"

"He's a scientist, not a candidate for a police commission."

"He's supposed to be responsible. Look at the other." The
General riffled through the other folder, not without relish.
"Bridger—Communist Party 1958 to '63. Then he swung right
round and started doing jobs for one of the international
cartels. But one of the dirtiest: Intel. You could lose him
anyway."

"Fleming won't work without him."

"That figures." The General gathered up the files. "I'd
say we're vulnerable in that area."

"All right," said Osborne wearily, and picked up the
Minister's phone. He spoke into it gently, as if ordering
flowers. "Bouldershaw Fell."

In the control room the message was coming through again. Harvey was out in the recording bay, looking after the tapes, and Fleming was alone at the control desk. They were short-handed: Whelan had suddenly been posted away and even Harries was absent. Bridger hovered about in corners looking petulant and uneasy and twitching a good deal. Finally he faced up to the other man.

"Look, John, this could go on for ever."

"Maybe."

The sound from the stars went on over the loudspeaker.

"I'm going to bale out." Fleming looked up at him. "The design's finished. There's nothing more for me to do here."

"There's everything for you to do!"

"I'd rather move on."

"How about that?"

They listened for a moment to the speaker. Bridger's nose twitched.

"Could be anything," he said off-handedly.

"But I've an idea what."

"What?"

"It could be a set of instructions."

"All right, you work on it."

"We'll work on it together."

At that moment Judy broke in on them. She marched across from the door, her high heels clicking on the flooring like a guardsman's, her face set and furious. She could hardly wait to get to them before she spoke.

"Which of you told the press?"

Fleming stared at her in amazement. She turned to Bridger.

"Someone has leaked the information—*all* the information —to the press."

Fleming clicked his tongue deprecatingly. Judy gave him a blazing look and turned back to Bridger.

"It wasn't Professor Reinhart and it wasn't me. It wasn't Harvey or the other boys—they don't know enough. So it must be one of you."

"Q.E.D." said Fleming. She ignored him.

"How much did they pay you, Dr. Bridger?"

"I—"

Bridger stopped. Fleming got up and barged his way between them.

"Is it your business?" he asked her.

"Yes. I—"

"Well, what are you?" He pushed his face close up to her and she realized that his breath smelled of drink again.

"I—" she faltered, "I'm the press officer. I'm carrying the can. I've just had the biggest rocket of all time."

"I'm very sorry," said Bridger.

"Is that all you can say?" Her voice rose unsteadily.

"Do yourself a favor, will you?" Fleming stood with his legs apart, swaying, and grinning contemptuously down on her. "Take your talons out of my friend Dennis."

"Why?"

"Because *I* told them."

"You!" She stepped back as if she had been slapped in the face. "Were you drunk?"

"Yes," said Fleming and turned his back on her. He walked to the door of the recording room and then looked round. "It wouldn't have made any difference if I'd been sober."

As he went out of the door he called back at her: "And they didn't pay me!"

Judy stood for a moment without hearing or seeing. The loudspeaker hissed and crackled, fluorescent lighting shone down on the sparse angular furniture. Outside the window, the arch of the telescope reared up into a darkening sky: only three evenings ago she had come to it, uninitiated and uninvolved ... She became aware of Bridger standing beside her, offering her a cigarette.

"Lost an idol, Miss Adamson?"

Judy, as press officer, had to report to Osborne, and Osborne reported to his Minister. Nothing was heard of Harries, and his disappearance was not announced. The press were persuaded that the whole thing was either a mistake or a hoax. After a series of painful meetings between ministers, the Ministry of Defense were able to assure General Vandenberg and his masters that nothing of the kind would occur again: they would take full responsibility. The search for Harries was intensified, and Fleming was summoned to London.

At first it seemed possible that Fleming was shielding Bridger, but it was soon established that he had in fact told the whole story over drinks in the Lion to an agency reporter called Jenkins. Although Bridger tendered his resignation, he had three months' notice to work out and he was left in charge of Bouldershaw Fell while Fleming was absent. The message continued to come in, and was printed out in a code of 0 and 1.

Fleming himself seemed quite unmoved by the commotion around him. He took all the printed sheets with him in the train to London and studied them hour after hour, making notes and calculations in the margin and on odd letters and envelopes that he found in his pockets. He appeared to be hardly aware of anything else. He dressed and ate absent-mindedly, he drank little; he burned with intense preoccupation and excitement. He ignored Judy, and hardly looked at the newspapers.

When he arrived at the Ministry of Science, he was shown up to Osborne's room, where Osborne was waiting for him with Reinhart and a stiff, middle-aged man with grey hair and impatient blue eyes. Osborne rose and shook hands.

"Dr. Fleming." He was very formal.

"Hi," said Fleming.

"You don't know Air Commodore Watling, Security Section, Ministry of Defense."

The stiff man bowed and looked at him without warmth. Fleming shifted and turned inquiringly to Reinhart.

"Hallo, John," said Reinhart, in a small, restrained voice, and looked down self-consciously at his fingers.

"Have a seat, Dr. Fleming."

Osborne indicated a chair facing the others, but Fleming stared from one to another of them before he sat, as though he were waking up in a strange place.

"Is this a court of inquiry?"

There was a small silence. Watling lit a cigarette.

"You were advised there was a security barrier on your work?"

"What does that mean?"

"That it was confidential."

"Yes."

"Then why—?"

"I don't go for gagging scientists."

"Take it easy, John," Reinhart said soothingly. Watling went on to another tack.

"You've seen the papers?"

"Some of them."

"Half the world believes little green men with feelers are about to land in our back gardens."

Fleming smiled, feeling the ground firmer beneath him.

"Do you?"

"I'm in possession of the facts."

"The facts are what I gave the press. The straight scientific facts. How was I to know they'd distort them?"

"It's not your job to assess these things, Dr. Fleming." Osborne had installed himself elegantly and judicially behind his desk. "Which is why you were told not to interfere. I warned you myself."

"So?" Fleming was bored already.

"We've had to send a full report to the Defense Co-ordination Committee," said Watling severely. "And the Prime Minister is making a statement to the United Nations."

"That's all right then."

"It's not the sort of position we like to be in, but our hand has been forced and we have to allay fear."

"Naturally."

"Our hand has been forced by you."

"Am I supposed to grovel?" Fleming began to be angry as well as bored. "What I do with my own discoveries is my own affair. It's still a free country, isn't it?"

"You *are* part of a team, John," Reinhart said, not looking at him.

Osborne leaned coaxingly forward across his desk.

"All we need, Dr. Fleming, is a personal statement."

"How will that help?"

"Anything which will reassure people will help."

"Particularly if you can discredit your informant."

"This isn't personal, John," said Reinhart.

"Isn't it? Then why am I here?" Fleming looked contemptuously round at them. "When I've made a statement to say I was talking out of the back of my head—what happens then?"

"I'm afraid . . ." Reinhart studied his fingers again.

"I'm afraid we've given Professor Reinhart no choice," said Watling.

"They want you to leave the team," Reinhart told him.

Fleming got up and thought for a moment, while they waited for an outburst.

"Well, it's easy, isn't it?" he said at last, smoothly.

"I don't want to lose you, John." Reinhart made a small, deprecating movement with his tiny hands.

"No, of course not. There's one snag."

"Oh?"

"You can't go any further without me."

They were prepared for that. There were other people, Osborne pointed out.

"But they don't know what it is, do they?"

"Do you?"

Fleming nodded and smiled. Watling sat up even straighter.

"You mean, you've deciphered it?"

"I mean, I know what it is."

"You expect us to believe that?"

Osborne obviously did not, nor Watling; but Reinhart was unsure. "What is it, John?"

"Do I stay with it?"

"What is it?"

Fleming grinned. "It's a do-it-yourself kit; and it isn't of human origin. I'll prove it to you."

He dug into his briefcase for his papers.

three
ACCEPTANCE

THE NEW Institute of Electronics was housed in what had once been a Regency square and was now a pedestrian precinct surrounded by tall concrete-and-glass buildings with mosaic faces. The Institute possessed several floors of computing equipment, and after intensive lobbying Reinhart was able to gain Fleming a reprieve and install him and the rest of the team there with access to the equipment. Bridger, nearing the end of his contract, was given a young assistant named Christine Flemstad, and Judy—to her and everyone else's disgust—was sent along with them.

"What," Fleming demanded, "is the point of a P.R.O. if we're so damn top-secret we have to stand on a ladder to brush our own teeth?"

"I'm supposed to learn, if you'll let me. So that when it *is* released . . . "

"You'll be *au fait?*"

"Do you mind?" Judy spoke tentatively, as though she, not Fleming, had been to blame before. She felt bound to him in an inexplicable way.

"I should worry!" said Fleming. "The more sex the better."

But, as he had said at Bouldershaw, he had no time. He spent all his days, and most of the night, breaking down the enormous mass of data from the telescope into comprehensible figures. Whatever deal he had made—or Reinhart had made for him—had sobered him and intensified his work. He drove Bridger and the girl with solid and unrelenting determination and suffered patiently all manner of supervision and routine. Nominally, Reinhart was in charge, and he took all his results obediently to him; but the defense people were never far away, and he even managed to be polite to Watling, whom they called "Silver-wings."

The rest of the team were less happy. There was a distinct coolness between Bridger and Judy. Bridger, in any case, was anxious to be gone, and the girl Christine was openly in the running to succeed him. She was young and pretty with something of Fleming's single-mindedness, and she patently regarded Judy as a hanger-on. As soon as she had an opportunity, she fought.

Shortly after they moved down from Bouldershaw, Harries had turned up: Watling revealed this on one of his visits to the unit. Harries had been set on at the bookie's, bundled into a car, beaten up and dumped in a disused mill, where he had nearly died. He had crawled around with a broken leg, unable to get out, living on water from a dripping tap and some chocolate he had in his pocket, until after three days he had been discovered by a rat-catcher. He did not return to them, and Watling told only Judy the details. She kept them to herself, but tried to sound Christine on Bridger's background.

"How long have you known him?"

They were in a small office off the main computer hall, Christine working at a trestle table littered with punched input cards, Judy pacing about and wishing she had a chair of her own.

"I was one of his research students at Cambridge." In spite of her Baltic parentage, about which Judy knew, Christine spoke like any English university girl.

"Did you know him well?"

"No. If you want his academic references . . ."

"I only wondered . . . "

"What?"

"If he ever behaved—oddly."

"I didn't have to wear a barbed wire girdle."

"I didn't mean that."

"What do you mean?"

"He never asked you to help him do anything, on the side?"

"Why should he?" She looked round at Judy with serious hostile eyes. "Some of us have real work to get on with."

Judy wandered into the computer hall and watched the machines clicking and flickering away. Each machine had its own attendant: neuter-looking young men and women in identical overalls. In the center was a long table where calculations from the computers were assembled in piles of punched cards or coils of tape or long screeds of paper from the output printers. The volume of figures they handled was prodigious, and it all seemed utterly unrelated to flesh and blood—a convocation of machinery, talking its own language.

Judy had learned a little of what the team were doing. The message from Andromeda had continued for many weeks without repeating itself, and then had gone back to the beginning and started all over again. This had enabled them to fill in most of the gaps in the first transmission; as the earth was turning, they were only able to receive it during the hours that the western hemisphere was facing the Andromeda constellation, and for twelve hours out of every twenty-four the source went below their horizon. When the message began again, the rotation of the earth was in a different phase to it, so that part of the lost passages could now be received; and by the end of the third repeat they had it all. The staff at Bouldershaw Fell went on monitoring, but there was no deviation. Whatever the source was, it had one thing to say and went on saying it.

No one concerned now doubted that it was a message. Even Air Commodore Watling's department referred to it as "the Andromeda broadcast" as if its source and identity were beyond doubt. The work on it they catalogued as Project A. It was a very long message, and the dots and dashes, when resolved into understandable arithmetic, added up to many million long groups of figures. Conversion into normal forms would have taken a lifetime without the computers, and took a good many months with them. Each machine had to be instructed what to do with the information given it; and this, Judy learned, was called programming. A program consisted of a set of calculations fed in on punched cards, which set the machine to do the job required. The group of figures to be analyzed—the data—was then put in, and the machine gave the answer in a matter of seconds. This process had to be repeated for every fresh consideration of every group of figures. Fortunately, the smaller computers could be used for preparing material for the larger ones, and all the machines possessed, as well as input, control, calculating and output units, a reasonable memory storage, so that new answers could be based on the experience of earlier ones.

It was Reinhart—kind, tolerant, wise, tactful Reinhart—who explained most of it to Judy. After the affair at Bouldershaw Fell he came to accept her with more grace, and to show that he liked her and felt sorry for her. Although he was deeply and precariously involved in the inter-departmental diplomacy which kept them going, his particular qualities of leadership were very apparent at this time. Somehow he kept Fleming on the rails and the authorities at bay and still had time to listen to everyone's ideas and problems; and all the while he remained discreetly in the background, hopping from issue to issue like some quiet, dainty, highly intelligent bird.

He would take Judy by the arm and talk to her quite simply about what they were doing, as though he had all the time and all the knowledge in the world. But there came a point in the understanding of computation where he had to hand over to Fleming, and Fleming went on alone. Computers, Judy realized, were Fleming's first and great love, and he communicated with them by a sort of intuitive magic.

It was not that there was anything cranky about him; he simply had a superhuman fluency in their language. He swam in binary mathematics like a fish in the sea, and made short cuts which it took Bridger and Christine many hours of solid plodding to check. But they never found him wrong.

One day, just before Bridger was due to leave, Reinhart took him and Fleming aside for a longer session than usual and at the end of it went straight to the Ministry. The following morning the Professor and Fleming went back to Whitehall together.

"Are we all met?"

Osborne's rather equine voice neighed down the length of the conference room. About twenty people stood round the long table, talking in groups. Blotters, notepads and pencils had been laid out for them on the polished mahogany and at intervals down the center of the table were silver trays bearing water jugs and glasses. At the end was one larger blotter, with tooled leather corners, for the Top Man.

Vandenberg and Watling were in one group, Fleming and

Reinhart in another, and a respectful circle of civil servants in charcoal-grey suits surrounded one dazzling matron in a flowered costume. Osborne surveyed them expertly and then nodded to the youngest charcoal-suited man who stood by the door. The young man disappeared into the corridor and Osborne took his place by the head of the table.

"Aheeem!" he whinnied. The others shuffled into their places, Vandenberg—at Osborne's invitation—at the right of the top chair. Fleming, accompanied by Reinhart, sat obstinately at the far end. There was a little silence and then the door opened and James Robert Ratcliff, Minister of Science, walked in. He waved an affable hand at one or two juniors who started to rise—"Sit down, dear boy, sit down!"—and took his seat behind the tooled leather. He had a distinguished, excessively well-groomed grey head and healthy pink-and-white face and fingers. The fingers were very strong, square and capable: one could imagine him taking large handfuls of things. He smiled genially upon the company.

"Good morning, lady and gentlemen. I hope I'm not late."

The more nervous shook their heads and muttered "No."

"How are you, General?" Ratcliff turned, slightly Caesarlike, to Vandenberg.

"Old and ailing," said Vandenberg, who was neither.

Osborne coughed. "Shall I go round the table for you?"

"Thank you. There are several fresh faces."

Osborne knew all the names, and the Minister gave a gracious inclination of his head or lift of his hand to each one. The flowered prima-donna turned out to be a Mrs. Tate-Allen from the Treasury, who represented the grants committee. When they got to Fleming the ministerial reaction changed.

"Ah—Fleming. No more indiscretions, I hope."

Fleming scowled the length of the table at him.

"I've had my mouth shut, if that's what you mean."

"It is." Ratcliff smiled charmingly and passed on to Watling.

"We'll try not to take too much of each other's time, shall we?" He raised his fine Roman head and looked down the table to Reinhart. "You have some more news for us, Professor?"

Reinhart coughed diffidently on to his little white hand.

"Dr. Fleming here has made an analysis."

"Excuse me," Mrs. Tate-Allen beamed, "but I don't think Mr. Newby here is entirely in the picture."

Mr. Newby was a small, thin man who looked used to humiliation.

"Oh, well," said Ratcliff, "perhaps you'd fill in the background, Osborne."

Osborne filled it in.

"And now?"

Twenty pairs of eyes, including the Minister's, turned to Fleming.

"We know what it is," said Fleming.

"Well done!" said Mrs. Tate-Allen.

"What is it?"

Fleming looked levelly at the Minister.

"It's a computer program," he said quietly.

"A computer program? Can you be sure about that?" Fleming merely nodded. Everyone else talked.

"Please!" said Osborne, banging his fist on the table. The hubbub subsided. Mrs. Tate-Allen held up a blue-gloved hand.

"I'm afraid, Minister, some of us don't know what a computer program is."

Fleming explained, while Reinhart and Osborne sat back and breathed relief. The boy was behaving well.

"Have you tried it in a computer?" asked Mrs. Tate-Allen.

"We've used computers to break it down. We've nothing that'll take all of it." He tapped the papers in front of him. "This is simply vast."

"If you had access to a bigger computer—" Osborne suggested.

"It isn't only size. It is, in fact, more than just a program."

"What is it then?" Vandenberg asked, settling more comfortably into his chair. It was going to be a long business.

"It's in three sections." Fleming arranged his papers as if that would make it clearer. "The first part is·a design—or rather, it's a mathematical requirement which can be interpreted as a design. The second part is the program proper, the order code as we call it. The third and last part is data—information sent for the machine to work on."

"I'd be glad of an opportunity . . . " Vandenberg extended a hand and the papers were passed to him. "I don't say you're wrong. I'd like our signals people to check your methodology."

"You do that," said Fleming. There was a respectful hush

as the papers were handed up the table, but Mrs. Tate-Allen evidently felt that some comment was required.

"I must say, this is very interesting."

"Interesting!" Fleming looked explosive. Reinhart laid a restraining hand on his sleeve. "It's the most important thing that's happened since the evolution of the brain."

"All right, John," said Reinhart. The Minister passed it over.

"What do you want to do next?"

"Build a computer that'll handle it."

"Are you seriously proposing," the Minister spoke slowly, choosing his words carefully, as though they were chocolates out of an assorted box, "that some other beings, in some distant part of the galaxy, who have never had any contact with us before, have now conveniently sent us the design and program for the kind of electronic machine—"

"Yes," said Fleming. The Minister sailed on: "Which we happen to possess on this earth?"

"We don't possess one."

"We possess the type, if not the model. Is it likely?"

"It's what happened."

Fleming made a dubious impression on the meeting. They had often seen it before: dedicated young scientists, obstinate and peevish, impatient of committee processes, and yet to be treated with great patience because they might have something valuable on them. These easily caricaturable officials were not fools; they were used to assessing people and situations. Much would depend on what Vandenberg and Osborne and Reinhart thought. Ratcliff inquired of the Professor.

"Arithmetic's universal," said Reinhart. "Electronic computing may well be."

"It may be the only form of computing, in the last analysis," put in Fleming.

Vandenberg looked up from the papers.

"I wonder—"

"Look," Fleming interrupted. "The message is being repeated all the time. If you've a better idea, you go and work on it."

Reinhart glanced uneasily across at Osborne, who was watching the state of play like a scorer at a cricket match.

"You can't use an existing machine?" Osborne asked.

"I said!"

"It seems a reasonable enough question," the Minister observed mildly. Fleming turned on him passionately.

"This program is simply enormous. I don't think you realize."

"Just explain, John," Reinhart said.

Fleming took a breath and continued more calmly. "If you want a computer to play you a decent game of draughts, it has to be able to accept a program of around five thousand order groups. If you want it to play chess—and you can; I've played chess with computers—you have to feed in about fifteen thousand orders. To handle this material," he waved towards the papers in front of Vandenberg, "you need a computer that can take in a thousand million, or, more accurately, tens of thousands of millions of numbers, before it can even *start* work on the data."

At last he had the meeting with him: this was a glimpse of a brain they could respect.

"It's surely a matter of assembling enough units," Osborne said.

Fleming shook his head.

"It isn't just size; it needs a new conception. There's no equipment on earth . . ." He searched his mind for an example, and they waited attentively until he found one. "Our newest computers still work in microseconds. This is a machine that must operate in milli-microseconds, otherwise we'd all be old men by the time it got round to processing the whole of the vast quantity of data. And it would need a memory—probably a low temperature memory—at least with the capacity of the human brain, and far more efficiently controlled."

"Is this proven?" asked Ratcliff.

"What do you expect? We have to get the means to prove it first. Whatever intelligence sent this message is way ahead of us. We don't know why they sent it, or to whom. But it's something we couldn't do. We're just *homo sapiens*, plodding along. If we want to interpret it—" He paused. "If . . ."

"This is theory, isn't it?"

"It's analysis."

The Minister appealed once more to Reinhart.

"Do you think it could be proved?"

"I can prove it," said Fleming.

"I was asking the Professor."

"I can prove it by making a computer that *will* handle it," said Fleming, undeterred. "That's what's intended."

"Is that realistic?"

"It's what the message is asking for."

The Minister began to lose patience. He drummed his square fingers on the table.

"Professor?"

Reinhart considered, not so much what he believed, but what to say.

"It would take a long time."

"But it's what is wanted?"

"Possibly."

"I shall need the best available computer to work with," said Fleming, as though it were all agreed. "And the whole of our present team."

Osborne looked anguished; the issue was very doubtful still, to anyone who knew, and the Minister showed signs of taking offense.

"We can make available university computers," he said, in tones that suggested matters of mere routine. Fleming's patience suddenly snapped.

"University nothing! Do you think universities have the best equipment in this day and age?" He pointed across the table at Vandenberg. "Ask your military friend where the only really decent computer in the country is."

A small frozen pause: the meeting looked at the American general.

"I'll need notice of that question."

"You won't, 'cause I'll tell you. It's at the rocket research establishment at Thorness."

"That's engaged on defense work."

"Of course it is," said Fleming contemptuously.

Vandenberg did not reply. This young man was the Minister's problem. The meeting waited while Ratcliff drummed his fingers on the tooled leather and Osborne totted up the score, not very hopefully. His master was undoubtedly impressed but not convinced: Fleming, like most men of sincerity, was a bad advocate; he had had his chance and more or less thrown it away. If the Minister did nothing, the whole thing would remain a piece of university theory. If he took action, he would have to negotiate with the military: he would have to convince not only the Minister of Defense but also Vandenberg's Allied committee that the effort was worth the candle. Ratcliff took his time. He liked to have people waiting for him.

"We could make a claim," he said at last. "It would be a Cabinet matter."

For some time after the meeting there was nothing for the team to do. Reinhart and Osborne took negotiations forward step by prudent step, but Fleming could go no further. Bridger cleared up his remaining work, Christine sat quietly in the office checking and re-checking the ground they had already been over; but Fleming turned his back on the whole thing, and took Judy with him.

"It's no good fiddling around until they've made up their minds," he told her and dragged her off to help him enjoy himself. Not that he made passes at her. He simply enjoyed having her around and was affectionate and surprisingly pleasant company. The mainspring of his discontent, she discovered, was irreverence of pomposity and humbug. When they got in the way of his job he was sour and sometimes violent, but when he put work behind him they became merely targets for his particular brand of bitten-off salted humor.

"Britain is sinking slowly in the west," he remarked once, when she asked him about the general state of things, and dismissed it with a grin. When she tried to apologize for her outburst at Bouldershaw Fell, he simply smacked her across the bottom.

"Forgive and forget, that's me," he said, and bought her a drink. She endured a good deal for his pleasure: he loved modern music, which she did not understand; he loved driving fast, which frightened her; and he loved looking at Westerns, which frightened her even more. He was deeply tired and restless. They rushed from cinema to concert, from concert to a long drive, from a long drive to a long drink, and by the end of it he was worn out. At least he seemed happy, although she was not. She felt she was sailing under false colors.

They only went occasionally to the little office in the Institute, and when they were there Fleming flirted with Christine. Not that Judy could blame him. He took no notice of her in any other way, and she was astonishingly pretty. She was, as she confided to Bridger, "In love with his brain," but she seemed not particularly to relish being hugged and pinched. She went on stolidly with her work. She did inquire, however, about Thorness.

"Have you ever been there, Dr. Fleming?"

"Once."

"What's it like?"

"Remote and beautiful, like you. Also high-powered, soulless, clueless—not like you."

It was assumed that, if Fleming were allowed to go there, she would go too. Watling had looked over her antecedents and found them impeccable. Father and mother Flemstad had fled from Lithuania when the Russian armies rolled over it towards the end of the Hitler war, and Christine had been born and brought up in England. Her parents had become naturalized British citizens before they died and she had been subjected to every possible check.

Dennis Bridger's activities seemed a good deal more interesting. As the date of his departure drew near, he received an increasing number of unexplained long-distance telephone calls which appeared to worry him a good deal, although he never talked about them. One morning, alone in the office with Judy, he seemed more harassed than usual. When the telephone rang he seized it practically out of her hand. It was obviously a summons; he made some sort of excuse and left the office. Judy watched him from the window as he walked across the precinct to the roadway where a very large, very expensive car was waiting for him.

As he approached, the driver's door opened and an immensely tall chauffeur stepped out wearing the sort of livery that one associated with a *coupé de ville* of the nineteen twenties, a pale mustard high-buttoned cross-over tunic, breeches and polished leather leggings.

"Dr. Bridger?"

He had on dark glasses and he spoke with a soft, indeterminate foreign accent. The car was shining and monstrously beautiful, like a new aircraft without wings. Twin radio masts sprung from its tail fins to above the height of a man—even that man. The whole outfit was quite absurdly larger than life.

The chauffeur held open the door to the back of the car while Bridger got in. There was an immensely wide seat, a deeply carpeted floor, blue-glazed windows and, on the far side of the seat, a short stocky man with a completely bald head.

The short man extended a hand with a ring on it.

"I am Kaufmann."

The chauffeur returned to his place in front of the glass partition and they moved off.

"You do not mind if we drive around?" There was no mistaking Kaufmann's accent: he was German, prosperous and tough. "There is so much tittle-tattle if one is seen in places."

There was a small buzz by his ear. He picked up an ivory telephone receiver that lay across a rack in front of him. Bridger could see the chauffeur speaking into a microphone by the steering wheel.

"Ja." Kaufmann listened for a moment and then turned and looked out of the rear window. "Ja, Egon, I see. Go in a circle, then, yes? Und Stuttgart ... the call for Stuttgart."

He replaced the phone and turned to Bridger.

"My chauffeur says we are being followed by a taxi." Bridger looked around nervously. Kaufmann laughed, or at least he showed his teeth. "Not to worry. There are always taxis in London. He will see we go nowhere. What is important is I have my call to Stuttgart." He produced a silver case containing miniature cigars. "Smoking?"

"No thank you."

"You send me a telex message to Geneva." Kaufmann helped himself to a cigarillo. "Some months ago."

"Yes."

"Since then, we do not hear from you."

"I changed my mind." Bridger twitched anxiously.

"And now, perhaps, comes the time to change it back. We have been very puzzled, you know, these past few months." He was serious but agreeable and relaxed. Bridger looked guiltily out of the back window again.

"Do not worry, I tell you. It is looked after." He held a jewelled silver lighter to the end of his cigarillo and inhaled. "There really was a message?"

"Yes."

"From a planet?"

"A very distant planet."

"Somewhere in Andromeda?"

"That's right."

"Well, that is a comfortable way away."

"What is this—?" Bridger twitched his nose as the cigar smoke drifted up it.

"What is this about? I come to that. In America—I was in America at the time—there was great excitement. Everyone was very alarmed. And in Europe—everywhere. Then your government say: 'Nothing. It is nothing. We will tell you later.' And so on. And people forget; months go by and gradually people forget. There are other things to worry about. But there is something?"

"Not officially."

"No, no—officially there is nothing. We have tried, but everywhere is a blank wall. Everybody's lips are sealed."

"Including mine."

They were by now half-way round Regent's Park. Bridger looked at his watch.

"I have to get back this afternoon."

"You are working for the British Government?" Kaufmann made it sound like a piece of polite conversation.

"I'm part of their team," said Bridger.

"Working on the message?"

"Why should that interest you?"

"Anything of importance interests us. And this may be of great importance."

"It might. It might not."

"But you are going on with the work? Please, do not look so secretive. I am not trying to pump you."

"I'm not going on with it."

"Why not?"

"I don't want to stay forever in government service."

They drove past the zoo and down towards Portland Place. Kaufmann puffed contentedly at his cigar while Bridger waited. As they turned west into Marylebone Kaufmann said:

"You would like something more lucrative? With us?"

"I did think so," Bridger said, blinking at his feet.

"Until your little fracas in Bouldershaw?"

"You knew about that?" Bridger looked at him sharply. "At Oldroyd's?"

"Naturally I knew."

He was very affable, almost sweet. Bridger studied his shoes again.

"I didn't want any trouble."

"You should not be so easy put off," said Kaufmann. "At

the same time, you must not lead people towards us. We may be busy with something else."

They turned north again, up Baker Street.

"I think you should stay where you are," he said. "But you should keep in touch with me."

"How much?"

Kaufmann opened his eyes wide.

"Excuse?"

"If you want me to give you information."

"Really, Dr. Bridger!" Kaufmann laughed. "You have no finesse."

The intercom buzzed. Kaufmann picked up the phone.

"Kaufmann. . . . Ja, ja. . . . Das ist Felix? . . ."

They did two more turns round the park and then dropped Bridger off a few hundred yards from the Institute. Judy watched his return but he said nothing to her. He thoroughly distrusted her anyhow.

Half an hour later the taxi which had followed Kaufmann's car drew up at a telephone box and Harries stepped out. His leg was still strapped and he moved stiffly, but he considered himself fit for work. He paid the driver and limped across to the phone box. As the taxi drove away another car drew up and waited for him.

The phone was answered by Watling's P.A., a bored Lieutenant from the Household Cavalry, the Ministry of Defense being, by that time, what was called "integrated."

"I see. Well, you'd better come round and report."

As he hung up, Watling swept in, brisk, and bothered from another meeting with Osborne.

"Jabber, jabber, jabber. That's all they do." He slung his briefcase on to a chair. "Anything new?"

"Harries has been on."

"And?"

Watling took possession of his desk, a severe metal table in a severe concrete room with fire instructions on the door. The P.A. raised a cavalry-trained eyebrow.

"He says Bridger has been seen with a Known Person."

"Who? You can ditch the jargon."

"Kaufmann, sir."

"Kaufmann?"

"Intel. The international cartel people."

Watling stared at the blank wall facing him. There were still a number of large cosmopolitan cartels in spite of the anti-trust laws and the administration of the Common Market. They were not palpably illegal but they were extremely powerful and in some cases they had very nearly a stranglehold over European trade. At a time when the West was liable to boycott by any or all of the countries it depended on for raw materials, there was a frightening amount of scope for unscrupulous trading agencies, and Intel was generally known and disliked for its lack of scruple. Anything which found its way into its hands was likely to be sold profitably in another capital the next time the market was good.

"Any more?"

"No. They did two or three circuits in Kaufmann's mobile gin-palace and then landed back at base."

Watling stroked his chin as he fitted pieces of thought neatly and methodically together.

"You think that's what he was up to at Bouldershaw?"

"Harries thinks so."

"Which is why Harries was hauled off and pranged and dumped?"

"Partly."

"Well, they're the last people we want genned up on this."

Once anything got into the hands of Intel it was extremely difficult to trace. They had a perfectly legal organization in London, registered offices in Switzerland and branches over at least three continents. Information slipped along their private wires like quicksilver and there was very little that could be done about it. There were no search warrants for that kind of operation. By the time you were ransacking a Piccadilly office, the thing you had lost was being swapped for manganese or bauxite behind some very unsympathetic frontier. Nothing was sacred, or safe.

"I suppose Bridger'll go on feeding 'em stuff," he said.

"He's supposed to be pulling out," his P.A. reminded him.

"I doubt if he will now. They'll have crossed his palm." He sighed. "Anyway, he'd get it all from Fleming. They're thick as condensed soup."

"You think Fleming's in it?"

"Ach!" Watling pushed his chair back and gave the thing up. "He's just a hopeless innocent. He'll blow the gaff to anyone to show how independent he is. Look at what happened last time. And now we're going to have them in our midst."

"How so?"

"How so? You ought to write a phrasebook. They're moving into W.D. quarters, that's how so. The whole boiling. Fleming wants to build his super-computer at the Rocket Research Establishment at Thorness."

"Oh?"

"That's Top Secret."

"Yes, sir." The P.A. looked languidly discreet. "Has it been agreed?"

"It will be. I can smell a nonsense when I'm down-wind of it. Vandenberg's furious. So are all the Allies, I wouldn't wonder. But Reinhart's all for it and so's Osborne, and so's their Minister. And so will the Cabinet be, I expect."

"Then we can't keep 'em out?"

"We can watch 'em. We'd better keep Harries on it for one."

"They've their own security staff at Thorness. Army," the P.A. added with pride.

The Air Commodore sniffed. "Harries can work in with them."

"Harries wants to come off it."

"Why?"

"He says he's sure they've rumbled him."

"How? Pardon." Watling flashed a smile at him. "How so?"

"Well, they beat him up at Bouldershaw. They probably think he's on to something bigger than this."

"He probably is. Where is he now?"

"Tailing them. He's coming in later to report."

But Harries did not report later, or at all. Judy and Fleming found his corpse the following morning, under the tonneau cover of Fleming's car.

When Judy had been sick and they had both been to the police station and the body had been taken away and dealt with, they went back to the office to find a message for Fleming to go straight round to the Ministry of Science. Judy, waiting with Christine, was interviewed by Watling and felt frightened and miserable. Christine went on with her work, only stopping to give Judy two aspirin with the air of one who dispenses charity regardless of merit.

Before he left for the Ministry, Fleming had kissed Judy on the cheek. She smiled queasily at him.

"Why should they dump it on me?" he said.

"They didn't dump it on you. They dumped it on me, as a warning."

She went to the Ladies and was sick again.

Fleming came back before lunch cock-o'-hoop and bubbling. He pulled Christine out of her chair and held her to him.

"It's through!"

"Through?" Judy remained dazed at the other side of the room.

"Authority in triplicate from Air Commodore Jet-Propelled's superior officers. They've opened wide their pearly barbed wire stockade."

"Thorness?" Christine asked, pushing him away. Fleming bounced his behind on to the trestle table.

"We're graciously allowed in to use their beautiful, beautiful tax-payers' equipment hitherto reserved for playing soldiers."

"When?" asked Judy.

Fleming slid off the table and went across and hugged her.

"As soon as we're ready. Priority A on the big computer— barring what is laughingly called a national emergency. We're excused morning parades, we shall be issued with passes, we shall have our fingers printed, our brains washed and our hair searched for small animals. And we shall build the marvel of the age." He left Judy and held out his arms to Christine. "You and I, darling! We'll teach 'em, won't we? 'Is it proven?' asks his Ministership. We'll prove 'em! 'Come the four corners of the world in arms, and we will shock them'—as the lady said in the strip club. Oh—and Silver-Wings is coming to give us our marching orders."

He started singing "Silver wings among the gold," and took them both out to a lunch which Judy could not eat. There was no sign of Bridger.

Watling called back in the afternoon, composed but severe, like a visiting headmaster. He made the three of them sit down while he lectured them.

"What happened to Harries followed directly from his work with you."

"But he was a lab cleaner!"

"He was Military Intelligence."

"Oh!"

This was news to Christine, and to Fleming. He reacted with a kind of savage flippancy.

"Ours, as they say?"

"Ours."

"Charming."

"Don't flatter yourselves that this was all on account of what you're doing. You're not that important yet." The girls sat and listened while Watling turned his attention exclusively on Fleming. "Harries probably ran into something else when he was covering for you."

"Why was he covering for us if we're not important?"

"People—other people—don't know whether it's important or not. They know something's on, thanks to you opening your mouth. It may or may not be of great strategic value."

"Do you know who killed Harries?" Fleming asked quietly. His own share in the death had perhaps come home to him.

"Yes."

"That's something."

"And we know who paid them to."

"Then you're home and dry."

"Except that we won't be allowed to touch them," said Watling stiffly. "For diplomatic reasons."

"Charming again."

"It isn't a particularly charming world." He looked round at them as if performing an unpleasant duty. He was a modest and unpompous man who disliked preaching. "You people who've been living a quiet, sheltered life in your laboratories have got to understand something: you're on ops now."

"On what?" asked Fleming.

"Operations. If this idea of yours comes off, it'll give us a very valuable piece of property."

"Who's 'us'?"

"The country."

"Ah yes, of course."

Watling ignored him. He had heard plenty about Fleming's attitude to the Establishment.

"Even if it doesn't work, it'll attract attention. Thorness is an important place and people will go to great lengths to find out what's going on there. This is why I'm warning you—all of you." He fixed them in turn with his brisk blue eyes. "You're not in the university any more—you're in the jungle. It may just look like stuffy old officialdom, with a lot of smooth talk and platitudinous statements by politicians and government servants like me, but it's a jungle all the same. I can assure you of that. Secrets are bought and sold, ideas are stolen, and sometimes people get hurt. That's how the world's business is done. Please remember it."

When he had gone, Fleming returned to the computers and Judy went down to Whitehall to get her next instructions. Bridger drifted in later in the day, anxious and looking for Fleming.

"Dennis"—Fleming bounced back in from the computer hall—"We're off!"

"Off?"

"Thorness. We're cooking with gas."

"Oh, good," said Bridger flatly.

"The Minister of Science hath prevailed. Mankind is about to take a small step forward into the jungle, according to our uninformed friends. Why don't you change your mind? Join the happy throng."

"Yes. Thank you, John." Bridger looked down at his feet and twitched his nose in an agony of shyness. "That's what I came to see you about. I *have* changed my mind."

By the time Judy reached Osborne, Osborne knew.

four
ANTICIPATION

NO ONE EVER went to Thorness for fun. The quickest way from London took twelve hours, by air to Aberdeen and then by fast diesel across the Highlands to Gairloch on the west coast. Thorness was the first station north of Gairloch, but there was nothing there but a small decaying village, the wild rocky coast and the moors. The Research Establishment covered a headland facing out to the wide gap of water between the Isle of Skye and the Isle of Lewis, and was fenced in to the landward side by tall link wiring topped with barbed wire. The entrance was flanked by guard-huts and guards, and the fence and cliff-top were patrolled by soldiers with dogs. To seaward lay the grey Atlantic water, an island inhabited by birds, and an occasional Royal Naval patrol launch. It was all green and grey and brown and prone to clouds, and apart from periodical noises from inside the camp, it was a silent place.

It was raining when Reinhart and Fleming arrived. A black staff car driven by a young woman in green uniform met them at the station and splashed along the open moorland road to the gates of the camp. There they were checked in by a sergeant of the Argyll and Sutherland Highlanders who phoned the Director to let him know they were on the way.

The main offices were in a long, narrow one-storey building standing in the middle of the open compound. Although it was new and modern in design, it still had something of the traditional, bleak look of a barracks; but the inside of

58

the Director's office was a very different matter. The ebony
floor shone, the lights were hooded by white streamlined
shapes, windows were curtained to the floor and maps and
charts on the walls were framed in polished wood. The
Director's desk was wide and beautiful: behind it sat a man
with a narrow, lined face, and on it stood a small plaque
stating, in neat black letters, DR. F.T.N. GEERS.

He greeted them with politeness but without enthusiasm,
and with a patently false deprecation of what he was doing.

"You'll find it a very dull place here," he said, offering
them cigarettes out of the polished nose-cap of a rocket.
"We know each other by repute of course."

Reinhart sat warily on one of the visitors' chairs, which
were so low that he could hardly see the Director behind
his desk.

"We've corresponded, I think, over missile tracking." He
had to crane up to speak; it was obviously done on purpose.
Fleming regarded the arrangement and smiled.

A physicist by training, Geers had for years been a senior
scientific executive on defense projects and was now more
like a commanding officer than a scientist. Somewhere beneath
the martinet's uniform a disappointed research man lay
hidden, but this only made him more envious of other people's
work and more irritated by the mass of day-to-day detail
that fell upon him.

"It's about time you got your job behind barbed wire, from
all I hear." He was peevish but able; he had plans worked
out for them. "It's going to be difficult, of course. We can't
give you unlimited facilities."

"We don't ask—" began Reinhart.

Fleming interrupted. "The priorities have been fixed, I
understood." Geers gave him a sharp, cold look and flicked
ash into a tray made from a piston casting.

"You'll have certain hours set aside on the main computer.
You'll have your own work block and living quarters for your
team. They'll be within our perimeter and you'll be under
our surveillance, but you'll have passes and you'll be free
to come and go as you wish. Major Quadring is in charge
of our security, and I'm in charge of all research projects."

"Not ours," said Fleming, without looking at Reinhart.

"Mine are more mundane but more immediate tasks."
Geers, so far as possible, tried to avoid Fleming and addressed
himself to the Professor. "Yours is a Ministry of Science

affair—more idealistic, though perhaps a little hit and miss."

There was a framed photograph, on one corner of his desk, of his wife and two small children.

"I wonder how they get on?" Fleming said to Reinhart when they left.

It was still pouring outside. One of Geers's assistants led them round the compound, across the wet grass, along concrete paths between rows of low bunker-like buildings half buried in the ground, and up to the launching area at the top of the headland.

"It's quite calm here today," he said, as they bent their heads against the sweeping rain. "It can blow a gale as soon as look at you."

Several small rockets rested on their tilted racks, swathed in nylon covers, pointing out to sea, and one larger one stood vertical on the main launching pad, looking heavy and earthbound lashed to its scaffold.

"We don't go in for the really big stuff here. These are all interceptors; a lot of ability packed into a little space. It's all highly classified, of course. We don't encourage visitors in the normal way."

The main computer was an impressive affair, housed in a big laboratory building. It was an American importation, three times the size of anything they had used before. The duty staff gave Fleming a timetable with his sessions marked on it; they seemed friendly enough though not particularly interested. There was also an empty office building for their own use, and a number of pre-fabricated chalets for living quarters—small and bare but clean and fitted out with service furniture.

They squelched in their sodden shoes across to the personnel area and were shown the senior staff mess and lounge, the shop, laundry and garage, the cinema and post office. The camp was completely self-supporting: there was nothing to go out for but views of weather and sky.

For the first two or three months only the basic unit moved up: Fleming, Bridger, Christine, Judy and a few junior assistants. The offices bulged with calculations, plans, blueprints and odd pieces of experimental lash-up equipment. Fleming and Bridger had long all-night sessions over wiring circuits and electronic components, and slowly the building filled up with more and more research and design assistants and with draftsmen and engineers.

Early the following spring a firm of Glasgow contractors appeared on the site and festooned the area with boards saying MACINTYRE & SONS. A building for the new super-computer, as Fleming's brain-child was called, was put up inside the perimeter but away from the rest of the camp, and truck-loads of equipment arrived and disappeared inside it.

The permanent staff viewed all this with lively but detached interest and went on with their own projects. Every week or so there would be a roar and a flash from the launching pads as another quarter of a million pounds of tax-payers' money went off into the air. The moorland sheep and cattle would stampede in a half-hearted sort of way, and there would be a few days of intense activity inside the plotting room. Apart from that it was as quiet as an undiscovered land and, when the rain lifted, incredibly beautiful.

The junior members of Reinhart's team mixed in happily with the defense scientists and the soldiers guarding them, eating and drinking and going on excursions together and sailing together in small boats on the bay; but Bridger and Fleming walked on their own and were known as the heavenly twins. When they were not either in the computer building or the offices they were usually in one or other of their huts, working. Occasionally Fleming shut himself up with a problem and Bridger took a motor-boat out to the bird island, Thor-holm, with a pair of field-glasses.

Reinhart operated from London, paying periodic visits but mostly orbiting round Whitehall, pushing through plans, permits, budgets and the endless reports required by the government. Somehow everything they wanted they got fast and there were few delays. Osborne, Reinhart said modestly, was a past master.

Only Judy was at a loose end. Her office was apart from the others, in the main administrative block, and her living quarters were with the women defense scientists. Fleming, though perfectly amiable, had no time to spend with her; Bridger and Christine went to some lengths to miss her. She managed to keep a general tally on what was going on, and she allowed some of the army officers to take her about, but otherwise there was nothing. During the long winter evenings she took to tapestry and clay modelling and acquired a reputation for being arty, but in reality she was just bored.

When the new computer was nearly finished, Fleming gave her a conducted tour of it. His own attitude was a mixture of deprecation and awe; he could be completely wrong about it, or it could be something unimaginable and uncanny. The chief impression he gave was of fatigue; he was desperately tired now, and tiredly desperate. The machine itself was indeed something. It was so big that instead of being housed in a room, the control room was built inside it.

"We're like Jonah in the belly of the whale," he told her, pointing to the ceiling. "The cooling unit's up there—a helium liquefier. There's a constant flow of liquid helium round the core."

Inside the heavy double fire-doors was an area the size of a ballroom, with a ceiling-high wall of equipment dividing it across the center. Facing that, and with its back to the doors, was the main control desk, with a sort of glorified typing desk on one side and a printing machine on the other. Both the typing desk and the printer were flanked by associated tape decks and punch-card equipment. The main lights were not yet working: there was only a single bulb on the control desk and a number of riggers' lamps hanging from the equipment rack. The room was semi-underground and had no windows. It was like a cave of mystery.

"All that," said Fleming, pointing to the wall of equipment facing them, "is the control unit. This is the input console."

He showed her the teletype keyboard, the magnetic tape scanner and the punched-card unit. "He was intended to have some sort of sensory magnetic system, but we've modified it to scan transcript. Easier for mortals with eyes."

"He?"

Fleming looked at her oddly.

"I call him 'he' because he gives me the sense of a mind. Of a person almost."

She had lived so long on the fringe of it that she had grown used to the idea. She had forgotten the shiver that went through her at Bouldershaw Fell when the message first came to them out of space. There had been so many alarms and excursions that the issue had become clouded, and in any case the message itself had been reduced to mundane terms of building and wiring and complicated man-made equipment. But standing there beside Fleming, who seemed not only tired but possessed and driven on by some kind of compulsion from outside, it was impossible not to sense an obscure, alien power lurking in the dim room. It merely touched her and passed away. It did not live in her brain as it seemed to live in his, but it made her shiver again.

"And this is the output unit," said Fleming, who did not appear to notice what she had felt. "His normal thought processes are in binary arithmetic, but we make him print out in denary so that we can read it straight off."

The wall of equipment in front of them was broken by a facia of display panels.

"What's that?" asked Judy, pointing to an array of several hundred tiny neon bulbs set in rows between two perspex-sheathed metal plates that stood out at right angles from the cabinet.

"That's all the control unit. The lamps are simply a progress display device. They show the state of data going through the machine."

"Have any gone through yet?"

"No, not yet."

"You seem sure it will all work."

"I'd never considered it not doing. It would be pointless for them to send a design for something that didn't work." The certainty in his voice was not simply his personal arrogance; there was the effect of something else speaking through him.

"If you understand it right."

"Yes, I understand it. Most of it." He waved a hand at the sheathed metal plates. "I don't quite know what those are for. They're electric terminals with about a thousand volts between them, which is why we put safety covers on. They were in the design and I expect we'll learn how to use them. They're probably some sort of sensing apparatus."

Again, he seemed quite sure of it all, and quite unbaffled by its complexity. It was as if his brain had long been prepared and waiting for it: Judy thought how aching and empty he must have felt the year before when he was talking about a breakthrough and knocking down the railings. Not that he looked any happier now. She remembered that Bridger had said, "John'll never be happy."

Everything else seemed comparatively matter-of-fact as they walked round the room.

"The way it works," said Fleming, "is, you teletype the data in—that's the quickest way we have. The control unit decides what to do. The arithmetic units do the calculating—calling on the memory storage as they need, and putting new information into memory—and the answer comes out on the printer. The highway ducts are under the floor and the arithmetic units are along the side walls. It's quite a conventional system really, but the conventionality ends there. It has a speed and capacity that we can hardly imagine."

There was complete silence around them. Shining rows of metal cabinets stood on each side of them, hiding their secrets, and the blank face of the control panel stared unseeingly at them in the dim light. Fleming stood casually looking round, seeming as much part of it as he was part of his car when driving.

"He'll look prettier when he's working," he said, and took her round to the area behind the control racks.

This was a large semi-circular room, as dimly lighted as the other, with a huge metal-clad column rising through the center.

"That's the real guts of it: the memory storage." He opened a panel in the lower wall of the column and shone an inspection lamp inside. "There's a nice little job in molecular electronics for you. The memory is in the core and the core is held in a total vacuum to within a degree or two of absolute zero. That's where the liquid helium comes in."

Judy, peering in, could see a cube of what looked like a metal about three feet square sealed in a glass tube and surrounded by cooling ducts. Fleming spoke mechanically, as if giving a lecture.

"Each core is built up of alternate wafers of conducting and non-conducting material half-a-thou thick, criss-crossed into a honeycomb. That gives you a complete yes-no gate circuit on a spot of metal you can hardly see."

"Is that the equivalent of a brain cell?"

"If you like."

"And how many are there?"

"The core's a three-meter cube. That makes several millions of millions. And there are six cores."

"It's bigger than a human brain."

"Oh yes. Much bigger. And faster. And more efficient."

He closed the door-panel and said no more about it. She tried to imagine how it would really work, but the effort was as far beyond her as the understanding of matter; it was too vast and unfamiliar to visualize. She congratulated him and went away. He looked, for a moment, lonely and haunted but made no attempt to stop her. Then he started checking figures again.

Dennis Bridger was not captivated in the same way. He did his work stolidly and morosely, and made no discernible attempt to follow up his contacts with Intel. Major Quadring and his security people kept a careful eye on him; periodic checks were made on all staff leaving the main gates, to see that they were not taking out documents or other classified material, but Bridger did nothing at all to arouse their suspicion. His only recreation was visiting the off-shore island of Thorholm, from which he would return with gulls' and gannets' eggs and endearing photographs of puffins. Whatever inducement Kaufmann had given him to stay on did not seem to involve him in anything.

Geers regarded the whole team with suspicion. He was never obstructive, but a state of hostility existed between him and them. It was clear he would feel in some way satisfied if the experiment failed. However, as the super-computer neared completion, and the interest of his staff and his superiors in it increased, he took care to identify himself with any possible success. It was he who suggested that there should be a formal, though necessarily private, opening, and the Minister of Science—foiled of his unveiling of Bouldershaw Fell the previous year—allowed himself to be persuaded to cut a ribbon in Scotland. Fleming tried to put off the opening for as long as possible, but it was finally fixed for a day in October, by which time the new computer was due to be programmed and ready to receive its data. General Vandenberg and a couple of dozen Whitehall officials told their secretaries to make notes in their diaries.

Judy, at last, had something to do. There would be no press, but there were arrangements to be made with the various ministries, and plans for the visit to be worked out with Geers's staff. She saw little of Fleming. When she had finished her work she would go for long, solitary walks across the moors in the blustery weather of early autumn.

About a week before the opening, she saw a white yacht

standing out to sea. It was a big, ocean-going yacht, a long way off. From the camp, it was hidden behind the island of Thorholm; it could only be seen from further along the coast. Judy noticed it as she walked back by the cliff-top path in the afternoon.

The following afternoon it was still there, and Judy, walking along the path between the cliff edge and the heather, thought she could see the blink of an Aldis lamp signalling from it. This in itself would not have made her curious, had she not suddenly heard the sound of a car engine from the moor above her. By instinct, she dodged down behind a gorse bush and waited. It was a powerful but smooth engine that purred expensively as it ticked over.

The next thing Judy noticed was that the signalling had stopped. A moment or two later the engine revved and she could hear a car drive heavily away. After it had gone some distance, she got up and walked to the top of the path. Where it came to the cliff-top, it met a rough cart-track which wound away inland to join the main road in a valley between the hills. A large, shining car was disappearing round the first bend, behind a coppice of firs. Judy stared after it: there was something familiar about it.

She said nothing to Quadring, but went there again next day. There was no yacht and no car. The landscape was empty and silent except for the gulls. The next day it rained, and after that she was too busy with the Minister's visit to go out at all. By tea-time on the day before the opening, she had everything fixed—drivers laid on to collect the party from the station, a landing-crew provided for the Minister's helicopter, drinks and sandwiches in the Director's office, a timetable of the tour agreed with Reinhart and the others. Fleming was surly and withdrawn; Judy herself had a headache.

The sun came out about four o'clock, so she put on a wind-cheater and went out. As she walked along the cliff path the ground all round her steamed and, far below, the green waves slopped against the rocks in the freshening wind and threw up lace edges of foam that sparkled in the sunlight.

There was no yacht, and again no car where the path met the track at the cliff-top; but there were tire marks, recent ones made after the rain. Judy was thinking about this when she became aware of another distant noise. This time it was an outboard motor and it came from the far

side of the island, a couple of miles away. Straining her
eyes against the sun, she watched the tiny distant shape
of a boat edge out from behind the island, making for the
bay below the camp at Thorness. It was Bridger's boat, and
she could just see one person—presumably Bridger—in it.

She saw no more. There was a whistle and a crack beside
her and a splinter of rock fell away from the cliff face by
her head. She did not wait to examine the bullet scar on
the rock; she simply ran. Another bullet whistled close to
her as she pelted headlong down the path, and then she
was round the first turn of the cliff and out of range. She
ran as far as she could, walked for a bit and then ran
again. Long before she got back to camp the sun had set
behind a bank of cloud. The wind rose and blew the day
away. She shivered, and her legs were shaking.

She felt safer when she got through the main gates, but
terribly lonely. Quadring's office was closed. There was no one
else she could talk to, and she did not want to meet Bridger
in the mess. Dusk was falling as she walked between the
chalets in the living quarters, and suddenly she found herself
at Fleming's. She could not bear to be outside a moment
longer. She knocked once at the door and walked straight
in.

Fleming was lying on his bed listening to a recording of
Webern on a high-fidelity set he had rigged for himself.
Looking up, he saw Judy standing in the doorway, panting,
her face flushed, her hair blown about.

"Very spectacular. What's it in aid of?" He was half way
through a bottle of Scotch.

Judy shut the door behind her. "John—"

"Well, what?"

"I've been shot at."

"Phui." He put down his glass and swung his feet to the
floor.

"I have! Just now, up on the moors."

"You mean whistled at."

"I was standing at the top of the cliff when suddenly a
bullet went close past me and smacked into the rock. I jumped
back and another one—"

"Some of the brown jobs at target practice. They're all
rotten shots." Fleming walked over to the record-player and

switched it off. He was quite steady, quite sober in spite of the whisky.

"There was no one," said Judy. "No one at all."

"Then they weren't bullets. Here, have a drink and calm yourself down." He foraged for a glass for her.

"They were bullets," Judy insisted, sitting on the bed. "Someone with a telescopic sight."

"You're really in a state, aren't you?" He found a glass, half-filled it and handed it to her. "Why should anyone want to take pot shots at you?"

"There could be reasons."

"Such as?"

Judy looked down into her glass.

"Nothing that makes any sense."

"What were you doing on the cliffs?"

"Just looking at the sea."

"What was on the sea?"

"Doctor Bridger's boat. Nothing else."

"Why were you so interested in Dennis's boat?"

"I wasn't."

"Are you suggesting that he shot at you?"

"No. It wasn't him." She held the footboard of the bed to stop her hand from trembling. "Can I stay here a bit? Till I get over the shakes."

"Do what you like. And drink that up."

She took a mouthful of the undiluted whisky and felt it stinging her mouth and throat. From the quietness outside came a long low howl, and a piece of guttering on the hut shook.

"What was that?"

"The wind," said Fleming as he stood watching her.

She could feel the spirit moving down, glowing, into her stomach. "I don't like this place."

"Nor do I," he said.

They drank in the silence broken only by the wind moaning round the camp buildings. The sky outside the window was almost dark, with blacker clouds blowing raggedly in from over the sea. She lowered her glass and looked Fleming in the eyes.

"Why does Doctor Bridger go to the island?" She never felt inclined to call Bridger by his first name.

"He goes bird-watching. You know jolly well he goes bird-watching."

"Every evening?"

"Look, when I'm flaked out at the end of the day I go sailing." This was true. Navigating a fourteenfooter was Fleming's one outside activity. Not that he did it very often; and he did it alone, not with the camp sailing club. "Except when I'm really flaked, like now."

He picked up the bottle by its neck and stood frowning, thinking of Dennis Bridger. "He goes snooping on sea-birds."

"Always on the island?"

"That's where they are," he said impatiently. "There's masses of stuff out there—gannets, guillemots, fulmars ... Have some more of this."

She let him pour some more into her glass. Her head was humming a little.

"I'm sorry I burst in."'

"Don't mind me." He rumpled her already tangled hair in his affectionate, unpredatory way. "I can do with a bit of company in this dump. Specially when it's a sweet, sweet girl."

"I'm not in the least sweet."

"Oh?"

"I don't like what I am." Judy looked away from him, down at her glass again. "I don't like what I do."

"That makes two of us." Fleming looked over her head towards the window. "I don't like what I do either."

"I thought you were completely taken up in it?"

"I was, but now it's finished I don't know. I've been trying to get myself sloshed on this, but I can't." He looked down at her in a confused way, not at all as he had done in the computer. "Perhaps you're what I need."

"John—"

"What?"

"Don't trust me too much."

Fleming grinned. "You up to something shady?"

"Not as far as you're concerned."

"I'm glad to hear it," he said, pushing up her chin with his hand. "You've an honest face."

He kissed her forehead lightly, not very seriously.

"No." She turned her head aside. He dropped his hand and turned away from her, as if his attention had moved to something else. The wind howled again.

"What are you going to do about this shooting?" he asked after a pause.

She shivered in spite of the warmth inside her, and he put a hand on her shoulder.

"Sometimes at night," he said, "I lie and listen to the wind and think about that chap over there."

"What chap?"

He nodded in the direction of the computer, the new computer which he had made.

"He hasn't a body, not an organic body that can breathe and feel like ours. But he's a better brain."

"It's not a person." She pulled Fleming down on the bed so that they were sitting side by side. She felt, for once, much older than he.

"We don't know what it is, do we?" said Fleming. "Whoever sent ye olde message didn't distribute a design like this for fun. They want us to start something right out of our depth."

"Do you think they know about us?"

"They know there are bound to be other intelligences in the universe. It just happens to be us."

Judy took hold of one of his hands.

"You needn't go further with it than you want."

"I hope not."

"All you're doing is building a computer."

"With a mental capacity way beyond ours."

"Is that really true?"

"A man is a very inefficient thinking machine."

"You're not."

"We all are. All computers based on a biological system are inefficient."

"The biological system suits me," she said. Her speech and vision were beginning to blur. Fleming gave her a short, bear-like hug.

"You're just a sexy piece."

He got up, yawned and stretched and switched on the light. Feeling a sudden loosening of tension, she lolled back on the bed.

"You need a holiday," she told him, slurrily.

"Maybe."

"You've been at it for months now without a break. That thing." She pointed towards the window.

"It had to be ready for his Ministership."

"If it did get out of control, you could always stop it."

"Could we? It was operational over a month ago. Did you know that?"

"No."

"We've been feeding in the order code so that the data can all be in by the time the gentry arrive."

"Did anything happen?"

"Nothing at first, but there was a small part of the order code I ignored. It arranged things so that when you switch on the current the first surge of electricity automatically sets the program working: at its own selected starting point. I deliberately left that out of the design because I didn't want him to have it all his own way, and he was furious."

Judy looked at him skeptically.

"That's nonsense."

"All right, he registered disturbance. Without any warning, before we'd even started putting in data, he started to print out: the missing section of the code. Over and over and over—telling me to put it in. He was very cross." He gazed earnestly into her unbelieving face. "I switched him off for a bit and then started feeding in the data. He was quiet after that. But he was designed to register disturbance. God knows what else he was designed for!"

She lay looking at him, not focusing.

"We shall put the last of the data in tomorrow," he went on. "Then heaven knows what'll happen. We get a message from two hundred light-years away—do you think all it gives us is a handy little ready-reckoner? Well, I don't. Nor do the people who killed Harries and shot at you and are probably tailing Dennis and me."

She started to interrupt him, but thought better of it.

"Remember?" he asked. "Remember I talked about a breakthrough?"

"Distinctly." She smiled.

"The kind of breakthrough you get once in a thousand years. I'll lay you any odds . . ."

He turned to the window and looked out, lost in some unthinkable speculation.

"You could always switch it off."

"Perhaps. Perhaps we could switch it off."

It was pitch black outside, with driving rain, and the wind continued to howl.

"It's dark," he said. He drew the curtain across and turned

back to her with the same haunted look in his eyes that she had seen before.

"That makes two of us who are scared," she said.

"I'll see you back to your hut if you like." He looked down at her and smiled. "Or you could spend the night here."

five
ATOMS

JUDY LEFT him at first light and went back to her own chalet. By midday the first contingent from London had arrived and was being entertained in the mess. She moved between the charcoal-grey suits distributing information sheets and feeling fresh and alive and happy. Fleming was at the computer building with Bridger and Christine, inputting the final section of data. Reinhart and Osborne were closeted with Geers.

Vandenberg, Watling, Mrs. Tate-Allen and the faithful and unspeaking Newby came on the two o'clock train and were met by the two best cars. The Minister was due to arrive by helicopter at three—a typically odd and showy whim which was politely passed over without comment by the rest of the party.

By that time the rain had cleared and a guard of honor was drawn up beside the parade-ground in the middle of the camp. Reinhart and Major Quadring waited with them, Quadring wearing his best battle-dress with clean medal-ribbons, Reinhart clutching a bedraggled plastic mac.

The other guests and hosts assembled on the porch of the new computer building and looked hopefully at the sky. Osborne made whinnying, diplomatic conversation.

"I don't expect you knew the British Isles extended so far north, eh General?" This to Vandenberg, who showed signs of restlessness and potential umbrage. "Eh Geers?"

Geers wore a new suit and stood unyieldingly in front of the others, very much the Director.

"Have they hatched a swan or an ugly duckling?" Mrs. Tate-Allen asked him.

"I wouldn't know. We only have time for practical work."

"Isn't this practical?" Osborne inquired.

Watling said, "I used to fly over here in the war."

"Really?" said Vandenberg, without interest.

"North Atlantic patrols. When I was in Coastal."

But nobody heard him: the helicopter had arrived. It hovered like a flustered bird over the parade-ground and then sank down on its hydraulic legs. Its rotors sliced the air for a minute and then stopped. The door opened, the Right Honorable James Ratcliff climbed down, the guard presented arms, Quadring saluted and Reinhart tripped forward on his dainty feet, shook hands and led the Minister to the assembled company in the porch. Ratcliff looked very well and newly bathed. He shook hands with Geers and beamed and smirked at the rest.

"How do you do, Doctor? It's very good of you to harbor our little piece of equipment in your midst."

Geers was transformed.

"We're honored, sir, to have work like this," he said with his best smile. "Pure research among us rude mechanicals."

Osborne and Reinhart exchanged glances.

"Shall we go in?" asked Osborne.

"Yes, indeed." The Minister smiled on all. "Hallo, Vandenberg, nice of you to come."

Geers stepped forward and grasped the door handle.

"Shall *I*?" He looked challengingly at Reinhart.

"Do," said Reinhart.

"It's this way, Minister." And Geers shepherded them in.

The lights were all working now in the computer room and Geers did the honors of display with some pride. Reinhart and Osborne left him to it and Fleming watched sourly from the control desk. Geers introduced Bridger and Christine and—quite casually—Fleming.

"You know Dr. Fleming, Minister, who designed it."

"The designers are in the constellation of Andromeda," said Fleming. Ratcliff laughed as if this was a very good joke.

"Well, you've done a pretty big job. I see why you all wanted so much money."

The party moved on. Mrs. Tate-Allen was much impressed by the neon lamps; the men in charcoal suits studied blue-painted cabinets of equipment with baffled interest, and Fleming was forced to fall in at the rear with Osborne.

"There's no business like show business."

"It's a compliment in fact," said Osborne. "They entrust it to you: the knowledge, the investment, the power."

"Bigger fools they."

But Osborne did not agree. After they had been round the memory cylinder, the whole group gathered in front of the control desk.

"Well?" said Ratcliff.

Fleming picked up a sheet of figures from the desk.

"These," he said, so quietly that hardly anyone could hear him. "These are the end groups of the data found in the message."

Reinhart repeated it for him, took the paper and explained. "We're now going to pass these in through the input consul and trigger the whole machine off."

He passed the sheet to Christine who sat down at the tele-type machine and started tapping the keys. She looked very deft and pretty: people admired. When she had finished, Fleming and Bridger threw switches and pressed buttons on the control desk and waited. The Minister waited. A steady hum came from the back of the computer, otherwise there was silence. Somebody coughed.

"All right, Dennis?" Fleming asked. Then the display lamps began to flicker.

It was very effective at first. Explanations were given: it showed the progress of the data through the machine; as soon as it had finished its calculations it would print out its finding on that wide roll of paper there. . . .

But nothing happened; an hour later they were still waiting. At five o'clock the Minister climbed unsmiling into his helicopter, rose into the sky and was carried southwards. At six o'clock the remaining visitors drove to the station to catch the evening train for Aberdeen, accompanied by a tight-lipped and crestfallen Reinhart. At eight o'clock Bridger and Christine went off duty.

Fleming stayed on in the empty control room, listening to the hum of the equipment and gazing at the endlessly flashing panel. As soon as she could, Judy joined him and sat with him at the control desk. He didn't speak, even to swear or complain, and she could think of nothing adequate to say.

The hands of the clock on the wall moved round to ten, and then the lamps on the panel stopped flickering. Fleming sighed and moved to get up to go. Judy touched his sleeve with her finger-tips to suggest some sort of comfort. He turned to kiss her, and as he did so the output printer clattered into life.

Reinhart stopped overnight in Aberdeen, where a Scottish Universities seminar was taking place. The seminar was an excuse; he did not want to spend the rest of the journey face to face with the politely condescending company from London. His one consolation was that he met an old friend, Madeleine Dawnay, professor of chemistry at Edinburgh. She was perhaps the best biochemist in the country, immensely capable and reassuring and with all the charm, her students said, of a test-tube-ful of dried skin. They talked for a long time, and then he went off to his hotel bedroom and worried.

In the morning he had a telegram from Thorness: FULL HOUSE. ACES ON KINGS. COME QUICK. FLEMING. He cancelled his plane reservation to London, bought a new railway ticket and set off north-west again, taking Dawnay with him.

"What does it mean?" she asked.

"I hope to heaven it means something's happened. The damn thing cost several million and I thought last night we were going to be the laughing-stock of Whitehall."

He did not know quite why he was taking her. Possibly to give himself some moral support.

When he telephoned the camp from Thorness station to ask for a car and an extra pass, his call was put straight through to Quadring's office.

"Damn scientists," said Quadring to his orderly. "They're in and out as if it were a fairground."

He took the pass the orderly had written and walked down the corridor to Geers's office. In the ordinary way he was a pleasant enough character, but Judy had been in to report the affair of the shooting and he was on edge and tetchy.

"I wonder if you'd sign this, sir?" He put the pass down on Geers's desk.

"Who is it?"

"Someone Professor Reinhart's bringing in."

"Have you checked him?"

"It's a 'her' actually."

"What's her name?" Geers squinted down at the card through his bifocals.

"Professor Dawnay."

"Dawnay! Madeleine Dawnay?" He looked with new interest. "You don't have to worry about her. I was at Manchester with her, before she moved on."

He smiled reminiscently as he signed the pass. Quadring shuffled uneasily.

"It's not easy keeping track of these Min. of Science bods."

"As long as they stick to their own building." Geers handed the pass back.

"They don't."

"Who doesn't?"

"Bridger for one. He goes out in his boat a lot to the island."

"He's a bird-watcher."

"We think it's something else. My own guess is he takes papers with him."

"Papers?" Geers looked up sharply with a glint of spectacles. "Have you any proof?"

"No."

"Well then—"

"Would it be possible to have him searched at the landing jetty?"

"Suppose he hadn't got anything?"

"I'd be surprised."

"And we'd look pretty foolish, wouldn't we?" Geers took off his glasses and stared discomfortingly at the major. "And if he was up to something we'd put him on his guard."

"He is up to something."

"Then get some facts to go on."

"I don't see how I can."

"You're responsible for the security of this establishment."

"Yes, sir."

Geers gave it his full attention for a moment.

"What about Miss Adamson?"

Quadring told him.

"Nothing since?"

"Not that we can see, sir."

"Hm." He closed the legs of his spectacles with a snap that dismissed the matter. "If you're going over to the computer building you might give Professor Dawnay her pass."

"I wasn't."

"Then send someone. And give her my regards. In fact, if they're through at a reasonable hour they might look in for a sherry."

"Very good, sir." Quadring backed gingerly away from the desk.

"And Fleming, I suppose, if he's with them."

"Yes, sir."

He got as far as the door. Geers was looking wistfully at the ceiling, thinking of Madeleine Dawnay.

"I wish we did more primary research ourselves. One gets tired of development work."

Quadring made his escape.

In the end it was Judy who took the pass. Dawnay was in the computer control room, being shown round by Reinhart and Bridger while Christine tried to raise Fleming on the camp phone. Judy handed over the pass and was introduced.

"Public Relations? Well, I'm glad they let girls do something," said Dawnay in a brisk, male voice. She looked hard but not unkindly at everyone. Reinhart fluttered a little; he seemed unusually nervous.

"What did John want?"

"I don't know," Judy told him. "At least, I don't quite follow it."

"He sent me a telegram."

After a minute Fleming hurried in.

"Ah, there you are."

Reinhart pounced on him.

"What's happened?"

"Are we alone?" Fleming asked, looking coolly at Dawnay.

Reinhart introduced them irritably and fidgeted from one tiny foot to the other while she quizzed Fleming about the computer.

"Madeleine's fully in the picture."

"She's lucky. I wish I were." Fleming fished from his pocket a folded sheet of paper and handed it to the Professor.

"What's this?" Reinhart opened it. Fleming watched him with amusement, like a small boy playing a trick on a grown-up. The paper bore several lines of typed figures.

"When did it print this?" Reinhart asked.

"Last night, after you'd all gone. Judy and I were here."

"You didn't tell me." Bridger edged in reproachfully.

"You'd gone off."

Reinhart frowned at the figures. "It means something to you?"

"Don't you recognize it?"

"Can't say I do."

"Isn't it the relative spacings of the energy levels in the hydrogen atom?"

"Is it?" Reinhart handed the paper to Dawnay.

"You mean," Bridger asked, "it suddenly came out with that?"

"Yes. It could be." Dawnay read slowly through the figures. "They look like the relative frequencies. What an extraordinary thing."

"The whole business is a little out of the ordinary," said Fleming.

Dawnay read through the figures again, and nodded.

"I don't see the point." Judy wondered if she was being unusually obtuse.

"It looks as if someone out there," Dawnay pointed up to the sky, "has gone to a lot of trouble to tell us what we already know about hydrogen."

"If that's really all." Judy looked at Fleming, who said nothing. Madeleine Dawnay turned to Reinhart.

"Bit of a disappointment."

"I'm not disappointed," Fleming said quietly. "It's a starting point. The thing is, do we want to go on?"

"How can you go on?" Dawnay asked.

"Well, hydrogen is the common element of the universe. Yes? So this is a piece of very simple universal information. If we don't recognize it, there's no point in the machine continuing. If we do, then he can proceed to the next question."

"What next question?"

"We don't know yet. But this, I bet you, is the first move in a long, long game of questions and answers." He took the paper from her and handed it to Christine. "Push this into the intake."

"Really?" Christine looked from him to Reinhart.

"Really."

Reinhart remained silent, but something had happened to him; he was no longer dejected and his eyes twinkled and were alert. The rest of them stood in a silent thoughtful group while Christine sat down to the input teletype and Bridger adjusted settings on the control desk.

"Now," he said. He was even quieter than Fleming, and Judy could not decide whether he was jealous or apprehensive or merely trying, like the others, to work it out.

Christine tapped rapidly at the keyboard and the computer hummed steadily behind its metal panelling. It really did seem to be all around them—massive, impassive and waiting. Dawnay looked at the rows of blue cabinets, the rhythmically oscillating lights with less awe than Judy felt, but with interest.

"Questions and answers—do you believe that?"

"If you were sitting up among the stars, you couldn't ask us directly what we know. But this chap could." Fleming indicated the computer control racks. "If it's designed and programmed to do it for them."

Dawnay turned to Reinhart again.

"If Dr. Fleming's on the right line, you really have something tremendous."

"Fleming has an instinct for it," said Reinhart, watching Christine.

When she had finished typing, nothing happened. Bridger fiddled with the control desk knobs while the others waited. Fleming looked puzzled.

"What's up, Dennis?"

"I don't know."

"You could be wrong," said Judy.

"We haven't been yet."

As Fleming spoke the lamps on the display panel started to flicker, and a moment later the output printer went into action with a clatter. They gathered round it watching the wide white streamer of paper inching up over its roller, covered in lines of figures.

One of the long low cupboards in Geers's office was a cocktail cabinet. The Director stood four glasses on top and produced a bottle of gin from the lower shelf.

"What Reinhart and his people are doing is terribly exciting." He was wearing his second-best suit but his best manner for Dawnay's benefit. "A little set-back yesterday, but I gather it's all right now."

Dawnay, submerged in one of the armchairs, looked up and caught Reinhart's eye. Geers went on talking as he sprinkled bitters into one of the glasses.

"We've nothing but ironmongery here, really, out in this wilderness. We do a good deal of the country's rocketry, of course, and there's a lot of complex stuff goes into that, but I wouldn't mind changing into some old clothes and getting back to lab work. Is that pink enough?"

He placed the filled glass on his desk on a level with Dawnay's ear. Its base was tucked into a little paper mat to prevent it from marking the polish.

"Fine, thanks." Dawnay could just see it and reach it

without getting up. Geers reached into the cabinet for another bottle.

"And sherry for you, Reinhart!" Sherry was poured. "One gets so stuck behind an executive desk. Cheers. . . . Nice to see you again, Madeleine. What have you been up to?"

"D.N.A., chromosomes, the origin of life caper." Dawnay spoke gruffly. She put her glass back on the desk and lit a cigarette, blowing the smoke down her nose like a man. "I've got into a bit of a cul-de-sac. I was just going away to think when I met Ernest."

"Stay and think here." Geers gave her a nice smile and then switched it off. "Where's Fleming got to?"

"He'll be over in a minute," said Reinhart.

"You've a bright boy, though an awkward one," Geers informed him. "In fact you've a bit of an awkward squad altogether, haven't you?"

"We've also got results." Reinhart was unruffled. "It's started printing out."

Geers raised his eyebrows.

"Has it indeed? What's it printing?"

They told him.

"Very odd. Very odd indeed. And what happened when you fed it back?"

"A whole mass of figures came out."

"What are they?"

"No idea. We've been going over them, but so far . . ." Reinhart shrugged.

Fleming walked in with a perfunctory sort of knock.

"This the right party?"

"Come in, come in," said Geers, as if to a promising but gauche student. "Thirsty?"

"When am I not?"

Fleming was carrying the print-out sheets. He threw them down on the desk to take his drink.

"Any joy?" Reinhart asked.

"Not a crumb. There's something wrong with him, or wrong with us."

"Is that the latest?" asked Geers, straightening the papers and bending over them to look. "You'll have to do a lot of analysis on this, won't you? If we can help in any way—"

"It ought to be simple." Fleming was subdued and preoccupied as though he was trying to see something just beyond him. "I'm sure there ought to be something quite easy. Something we'd recognize."

"There was a section here—" Reinhart took the sheets and shuffled through them. "Seems vaguely familiar. Have another look at that lot, Madeleine."

Madeleine looked.

"What sort of thing do you expect?" Geers asked Fleming, as he poured a drink.

"I don't know. I don't know what the game is yet."

"You wouldn't be interested in the carbon atom, would you?" Dawnay looked up out of her chair with a faint smile.

"The carbon atom!"

"It's not expressed the way we'd put it; but, yes, it could be a description of the structure of carbon." She blew smoke out of her nose. "Is that what you meant, Ernest?"

Reinhart and Geers bent over the sheets again.

"I'm a bit rusty, of course," said Geers.

"But it could be, couldn't it?"

"Yes, it could be. I wonder if there's anything else."

"There won't be anything else," Fleming said. He seemed very sure, and no longer preoccupied. "Take it from the beginning. Think of the hydrogen question. He's asking us what form of life we belong to. All these other figures are other possible ways of making living creatures. But we don't know anything about them, because life on this earth is based on the carbon atom."

"Well, it's a theory," said Reinhart. "What do we do now? Feed back the figures relating to carbon?"

"If we want him to know what stuff we're made of. He won't forget."

"Aren't you presupposing an intelligence?" said Geers, who had no time for fancy stuff.

"Look," Fleming turned to him. "The message we picked up did two things. It stipulated a design. It then gave us a lot of basic information to feed into the computer when we'd built it. We didn't know what that information was at the time, but we're beginning to know now. With what was in the original program, and what we tell him, he can learn anything he likes about us. And he can learn to act upon it. If that's not an intelligence, I don't know what is."

"It's a very useful machine," Dawnay said. Fleming turned on her.

"Just because it doesn't have protoplasm, no chemist can imagine it as a thinking agency!"

Dawnay sniffed.

"What are you afraid of, John?" Reinhart asked.

"Its purpose. It hasn't been put here for fun. It hasn't been put here for our benefit."

"You've a neurosis about it," said Dawnay.

"You think so?"

"You've been given a windfall; use it." She appealed to Reinhart. "If you use Dr. Fleming's method and feed back the carbon formula, you may get something else. You may build up to more complicated structures, and you've got a marvellous calculating machine to handle them. That's all it is. Apply it."

"John?" Reinhart turned to Fleming.

"You can count me out."

"Would you like to tackle it, Madeleine?" said the Professor.

"Why don't you?" she asked him.

"It is a long step from astronomy to bio-synthesis. If your university can spare you. . . ."

"We can accommodate you." Geers, when he moved, moved in quickly. "You said you were at a dead end."

Dawnay considered.

"Would you work with me, Dr. Fleming?"

Fleming shook his head. "There's something needs thinking out first—before we start at all."

"I don't think so."

"I've gone as far as I want. Further, in fact, to show I could deliver the goods. But for me the road ends here."

Reinhart opened his mouth to speak, but Fleming turned away.

"All right," Reinhart said. "Will you tackle it, Madeleine?"

They made the rest of the arrangements when Fleming had gone.

Dawnay moved in the following week and set to work on the computer, with Bridger and Christine helping her and Geers now full of enthusiasm and attention. Fleming returned to London and Judy saw nothing of him; being a serving officer tied by oath, she had to stay where she was ordered. In a way it was a relief to be free of their equivocal relationship. After their one night in his chalet she had kept him, as far as possible, at arm's length, for she was torn between the instinct of being in love and the feeling that she did not want him to take her for something other than she was. At least while he was away she did not have to report on him—only on Bridger, and that she minded less.

Bridger gave no clue to any of them. Judy kept away from the moor and Quadring's patrols found nothing. Bridger himself grew steadily more miserable and withdrawn. He worked competently but without enthusiasm, spending his spare time watching the late migrations from the Thorholm nestings.

Autumn darkened into winter. Back in London, Fleming settled down to check the entire message and all his original calculations. Monitoring of the signal went on from Boulder-shaw Fell, but it was now only routine. The code was always the same; Fleming could find nothing in all his workings to give him a line on what he feared.

At Thorness Dawnay made better progress.

"The boy was right about one thing," she told Reinhart. "The question and answer business. We fed in the carbon atom figures and immediately it began to print out stuff on the structure of protein molecules."

When she fed that back, it started asking more questions. It offered the formulas of a variety of different structures based on proteins, and it clearly wanted to be given more information about them. Dawnay set her department at Edinburgh to work. Between them they put back into the machine everything they knew about cell formation. By the New Year it had given them the molecular structure of hemoglobin.

"Why hemoglobin?" asked Judy, who had followed her to Edinburgh in an attempt to understand what was happening.

"The hemoglobin in the blood carries the electricity supply to your brain."

"He offered you that as one of a set of alternatives?" Reinhart asked. They had all three met in Dawnay's study in one of the old grey university buildings because she had told them she wanted a Ministry decision.

"Yes," she said. "As before. And we fed that one back."

"So now it knows what our brains run on."

"It knows a great deal more than that by now."

Reinhart stroked his chin with his little fingers.

"Why does it want to?"

"You're under Fleming's influence, aren't you?" Dawnay said reprovingly. "It doesn't 'want to know' anything. It calculates logical responses from information which we give it, and from what it already possesses. Because it's a calculating machine."

"Is that all?" Judy, from what little she knew, shared Reinhart's doubts.

"Let's try to be scientific about it, shall we?" Dawnay said. "Not mystical."

"Professor Reinhart, do you ...?"

Reinhart looked uncomfortable. "Fleming would say it wants to know what sort of intelligence it's up against—what sort of computers we are, how big our brains are, how we feed them, what sort of beings we house them in."

"Young Fleming's emotionally disturbed, if you ask me," said Dawnay. She waved her hand towards shelves piled with folders of paper. "We've got so much now we can hardly see daylight, but I've an idea what it's all about, which is why I wanted you. I think it's given us the basic plan of a living cell."

"A what?"

"Not that it's any good to us. We have this huge amount of numbers. It's far too complex for us ever to understand fully."

"Why should it be?"

"Look at the size of it! We can recognize odd bits—odd bits of chromosome structure and so on—but it would take years to analyze it all."

"If that's what you're meant to do."

"What do you mean?"

Reinhart stroked his chin again. His fingers, Judy noticed, had little dimples on them. There was something very comforting and humane about him, even when he was out of his depth in theory.

"I want to talk to Fleming and Osborne," he said.

He got them together, eventually, in Osborne's office. By that time he had all the facts at his fingertips and he wanted action. Fleming looked older and slack, as though the elastic inside him had run down. His face was pouchy and his eyes bloodshot.

Osborne sat back elegantly and listened to Reinhart.

"Professor Dawnay's come up with what appears to be the detailed chromosome structure of a cell."

"A living cell?"

"Yes. It's something we've never known before: the order in which the nucleic acid molecules are arranged."

"So you could actually build one up?"

"If we can use the computer as a control, and if we can make a chemical device to act on the instructions as they come up—in fact, if we can make a D.N.A. synthesizer—then I think we can begin to build living tissue."

"That's what the biologists have been after for years, isn't it?"

"You really want to let it make a living organism?" Fleming asked.

"Dawnay wants to try," said Reinhart. "Fleming doesn't. What do we do?"

"Why don't you?" Osborne asked Fleming quite casually, as though it was a matter of passing interest.

"Because we're being pushed into this by a form of compulsion," said Fleming wearily. "I've been saying that ever since the day we built the damn thing, and I can find nothing to make me think otherwise. Madeleine Dawnay imagines you can just use it as a piece of lab equipment: she's a cheerful optimist. If she wants to play with D.N.A. synthesis, let her stay in her university and do it. Don't let her use the computer. Or, if you must, at least wipe the memory first."

"Reinhart?" Osborne turned languidly to the Professor. Whatever impression Fleming had made on him did not show.

"I don't know," said Reinhart. "I simply don't know. It comes from an alien intelligence, but—"

" 'We can always pull out the plug'?" Fleming quoted for him. "Look, we built it to prove the content of the message. Right? Well, we've done that. We operated it to discover its purpose. Now we know that too."

"Do we?"

"I do! It's an intellectual fifth column from another world—from another form of existence. It's got the seeds of life in it, and also the seeds of destruction."

"Have you any grounds at all for saying that?" asked Osborne.

"No tangible grounds."

"Then how can we—?"

"All right, go on!" Fleming heaved himself up and made for the door. "Go on and see what happens—but don't come crying to me!"

six

ALERT

FOR ALL THAT, he went to Thorness in the spring—he said, to visit Judy, but in fact from morbid curiosity. He kept away from the computer block but Judy and Bridger, separately, told him what was happening. A new bay added to the building was filled by Dawnay with elaborate laboratory equipment, including a chemical synthesizer and an electron microscope. As well as Christine, she had several post-graduate students of her own at work on the project, and all the money she could reasonably need. Reinhart and Osborne between them had got substantial backing.

"And what about you?" Fleming asked Judy.

They sat on the cliff-top, inside the camp, above the jetty.

"I go round with the seasons." She smiled at him tenderly but warily. She was shocked by the change in him, by his blotchiness and general deterioration, and the look of utter defeat that hung about him. She longed to hold him and to give herself to him. At the same time she wanted to keep him away at the distance of their original friendship, which seemed to her the limit to which she could honorably go so long as she was acting a part of which she was ashamed. She had even tried to resign her commission when she heard he was coming back, but it had not been allowed. She knew too much by now to be released, and far too much to be able to tell him the truth.

Bridger had stayed in the camp, working all winter, and had made no suspicious move; but Kaufmann's car had been seen several times in the neighborhood and the tall, im-probably-dressed chauffeur had been watching arrivals and departures at the station and on at least one occasion had telephoned Bridger. After this Bridger had looked more unhappy than ever and had taken to having copies of the computer's output retyped for his own use. Judy had not spotted that, but Quadring had. Nothing had come of it, however. The white yacht had not reappeared, and indeed could hardly have been expected to during a winter of gales and blizzards and wild storm-swept seas. Early in the spring Naval patrols were stepped up and reinforced by helicopters, and the yacht, if it ever had anything to do with it, was scared away. But if security was increasing, so was the value of the information, and there was a general feeling among Judy's superiors that the stakes were rising.

Judy, having nothing to do but watch, had time—as usual—on her hands, and it suited Quadring to have Fleming covered. So she sat on the top of the cliff with him, pretending to be happy to see him and feeling bitterly divided against herself.

"When are you going to hold a press conference?" was his next question.

"I don't know. This year, next year, sometime."

"All this ought to have been referred to the public months ago."

"But if it's a secret?"

"It's a secret because it suits the politicians. That's why it's going the wrong way. Once you take science out of the hands of scientists and hand it over to them, it's doomed." He jerked his shoulder at the compound. "If that lot isn't doomed already."

"What are you going to do about it?" she asked him.

He gazed down at the waves breaking a hundred and fifty feet below them and then turned and grinned at her for the first time in a very long while.

"Take you sailing," he said.

It was one of those early false springs which sometimes come unexpectedly at the beginning of March. The sun shone, a light breeze blew from the south-west and the sea was beautiful. Fleming assumed that Judy had nothing else to do and they sailed every day on the bay and up the coast as far as Greenstone Point and down to the mouth of Gairloch. The water was freezing cold but the sands were warm and in the afternoons they used to beach the boat in any likely-looking cove, splash ashore and lie basking in the sun.

After a few days, Fleming looked healthier. He grew more cheerful and seemed able to forget for hours at a time the cloud that hung over his mind. He obviously sensed that she no longer wanted to be made love to and fairly soon fell back into the role of affectionate and dominating big brother. Judy held her breath and hoped for the best.

Then, one hot and glinting afternoon, they pulled into a tiny bay on the seaward side of the island, Thorholm. The rocks rose sheer behind, reflecting the heat of the sun back on to them as they lay side by side on the sand. All they could see was the blue sky above. The only things to be heard were the heavy, gentle sound of the waves and the calling of sea-birds. After a while Fleming sat up and pulled off his thick sweater.

"You'd better take yours off, too," he told her.

She hesitated, then pulled it off over her head and lay in her shorts and bra, feeling the breeze and sun playing on her body. Fleming took no notice of her at first.

"This is better than computers." She smiled with her eyes shut. "Is this where Bridger comes?"

"Yeah."

"I don't see any birds."

"I can see one." He rolled over and kissed her. She lay unresponsively and he turned away again, leaving a hand on her midriff.

"Why doesn't he go round with you?" she asked.

"He doesn't want to barge in on us."

She scowled up into the sun.

"He doesn't like me."

"It's mutual, isn't it?"

She did not answer. His hand moved down to her thigh.

"Don't, John."

"Signed a pledge for the Girl Guides?" He sounded suddenly cross and peevish.

"I'm not being prissy, only . . ."

"Only what?"

"You don't know me."

"Hell! You don't give me much chance, do you?"

She got up abruptly and looked about her. There was a cleft in the rocks behind them.

"Let's explore."

"If you like."

"Is that a cave there?"

"Yes."

"Let's go and look."

"We're not dressed for it."

"Aren't you formal?" She smiled at him and pulled on her sweater, and threw him his. "Here!"

"They go hellish deep into the cliff. You need caving gear, like pot-holers."

"We won't go far."

"O.K." He hoisted himself to his feet and shook off his bad temper. "Come on."

The cave widened inside and then tapered off as it went deeper into the rock. The floor was sandy at first and strewn with stones. As they went further in they found themselves scrambling over boulders. It was cold and very quiet inside. Fleming brought a torch from the boat and shone it on the rock walls ahead of them; patches of seeping water glittered in its light. After a few dozen yards they came to another chamber with a large pool at the far end. Judy knelt down and gazed into the water.

"There's a piece of cord here."

"What?" Fleming crouched beside her and looked down over the pool's lip. One end of a length of white cord was knotted and held down by a boulder at the edge while the rest of it ran down into the water. Fleming pulled on it: it was quite taut.

"Is it deep?" Judy peered down the beam of the torch but could see nothing but blackness beneath the pool's surface.

"Hold the torch, will you?"

Fleming took both hands to the cord and pulled it slowly up. On the end was a large thermos-type canister weighted with stones. Judy shone the torch on to the lid.

"It's Dennis's!" Fleming exclaimed.

"Dennis Bridger's?"

"Yes. He bought it for picnics. It has that mark like a zig-zag on it."

"Why should he leave it?" Judy spoke more to herself than Fleming.

"I don't know. Better ask him."

Judy opened the lid and felt inside.

"For goodness sake!"

"It's full of papers." She pulled some out and held them under the torch. "Do you recognize them?"

"It's our stuff." Fleming looked at them incredulously. "Copied. We'd better take them back to him."

"No." Judy put the papers back in the flask and fastened it.

"What are you going to do?"

"Leave it where we found it."

"But that's absurd."

"Please, John, I know what I'm doing." She picked up the canister and threw it back into the water, while he watched sulkily, holding the torch.

"What *are* you doing?" he demanded, but she would not tell him.

When they got back to camp they found Reinhart there. He buttonholed Fleming outside the office block.

"Can you spare me a minute, John?"

"I'm not here."

"Look, John," the Professor looked hurt. "We're stuck."

"Good."

"Madeleine's managed a D.N.A synthesis. Cells have actually formed."

"You must be proud of her."

"Single cells. But they don't live, or only a few minutes."

"Then your luck's in. If they did live they'd be under the control of the machine."

"How?"

"I don't know how. But they'd be no friends of ours."

"A single cell can't do much damage." Judy had never heard Reinhart openly pleading before. "Come anyway."

Fleming stuck his lower lip out obstinately.

"Go on, John." Judy faced round to him. "Or are you afraid they'll bite you?"

Fleming hunched up his shoulders and went with the Professor.

Judy walked straight into Quadring's office and reported.

"Ah," said Quadring. "That makes sense. Where is he now?"

They phoned the computer room, but Bridger had just left.

"Tell the F.S.P. boys to find him and tail him," Quadring told his orderly. "But he's not to see them."

"Very good, sir." The orderly swivelled his chair round to the switchboard.

"Who's on cliff patrol?"

"B Section, sir."

"Tell them to watch the path down to the jetty."

"Are they to stop him?"

"No. They're to let him go out if he wants to, and tell us." Quadring turned to Judy. "His friend phoned him today. They must want something urgently to run a risk like that."

"Why should they?"

"Maybe they've a deal on. We listened, of course. It was mostly pretty guarded, but they said something about the new route."

Judy shrugged. This was beyond her. Quadring waited until the orderly had telephoned the field security corporal and gone out to deliver his message to the B Section commander. Then he led Judy over to a wall-map.

"The old route was via the island. Bridger could take stuff there and dump it without having to check out of camp. When needed it could be picked up by the yacht. One of Kaufmann's colleagues probably has an ocean-going jog that can anchor well off and send a boat in to rendezvous with Bridger."

"The white one?"

"The one you saw."

"Then that's why—?" It was a long while since the shooting on the moor, but it came back clearly to her as she looked at the map.

"Kaufmann had to have someone to tip off Bridger and keep in touch with the yacht. He used his chauffeur, who used the car."

"And shot at me?"

"It was probably he. It was a silly thing to do, but I expect he thought he could lose the body in the sea."

Judy felt herself turn cold inside her thick sweater.

"And the new route?"

"What with the weather and us, they can't use the yacht any more, so they can't get to the island. Bridger still uses it as a hiding-place, as you've found out, but he'll have to bring the stuff back and smuggle it out of the main gate, which is riskier."

Judy looked out into the cold dusk that was falling on the warmth of the day. Low square roofs of research buildings jutted blackly from the darkening grass of the headland. Lights shone in a few hut windows, and above them the enormous arch of the sky began to dim and disappear.

Somewhere Dawnay was working in a lighted underground room, dedicated and unaware of the consequences of what she was doing. Somewhere Fleming was arguing with Reinhart about the future. And somewhere, alone and miserable and perhaps shaking with hidden fear, Bridger was changing into oilskins, fisherman's jersey and wading boots, to go out into the night.

"You'd better put on something thicker," said Quadring. "I'm going too."

It was warm in Dawnay's laboratory. Lights and equipment had been on for weeks and were slowly beating the air-conditioning.

"It smells of biologist," said Fleming as he and Reinhart walked in. Dawnay was peering down the eyepiece of a microscope. She glanced up casually.

"Hallo, Dr. Fleming." She spoke as though he had been out simply for a cup of tea. "It looks a bit like a witch's soup-kitchen, I'm afraid."

"Anything in the broth?" Reinhart asked.

"We've just been preparing a new batch. Like to stop and see?" The microscope had an electronic display tube, like a television screen. "You can watch on there if anything should happen."

"New culture?" asked one of her assistants, fitting a needle to a hypodermic syringe.

"Take some from there, and watch the temperature of your needle."

Dawnay explained her progress to Fleming while the assistant took a small bottle from a refrigerator.

"We do the synthesis round about freezing-point, and they come to life at normal temperature." She seemed perfectly friendly and untouched by what Fleming thought. The assistant pierced the rubber cap of the bottle with the hypodermic needle and drew up some fluid into the syringe.

"What form of life have they?" asked Fleming.

"They're a very simple piece of protoplasm, with a nucleus. What do you want—feelers and heads?"

She took the syringe, squeezed a drop of fluid out on to a slide and clipped the slide on the viewing plate.

"How do they behave?"

"They move about for a bit, then they die. That's the trouble. We probably haven't found the right nutrients yet."

She put her eye to the microscope and focused up. As she moved the slide under the lens they could see individual cells forming—pale discs with a darker center—and swimming about in the screen for a few seconds. They stopped moving and were obviously dead by the time Dawnay changed to a higher magnification. She pulled the slide out.

"Let's try the other batch." She looked round at them with a tired smile. "This is liable to go on all night."

Soon after midnight Bridger was seen leaving his chalet. The cliff patrol watched him go down the path to the jetty. They did not challenge him, but telephoned through to the guard-room from an old gun emplacement at the top of the path. Quadring and Judy had joined them by the time Bridger pushed out from the jetty. His outboard motor sneezed twice, then spluttered steadily away across the water. There was some moonlight, and they could see the boat moving out over the bay.

"Aren't you going to follow him?" asked Judy.

"No. He'll be back." Quadring called softly to the sentries. "Stay up top and keep out of sight. It may be a long time."

Judy looked out to sea, where the little boat was losing itself among the waves.

The moon went long before dawn, and although they were wearing greatcoats they were bitterly cold.

"Why doesn't he come back?" she asked Quadring.

"Doesn't want to navigate in the dark."

"If he knows we're here . . ."

"Why should he? He's only waiting for a spot of daylight."

At four o'clock the sentries changed. It was still dark. At five the first pearl-pale greyness began to appear in the sky. The night duty cook clanked round with containers of tea. He left one in the guard-room, another at the main gate, another at the computer building.

Dawnay pushed her glasses up on to her forehead and drank noisily.

"Why don't you pack it in, Madeleine?" Reinhart yawned.

"I will soon." She pushed another slide under the lens. There was a tray half-full of used slides on the table beside her, and Fleming sat perched on the corner, disapproving but intrigued.

"Wait." She moved the slide a fraction. "There's one!"

On the display tube a cell could be seen forming.

"He's doing better than most," said Reinhart.

"He's getting pretty big." Dawnay switched the magnification. "Look—it's beginning to divide!"

The cell elongated into two lobes which stretched and broke apart, and then each lobe broke again into new cells.

"It's reproducing!" Dawnay leaned back and watched the screen. Her face was puckered with fatigue and happiness. "We've made life. We've actually made a reproductive cell. Look—there it goes again . . . How about that, Dr. Fleming?"

Fleming was standing up and watching the screen intently.

"How are you going to stop it?"

"I'm not going to stop it. I want to see what it does."

"It's developing into quite a coherent structure," Reinhart observed.

Fleming clenched his fists upon the table. "Kill it."

"What?" Dawnay looked at him in mild surprise.

"Kill it while you can."

"It's perfectly well under control."

"Is it? Look at the way it's growing." Fleming pointed at the rapidly doubling mass of cells on the screen.

"That's all right. You could grow an amoeba the size of the earth in a week if you could feed it fast enough."

"This isn't an amoeba."

"It's remarkably like one."

"Kill it!" Fleming looked round at their anxious unyielding faces, and then back at the screen. He picked up the heavy container in which the tea had been brought and smashed it down on the viewing plate of the microscope. A clatter of metal and glass rang through the hushed room. The viewing panel went dead.

"You young fool!" Dawnay almost cried.

"John—what are you doing?" Reinhart moved forward to stop him, but too late. Fleming pulled the splintered remains of the slide out of the microscope, threw them to the floor and ground his heel into them.

"You're mad! All mad! All blind raving mad!" he shouted at them, and ran to the door.

He ran out through the computer room, along the entrance corridor and on to the porch. There he stood for a minute, panting, while the cold air hit him in the face. To come into the open at the pale beginning of day, after a night in the concentration of Dawnay's room, was like waking from a nightmare. He took several gulps of air and strode off across the grass to the headland, trying to clear his brain and his lungs.

In the distance, he could hear an outboard motor.

He changed direction and walked furiously towards the spot where the path from the jetty reached the top of the cliff. The sound of the boat came steadily nearer in the growing light, drawing him like a magnet; but at the cliff-top he stumbled upon Quadring, Judy and two soldiers who were lying in wait on the grass. He drew up short.

"What the devil's going on?" He gazed at them wildly and uncomprehendingly. Quadring stood up, binoculars swinging from his chest.

"Get back. Get away from here."

The motor had stopped. The boat was gliding into the quay below them. Judy started to scramble to her feet, but Quadring motioned her down.

"Go away, John, please!" she said in an agonized voice.

"Go away? Go away? What the hell's everyone up to?"

"Be quiet," ordered Quadring. "And keep back from the edge."

"We're waiting for Dennis Bridger," Judy said.

"For Dennis?" He was in a state of shock and only took in slowly what was happening.

"I'd push off," Quadring advised him. "Unless you want to witness his arrest."

"His arrest?" Fleming pivoted slowly from Quadring back to Judy as the meaning dawned on him.

"You *are* all mad!"

"Keep back and keep quiet," said Quadring.

Fleming moved towards the edge of the cliff, but on a nod from Quadring the two soldiers took an elbow each and pulled him back. He stood piniomed between them, frustrated and desperate. Cold sweat trickled down his face, and all he could see was Judy.

"Are *you* in on this?"

"You know what we found." She avoided his eyes.

"*Are* you?"

"Yes," she said, and walked away to stand beside Quadring.

They let Bridger get right to the top of the path, lugging the heavy canister from the cave. As his head came up over the edge, Fleming shouted to him:

"Dennis!"

One of the soldiers clamped his hand over Fleming's

mouth, but by that time Bridger had seen them. Before Quadring could get on to him, he dropped the canister and ran.

He ran fast for a man in sea-boots, along the path at the edge of the cliff. Quadring and the soldiers pounded after him. Fleming ran after them, and Judy after him. It was like a stag-hunt in the cold, early light. They could not see where Bridger was going. He got to the end of the headland, and then turned and slipped. His wet rubber boots flailed at the grass at the edge, and then he was over. Five seconds later, he was a broken body on the rocks at the sea's edge.

Fleming joined the soldiers on the cliff-top, looking down. As Judy came up to him he turned away without speaking and walked slowly back towards the camp. He still had a splinter of glass from the microscope in his finger. Stopping for a moment, he pulled it out, and then walked on.

seven

ANALYSIS

GENERAL Vandenberg by this time had his allied headquarters accommodated in a bomb-proof bunker under the Ministry of Defense. His functions as co-ordinator had gradually expanded until he was now virtual director of local air strategy. However little they liked this, Her Majesty's Government submitted to it in the face of an international situation growing steadily worse: the operations room next to his private office was dominated by a wall map of the world showing traces of an alarming number of orbital satellites of unknown potentiality. As well as the American and Russian vehicles, some of which certainly carried nuclear armament, there was an increasing traffic put up by other powers whose relations with each other and with the West were often near sparking-point. Public morality thinned like the atmosphere as men and machines rose higher, and year by year the uneasy truce which was supposed to control the upper air and the spaces above it came nearer to falling into anarchy.

Vandenberg, through the Ministry of Defense, now had call on all local establishments, including Thorness. He rode gently but with determination, and watched carefully what went on. When he received reports of Bridger's death, he sent for Osborne.

Osborne's position was now very different from what it had been in the early days of Bouldershaw Fell. Far from representing a ministry in the ascendant, he and Ratcliff now had to bow before the wishes of the war men, contriving as best they could to keep some say in their own affairs. Not that Osborne was easily ruffled. He stood before Vandenberg's desk as immaculate and suave as ever.

"Sit down," Vandenberg waved him to a chair. "Rest your feet."

They went over the circumstances of Bridger's death move by move as though they were playing a game of chess; the general probing, and Osborne on the defensive but denying nothing and making no excuses.

"You have to admit," said Vandenberg at the end of it, "your Ministry's snarled it up good and hard."

"That's a matter of opinion."

Vandenberg pushed back his chair and went to look at his wall map.

"We can't afford to play schools, Osborne. We could use that machine. It's built on military premises, with military aid. We could use it in the public interest."

"What the hell do you think Reinhart's doing?" Osborne was eventually ruffled. "I'm sure your people would like to get your hands on it. I'm sure we all seem anarchistic to you because we haven't got drilled minds. I know there's been a tragedy. But they're doing something vitally important up there."

"And we're not?"

"You can't suddenly stop them in their tracks."

"Your Cabinet would say we can."

"Have you asked them?"

"No. But they would."

"At least—" Osborne calmed down again—"at least let us finish this present project, if we give you certain guarantees."

As soon as he was back in his own office he telephoned Reinhart.

"For heaven's sake patch up some sort of a truce with Geers," he told him.

Reinhart's meeting with the Director was depressingly similar to Osborne's with Vandenberg, but Reinhart was a better strategist than Geers. After two grinding hours they sent for Judy.

"We've got to strengthen the security here, Miss Adamson."

"You don't expect me—?" She broke off.

Geers glinted at her through his spectacles and she turned for understanding to Reinhart.

"My position here would be intolerable. Everyone trusted me, and now I turn out to be a security nark."

"I always knew that," said Reinhart gently. "And Professor Dawnay has guessed. She accepts it."

"Dr. Fleming doesn't."

"He wasn't meant to," said Geers.

"He accepted me as something else."

"Everyone knows you had a job to do," Reinhart looked unhappily at his fingers. "And everyone respects it."

"I don't respect it."

"I beg your pardon?" Geers took off his glasses and blinked at her as if she had gone out of focus. She was trembling.

"I've hated it from the start. It was perfectly clear that everyone here was perfectly trustworthy, except Bridger."

"Even Fleming?"

"Dr. Fleming's worth ten of anyone else I've met! He needs protecting from his own indiscretion, and I've tried to do that. But I will not go on spying on him."

"What does Fleming say?" Reinhart asked.

"He doesn't talk to me since . . ."

"Where is he?" asked Geers.

"Drinking, I suppose."

"Still on that, is he?" Geers raised his eyes to display hopelessness, and the gesture made Judy suddenly, furiously angry.

"What do you expect him to take to, after what's happened? Bingo?" She turned again, with faint hope, to Reinhart. "I've grown very fond of—of all of them. I admire them."

"My dear girl, I'm in no position . . ." Reinhart avoided her eyes. "It's probably as well it is out in the open."

Judy found she was standing to attention. She faced Geers.

"Can I be relieved?"

"No."

"Then may I have a different assignment?"

"No."

"Then may I resign my commission?"

"Not during a state of National Emergency." Geers's eyes, she noticed, were set too close together. They stared straight at her, expressionless with authority. "If it weren't for your very good record, I'd say you were immature for this job. As it is, I think you're merely unsettled by exposure to the scientific mind, especially such an ebullient and irresponsible mind as Fleming's."

"He's not irresponsible."

"No?"

"Not about important things."

"The important things at this establishment are the means of survival. We're under very great pressure."

"To the military, all things are military," said Reinhart icily. He walked across the room and looked out of the window, his little hands clasped uneasily behind his back. "It's a bleak place here, you know. We all feel the strain of it."

For some time after this outburst Geers was unusually agreeable. He did everything he possibly could for Dawnay, rushing through new equipment to replace what Fleming had damaged and generally identifying himself with what she was doing. Reinhart fought hard to retain his foothold and Judy went back to her duty with a sort of glum despair. She even screwed up her courage to see Fleming, but his room was empty and so were the three whisky bottles by his bed. With one exception, he spoke to no one in the days that followed Bridger's death.

Dawnay had gone straight back to work, with Christine to help her with the relatively simple calculations needed from the computer. Within a week they had another successful synthesis, and they were watching it, late in the evening, in the repaired microscope, when the door of the laboratory was pushed open and Fleming stood unsteadily inside.

Dawnay straightened up and looked at him. He wore no jacket or tie, his shirt was crumpled and dirty and he had seven days' growth of stubble round his jaw. He might have been on the verge of *delirium tremens*.

"What do you want?"

He gave her a glazed stare and swayed a step forward into the room.

"Keep out of here, please."

"I see you've new equipment," he said thickly, with a fatuous twitching smile.

"That's right. Now will you leave us?"

"Bridger's dead." He smiled stupidly at her.

"I know."

"You go on as though nothing had happened." It was difficult to understand what he said. "But he's dead. He won't come back any more."

"We've all heard, Dr. Fleming."

He swayed another pace into the room. "What you doing here?"

"This is private. Will you please go?" She got up and advanced grimly towards him. He stood blinking at her, the smile fading from his face.

"He was my oldest friend. He was a fool, but he was my—"

"Dr. Fleming," she said quickly. "Will you go, or do I call the guards?"

He looked at her for a moment, as if trying to see her through mist, then shrugged and shuffled out. She followed him to the door and locked it behind him.

"We can do without that," she said to Christine.

Fleming found his way back to his hut, took an unfinished bottle of whisky from his desk drawer and poured it down the sink. Then he fell on to his bed and slept for twenty-four hours. The following evening he shaved and bathed and started to pack.

The new experiment grew fantastically. Within a few hours Dawnay had to transfer it from its microscope slide to a small nutrient bath, and the following morning it had to be moved into a larger bath. It continued to double itself during the whole of the day that Fleming slept, and by the evening Dawnay was forced to appeal for help to Geers, who took over the problem with a proprietary air and caused his workshop wing to build a deep, electrically-heated tank with a drip-feed channel into its open top and an inspection window in the middle of its front panel. Towards dawn the new creature was lifted by four assistants from its outgrown bath and placed in the tank.

In its new environment it grew to about the size of a sheep and then stopped. It seemed perfectly healthy and harmless, but it was not pretty.

Reinhart came to a decision that morning and went to see Dawnay. She was in her laboratory still, checking the feed control at the top of the tank. He hovered around until she had finished.

"Is it still alive?"

"And kicking." Apart from looking pale and taut around the eyes and mouth, she showed no sign of tiredness. "A day and a half since it was a smear on a slide: I told you there was no reason an organism shouldn't grow as fast as you like if you can get enough food into it."

"But it's stopped growing now?" Reinhart peered respectfully into the inspection port, through which he could see a dark form moving in the murk of the tank.

"It seems to have a pre-determined size and shape," Dawnay said, picking up a set of X-rays and handing them to him. "There's nothing much to see from there. There's no bone formation. It's like a great jelly, but it's got this eye and some sort of cortex—which looks like a very complicated nerve ganglia."

"No other features?" Reinhart held up the X-rays and squinted at them.

"Possibly some rudimentary attempt at a pair of legs, though you could hardly call them more than a division of tissue."

Reinhart put down the plates and frowned.

"How does it feed?"

"Takes it in through the skin. It lives in nutrient fluid and absorbs straight into its body cells. Very simple, very efficient."

"And the computer?"

Dawnay looked surprised.

"What about the computer?"

"Has it reacted at all?"

"How could it?"

"I don't know." Reinhart frowned at her anxiously. "Has it?"

"No. It's been entirely quiet."

The Professor walked into the computer control room and back again, his head down, his gaze on his neat shoecaps as they twinkled before him. It was as yet early morning and very quiet. He clasped his hands behind him and spoke without looking up at Dawnay.

"I want Fleming back on this."

Dawnay did not answer for a moment, then she said: "It's perfectly under control."

"Whose control?"

"Mine."

He looked up at her with an effort.

"We're on borrowed time, Madeleine. The people here want us out."

"In the middle of this?"

"No. The Ministry have fought for that, but we've got to work as a team and show results."

"Good grief! Aren't those results?" Dawnay pointed a short, bony finger at the tank. "We're in the middle of the biggest thing of the century—we're making life!"

"I know," Reinhart said, shifting uncomfortably from foot to foot. "But where is it taking us?"

"We've a lot to find out."

"And we can't afford any more accidents."

"I can manage."

"You're not on your own, Madeleine." Reinhart spoke with a kind of soft tenseness. "We're all involved in this."

"I can manage," she repeated.

"You can't divorce it from its origin—from the computer."

"Of course I can't. But Christine understands the computer, and I have her."

"She understands the basic arithmetic, but there's a higher logic, or so I think. Only Fleming understands that."

"I'm not having John Fleming reeling in here, breaking up my work and my equipment." Dawnay's voice rose. Reinhart regarded her quietly. He was still tense, but with a determination which had carried him a long way.

"We can't all do what we want entirely." He spoke so brusquely that Dawnay looked at him again in surprise. "I'm still in charge of this program—just. And I will be so long as we work as a team and make sense. That means having Fleming here."

"Drunk or sober?"

"Good God, Madeleine, if we can't trust each other, who can we trust?"

Dawnay was about to protest, and then stopped.

"All right. So long as he behaves himself and sticks to his own side of the job."

"Thank you, my dear." Reinhart smiled.

When he left the laboratory he went straight to Geers.

"But Fleming has notified me that he's leaving," Geers said. "I just sent Miss Adamson over to the computer to make sure he doesn't deliver a parting shot."

Fleming, however, was not at the computer. Judy stood in the control room, hesitating, when Dawnay came out to her.

"Hallo. Want to see Cyclops?"

"Why do you call it Cyclops?"

"Because of his physical characteristics." Dawnay seemed completely relaxed. "Don't they educate girls nowadays? Come along, he's in here."

"Must I?"

"Not interested?"

"Yes, but—"

Judy felt dazed. She had not taken in the progress of the experiment. For the past two days she had thought of almost nothing but Fleming and Bridger and her own hopeless position, and so far as she had any image at all of Dawnay's creation, it was microscopic and unrelated to her own life. She followed the older woman through into the laboratory without thinking and without expecting anything.

The tank confused her slightly. It was something she had not reckoned with.

"Look inside," said Dawnay.

Judy looked down in through the open top of the big tank, quite unprepared for what she was going to see. The creature was not unlike an elongated jellyfish, without limbs or tentacles but with a vague sort of bifurcation at one end and an enlargement that might be a head at the other. It floated in liquid, a twitching, quivering mass of protoplasm, its surface greeny-yellow, slimy and glistening. And in the middle of what might be its head was set—huge, lidless and colorless—an eye.

Judy felt violently sick and then panic-stricken. She turned away retching and stared at Dawnay as if she too were something in a nightmare, then she clamped her hand over her mouth and ran out of the room.

She ran straight across the compound to Fleming's hut, flung the door open and went inside.

Fleming was pushing some last things into a hold-all, his cases packed and standing on the floor. He looked across coldly at her as she stood panting and heaving in the doorway.

"Not again," he said.

"John!" She could hardly speak at first. Her head was turning and singing and her throat felt full of phlegm. "John, you must come."

"Come where?" He looked at her with blank hostility. The toll of the past week still showed in his pale skin and the dark pouches under his eyes, but he was calm and kempt and clearly again in full charge of himself. Judy tried to steady her voice.

"To the lab."

"For you?" It was a quiet sneer.

"Not for me. They've made something terrible. A sort of creature."

"Why don't you tell M.I.5?"

"Please." Judy went up to him; she felt completely defenseless but she did not care what he said or did to her. He turned away to go on with his packing. "Please, John! Something horrible's happening. You've got to stop it."

"Don't tell me what to do and what not to do," he said.

"They've got this thing. This monstrous-looking thing with an eye. An eye!"

"That's their problem." He pushed an old sweater into the top of the bag and pulled the strings together to close it.

"John—you're the only one . . ."

He pulled the bag off his bed and brushed past her with it to stack it with his cases. "Who's fault's that?"

Judy took a deep breath.

"I didn't kill Bridger."

"Didn't you? Didn't you put your gang on him?"

"I tried to warn you."

"You tried to fool me! You made love to me—"

"I didn't! Only once. I'm only human. I had a job—"

"You had a filthy job, and you did it marvellously."

"I never spied on you. Bridger was different."

"Dennis Bridger was my oldest friend and my best helper."

"He was betraying you."

"Betraying!" He looked at her briefly and then moved away and started sorting a collection of old bottles and glasses from a cupboard. "Take your official clichés somewhere else. Half this thing was Dennis's. It was the work of his mind, and mine; it didn't belong to you, or your bosses. If Dennis wanted to sell his own property, good luck to him. What business was it of yours?"

"I told you I didn't like what I had to do. I told you not to trust me. Do you think I haven't . . ."

Judy's voice shook in spite of her.

"Oh, stop snivelling," said Fleming. "And get out."

"I'll get out if you'll go and see Professor Dawnay."

"I'm leaving."

"You can't! They've got this horrible thing." Judy put out a hand and held desperately on to his sleeve, but he shook her off and walked across to the door.

"Good-bye." He turned the handle and opened it.

"You can't walk out now."

"Good-bye," he said quietly, waiting for her to go. She stood for a moment trying to think of something else to say, and at that moment Reinhart appeared in the doorway.

"Hallo, John." He looked from one to the other of them. "Hallo, Miss Adamson."

She walked out between them without speaking, blinking her eyes to stop herself from crying. Reinhart turned after her as she went, but Fleming shut the door.

"Did you know about that woman?"

"Yes."

Reinhart walked across to the bed and sat down on it. He looked old and tired.

"You couldn't have told me?" Fleming said accusingly.

"No, John, I couldn't."

"Well." Fleming opened drawers and shut them again, to make sure they were empty. "You can hire someone you can trust in my place."

The Professor looked round the room.

"Can I have a drink?" He stroked the tiny fingers of one hand across his forehead to revive himself. The second interview with Geers had not been easy. "What makes you think I don't trust you?"

"Nobody trusts us, do they?" Fleming routed about among the discarded bottles. "Nobody takes a blind bit of notice what we say."

"They take notice of what we do."

"Brandy be all right?" Fleming found a drop in the bottom of a flask, and slopped it into a tumbler. "Oh yes, we're very useful mechanics. But when it comes to the meaning of it—having an idea of what it's about—they don't want to know."

He held the glass out.

"Have you a drop of water?" Reinhart asked.

"That we can do."

"And you?" Reinhart nodded to the bottle. Fleming shook his head.

"They think they've just got a convenient windfall," he said, running water from his wash-basin tap. "And when we say this is the beginning of something much bigger they treat us like criminal lunatics. They put their watch-dogs on us—or their watch-bitches."

"There's no need to take it out on the girl." Reinhart took the glass and drank.

"I'm not taking it out on anyone! If they can't see that what we picked up by a sheer fluke is going to change all our lives, then let them find out in their own way. With any luck they'll foul it up and nothing will come of it."

"Something *has* come of it."

"Dawnay's monster?"

"You know about that?"

"It's a sub-program, merely—an extension of the machine." Fleming looked into an empty cupboard, but his attention was beginning to drift. "Dawnay thinks the machine's given her power to create life; but she's wrong. It's given itself the power."

"Then you must stay and control it, John."

"It's not my job." He slammed the cupboard door. "I wish to God I'd never started it!"

"But you did. You have a responsibility."

"To whom? To people who won't listen to me?"

"I listen to you."

"All right." He roamed round the room, picking up odd-ments and throwing them into the waste-paper basket. "I'll tell you what you're up against: and then I go."

"If you've anything constructive to say—" The drink had put some strength back into Reinhart's voice.

"Look—" Fleming came to rest at the end of the bed and bent over it with his hands on the board at its end, leaning his weight on his arms and concentrating, at last, not on the room, but on what he was saying. "You're all so busy asking 'What?'—'What have we got?', 'What does it do?'—no one except me asks 'Why?'. Why does an alien intelligence two hundred light-years away take the trouble to start this?"

"We can't tell that, can we?"

"We can make deductions."

"Guesses."

"All right—if you don't want to think it out!"

He straightened up and let his arms flop down to his sides. Reinhart sipped his brandy and waited for him. After a minute Fleming relaxed and grinned at him a little sheepishly.

"You old devil!" He sat down beside the Professor on the bed. "It's a logical intelligence, wherever and whatever it is. It sends out a set of instructions, in absolute terms, which postulate a piece of technology, which we interpret as this computer. Why? Do you think they said: 'Now, here's an interesting piece of technical information. We'll radio it out to the rest of the universe—they might find it useful'?"

"You obviously don't think so."

"Because where there's intelligence, there's will. And where there's will there's ambition. Supposing this was an intelligence which wanted to spread itself?"

"It's as good a theory as the next."

"It's the only *logical* theory!" Fleming banged his fist on his thigh. "What does it do? It puts out a message that can be picked up and interpreted and acted upon by other intelligences. The technique we use doesn't matter, just as it doesn't matter what make of radio set you buy—you get the same programs. What matters is, we accept their program: a program which uses arithmetical logic to adapt itself to our conditions, or any other conditions for that matter. It knows the bases of life: it finds out which ours is. It finds out how our brains work, how our bodies are built, how we get our information—we tell it about our nervous system and our sensory organs. So then it makes a creature with a body and a sensory organ—an eye. It's got an eye, hasn't it?"

"Yes."

"It's probably pretty primitive, but it's the next step. Dawnay thinks she's using that machine, but it's using her!"

"The next step to what?" Reinhart asked casually.

"I don't know. Some sort of take-over."

"Of us?"

"That's the only possible point."

Reinhart rose and, walking slowly and thoughtfully across the room, put his empty glass down with the others.

"I don't know, John."

Fleming appeared to understand his uncertainty.

"The first explorers must have seemed harmless enough to the native tribes." He spoke gently. "Kind old missionaries with ridiculous topees, but they finished up as their rulers."

"You may be right." Reinhart smiled at him gratefully; it was like old times, with both of them thinking the same way. "It seems an odd sort of missionary."

"This creature of Dawnay's: what sort of brain has it?" Reinhart shrugged and Fleming went on, "Does it think like us, or does it think like the machine?"

"If it thinks at all."

"If it has an eye, it has nerve centers—it certainly has a brain. What kind of brain?"

"Probably primitive too."

"Why?" Fleming demanded. "Why shouldn't the machine produce an extension of its own intelligence: a sub-computer that functions the same way, except that it's dependent on an organic body?"

"What would be the value?"

"The value of an organic body? A machine with senses? A machine with an eye?"

"You won't persuade anyone else," said Reinhart.

"You needn't rub that in."

"You'll have to stay with it, John."

"To do what?"

"To control it." Reinhart spoke flatly: he had made the decision some hours before. Fleming shook his head.

"How can we? It's cleverer than we are."

"Is it?"

"I don't want any part of it."

"That would suit it, according to your theory."

"If you don't believe me—"

Reinhart half raised a little hand. "I'm prepared to."

"Then destroy it. That's the only safe thing."

"We'll do that if necessary," Reinhart said, and he walked to the door as if the matter were settled. Fleming swung round to him.

"Will you? Do you really think you'll be able to? Look what happened when I tried to stop it: Dawnay threw me out. And if you try to they'll throw you out."

"They want to throw me out anyhow."

"They want *what?*" Fleming looked as if he had been hit.

"The powers that be want us all out of the way," Reinhart said. "They just want to know we're breaking up and they'll move in."

"Why, for God's sake?"

"They think they know better how to use it. But as long as we're here, John, we can pull out the plug. And we will, if it comes to it." He looked from Fleming's troubled face to the cases lying on the floor. "You'd better unpack those things."

The meeting between Fleming and Dawnay was electrically charged, but nothing dramatic happened. Fleming was quiet enough, and Dawnay treated him with a kind of tolerant amusement.

"Welcome the wandering boy," she said, and led him off to see the thing in the tank.

The creature floated peacefully in the middle of its nutrient bath; it had found the porthole and spent most of its time gazing out with its one huge lidless eye. Fleming stared back at it, but it gave no sign of registering what it saw.

"Can it communicate?"

"My dear boy," Dawnay spoke as though she were humoring a very young student. "We've hardly had time to learn anything about him."

"It has no vocal chords or anything?"

"No."

"Um." Fleming straightened up and looked in the top of the tank. "It might be a feeble attempt at a man."

"A man? It doesn't look like a man."

Fleming strolled through to the computer room, where Christine was watching the display panel.

"Anything printing out?"

"No. Nothing." Christine looked puzzled. "But there's obviously something going on."

The display lamps were winking steadily: it seemed that the machine was working away by itself without producing results.

For the next two or three days nothing happened, and then Fleming laid a magnetic coil from the machine round the tank. He did not—in fact, he could not—explain why he did it, but immediately the computer display began flashing wildly. Christine ran in from the laboratory.

"Cyclops is terribly excited! He's threshing about in his tank."

They could hear the bumping and slopping of the creature and its fluid from the other room. Fleming disconnected the coil and the bumping stopped. When they reconnected the coil, the creature reacted again, but still nothing came through on the output printer. Reinhart came over to see how they were getting on, and he and Dawnay and Fleming went over the routine once more; but they could make nothing of it.

The next day Fleming got them together again.

"I want to try an experiment," he said.

He walked across to the display panel and stood with his back to it, between the two mysterious terminals which they had never used. After a minute he took the perspex safety-guards off the terminals and stood between them again. Nothing happened.

"Would you stand here a moment?" he asked Reinhart, and moved away to let the Professor take his place. "Mind you don't touch them. There's a thousand volts or more across there."

Reinhart stood quite still with his head between the terminals and his back to the display panel.

"Feel anything?"

"A very slight—" Reinhart paused. "A sort of dizziness."

"Anything else?"

"No."

Reinhart stepped away from the computer.

"All right now?"

"Yes," he said. "I can't feel anything now."

Fleming repeated the experiment with Dawnay, who felt nothing.

"Different people's brains give off different amounts of electrical discharge," she said. "Mine's obviously low, so's Fleming's. Yours must be higher, Ernest, because it induces a leak across the terminals. You try, Christine."

Christine looked frightened.

"It's all right," said Fleming. "Stand with your head between those things, but don't touch them or they'll roast you."

Christine took her place where the others had stood. For a moment it seemed to have no effect on her, then she went rigid, her eyes closed and she fell forward in a dead faint. They caught her and pulled her into a chair, and Dawnay lifted up her eyelids to examine her eyes.

"She'll be all right. She's only fainted."

"What happened?" asked Reinhart. "Did she touch one?"

"No," Fleming said. "All the same, I'd better put the guards back on." He did so, and stood thinking while Dawnay and Reinhart revived Christine, ducking her head between her legs and dabbing her forehead with cold water.

"If there's a regular discharge between those terminals and you introduce the electrical field of a working brain into it . . ."

"Hold on," said Dawnay impatiently. "I think she's coming round."

"Oh, she'll be O.K." Fleming looked thoughtfully at the panel and the two sheathed contacts that stuck out from it. "It'll change the current between them—modulate it. The brain will feel a reaction; there could be some pick-up, it could work both ways."

"What are you talking about?" Reinhart asked.

"I'm talking about these!" Fleming flared up with excitement. "I think I know what they're for. They're a means of inputting and picking up from the machine."

Dawnay looked doubtful. "This is just a neurotic young woman. Probably a good subject for hypnosis."

"Maybe."

Christine came round and blinked.

"Hallo." She smiled at them vaguely. "Did I faint?"

"I'll say you did," said Dawnay. "You must have a hell of an electrical aura."

"Have I?"

Reinhart gave her a glass of water. Fleming turned to her and grinned.

"You've just done a great service to science." He nodded to the terminals. "You'd better keep away from between there."

He turned back to Reinhart.

"The real point is that if you have the right sort of brain—not a human one—one that works in a way designed by the machine—then you have a link. That's how it's meant to communicate. Our way of feeding back questions as answers is terribly clumsy. All this business of printers—"

"Are you saying it can thought-read?" Dawnay asked scornfully.

"I'm saying two brains can communicate electrically if they're of the right sort. If you get your creature and push his head between those terminals—"

"I don't see how we can do that."

"It's what it wants! That's why it's restless—why they're both restless. They want to get in touch. The creature's in the machine's electromagnetic field, and the machine knows the logical possibilities of it. That's what he's been working out, without telling us."

"You can't drag Cyclops out of his nutrient bath," Dawnay said. "He'll die."

"That must have been thought of."

"You could rig up an electro-encephalograph," said Reinhart. "The kind they use for mental analysis. Put a set of electric pads on Cyclops's head and run a co-axial cable from there to the terminals to carry the information. You'll have to put it through a transformer, or you'll electrocute him."

"What does that do?" Dawnay looked at him skeptically.

"It puts the computer in touch with its sub-intelligence," said Fleming.

"To serve what purpose?"

"To serve *its* purpose." He turned away from them and paced up the room. Dawnay waited for Reinhart to speak, but the old man stood obstinately, frowning down at his hands.

"Feeling better now?" he asked Christine.

"Yes, thank you."

"Do you think you could rig up something like that?"

"I think so."

"Dr. Fleming will help you. Won't you, John?"

Fleming stood at the far end of the room, the banks of equipment rising massively behind him.

"If that's what you really want," he said.

"The alternative," said Reinhart, more to Dawnay and himself than to Fleming, "is to pack up and hand over. We haven't much choice, have we?"

eight

AGONY

JUDY KEPT as far from Fleming as she could, and when she did see him he was usually with Christine. Everything had changed since Bridger died; even the early burst of spring weather was soon ended, leaving a grey pall of gloom over the camp and over herself. With an additional pang she realized that Christine was likely to take not only her place but Dennis Bridger's as well in Fleming's life, working and thinking with him as she herself had never been able to do. She thought at first that she would not be able to bear it and, going over Geers's head, wrote direct to Whitehall begging to be removed. The only result was another lecture from Geers.

"Your job here has hardly begun, Miss Adamson."

"But the Bridger business is over!"

"Bridger may be, but the business isn't." He seemed quite unaware of her distress. "Intel have had enough to whet their appetite, and now they've lost him they'll be looking for someone else—perhaps one of his friends."

"You think Dr. Fleming would sell out?" she asked scornfully.

"Anyone might, if we let them."

In the event it was Fleming, not Judy, who reported the first move from Intel.

He, Christine and Dawnay had found a way of securing the contact plates of an encephalograph on to what seemed to be the head of Cyclops, and Christine had helped him to link them by cable to the high-voltage terminals of the

116

computer. They added a transformer to the racks below the
display panel and ran the circuit through there, so that the
current reaching Cyclops had only about the strength of a
torch battery. All the same, the effect was alarming. When
the first connection was made the creature went completely
rigid and the control display lamps of the computer jammed
full on. After a little, however, both the creature and the
machine appeared to adjust themselves; data processing went
on steadily, although nothing was printed out, and Cyclops
floated quietly in his tank, gazing out of the port-hole with
his single eye.

All this had taken several days, and Christine had been
left in charge of the linked control room and laboratory with
instructions to call Dawnay and Fleming if anything fresh
happened. Dawnay took some hard-earned rest, but Fleming
visited the computer building from time to time to check
up and to see Christine. He found her increasingly strung-up
as days went by, and by the end of a week she had become
so nervous that he tackled her about it.

"Look—you know I'm dead scared of this whole business,
but I didn't know you were."

"I'm not," she said. They were in the control room, watching
the lights flickering steadily on the panel. "But it gives me
an odd feeling."

"What does?"

"That business with the terminals, and . . ." She hesitated
and glanced nervously towards the other room. "When I'm
in there I feel that eye watching me all the time."

"It watches all of us."

"No. Me particularly."

Fleming grinned. "I don't blame it. I look at you myself."

"I thought you were otherwise occupied."

"I was." He half raised his hand to touch her, then changed
his mind and walked away to the door. "Take care of
yourself."

He walked down the cliff path to the beach, where he
could be quiet and alone and think. It was a grey, empty
afternoon, the tide was out and the sand lay like dull grey
slate between the granite headlands. He wandered out to
the sea's edge, head down, hands in pockets, trying to work
through in his mind what was going on inside the computer.
He walked slowly back to the rocky foreshore, too deep in

his thoughts to notice a squat, bald man sitting on a boulder smoking a miniature cigar.

"One moment, sir, please." The guttural voice took him by surprise.

"Who are you?"

The bald man took a card from his breast pocket and held it out.

"I can't read," said Fleming.

The bald man smiled. "You, however, are Dr. Fleming."

"And you?"

"It would mean nothing." The bald man was slightly out of breath.

"How did you get here?"

"Around the headland. You can, at low tide, but it is quite a scramble." He produced a silver case of cigarillos. "Smoking?"

Fleming ignored it. "What do you want?"

"I come for a walk." He shrugged and put the case back in his pocket. He seemed to be recovering his breath. "You often come here yourself."

"This is private."

"Not the foreshore. In this free country the foreshore is . . ." He shrugged again. "My name is Kaufmann. You have not heard it?"

"No."

"Your friend Herr Doktor Bridger—"

"My friend Bridger is dead!"

"I know. I heard." Kaufmann inhaled his small cigar. "Very sad."

"Did you know Dennis Bridger?" Fleming asked, perplexed and suspicious.

"Oh yes. We had been associated for some time."

"Do you work for—?" The light dawned and he tried to remember the name.

"Intel? Yes."

Kaufmann smiled up at Fleming and blew out a little wraith of smoke. Fleming took his hands from his pockets.

"Get out."

"Excuse?"

"If you're not off this property in five minutes, I shall call the guards."

"No, please." Kaufmann looked hurt. "This was so happy a chance meeting you."

"And so happy for Bridger?"

"No one was more sorry than I. He was also very useful."

"And very dead." Fleming looked at his wristwatch. "It'll take me five minutes to climb the cliff. When I get to the top I shall tell the guards."

He turned to go, but Kaufmann called him back.

"Dr. Fleming! You have much more lucrative ways of spending the next five minutes. I am not suggesting you do anything underhand."

"That's dandy, isn't it?" said Fleming, keeping his distance.

"We were thinking, rather, you might like to transfer from government service to honorable service with us. I believe you are not too happy here."

"Let's lay this on the line shall we, my herr friend?" Fleming walked back and stood looking down at him. "Maybe I don't love the government, maybe I'm not happy. But even if I hated their guts and I was on my last gasp and there was no one else in the world to turn to, I'd rather drop dead before I came to you."

Then he turned away and climbed up the cliff path without looking back.

He went straight to Geers's office and found the Director dictating reports into a tape-machine.

"What did you tell him?" asked Geers when Fleming had reported.

"Do you mind!" A look of disgust came over Fleming's face. "It's bad enough keeping it out of the hands of babes and sucklings, without feeding it to sharks."

He left the office wondering why he had bothered; but in fact it was one of the few actions that told in his favor during the coming months.

Patrols were set on the beach, concertina wire was staked down from the headlands into the sea. Quadring's security staff did a comb-out of the surrounding district, and nothing more was heard of Intel for a long time. The experiment in the computer building continued without any tangible result until after Dawnay came back from her holiday; and then, one morning, the computer suddenly started printing out. Fleming locked himself up in his hut with the print-out, and after about a hundred hours' work he telephoned for Reinhart.

From what he could make out, the computer was asking an entirely new set of questions, all concerning the appearance, dimensions and functions of the body. It was possible, as

Fleming said, to reduce any physical form to mathematical terms and this, apparently, was what it was asking for.

"For instance," he told Reinhart and Dawnay when they sat down together to work on it, "it wants to know about hearing. There's a lot here about audio frequencies, and it's obviously asking how we make sounds and how we hear them."

"How could it know about speech?" Dawnay inquired.

"Because its creature can see us using our mouths to communicate and our ears to listen. All these questions arise from your little monster's observation. He can probably feel speech vibrations, too, and now that he's wired to the machine he can transmit his observations to it."

"You assume."

"How else do you account for this?"

"I don't see how we can analyze the whole human structure," Reinhart said.

"We don't have to. He keeps making intelligent guesses, and all we have to do is feed back the ones that are right. It's the old game. I can't think, though, why it hasn't found some quicker method by now. I'm sure it's capable of it. Perhaps the creature hasn't come up to expectations."

"Do you want to try it?" Reinhart asked Dawnay.

"I'll try anything," she said.

So the next stage of the project went forward, while Christine stayed with the computer, taking readings and inputting the results. She seemed all the time in a state of nervous tension, but said nothing.

"Do you want to move over to something else?" Fleming asked her when they were alone together one evening in the computer building.

"No. It fascinates me."

Fleming looked at her pensive and rather beautiful face. He no longer flirted with her as he used to before he was interested, when she was just a girl in the lab. Pushing his hands into his pockets, he turned from her and left the building. When he had gone she walked across the control room to the laboratory bay. It took her an effort to go through into the room where the tank was, and she stood for a moment in the doorway, her face strained, bracing herself. There was no sound except for the steady mains hum of the computer, but when she came within range of the port-hole in the side of the tank the creature began to move about, thumping against the tank walls and slopping fluid out of the open top.

"Steady," she said aloud. "Steady on."

She bent down mechanically and looked in through the port-hole: the eye was there looking steadily back at her, but the creature was becoming more and more agitated, threshing about with the fringes of its body like a jellyfish. Christine passed a hand across her forehead; she was slightly dizzy from bending down, but the eye held her as if mesmerically. She stayed there for a long minute, and then for another, growing incapable of thought. Slowly, as if of its own volition, her right hand moved up the side of the tank and her fingers sought the wire leading in to the encephalograph cable. They touched the wire and tingled as the slight current ran through them.

The moment she touched the wire, the creature grew quiet. It still looked steadfastly at her but no longer moved. The whole building was utterly quiet except for the hum of the computer. She straightened slowly, as if in a trance, still holding the wire. Her fingers ran along it until they touched the sheath of the cable and then closed on that, sliding it through the hollow of her hand. The cable was only loosely rigged; it looped across from the tank to the wall of the laboratory and was slung along the wall from pieces of tape tied to nails at intervals of a few yards. As her hand felt its way along the cable, she walked stiffly across to the wall and along beside it to the doorway to the computer room. Her eyes were open, but fixed and unseeing. The cable disappeared into a hole drilled in the wooden facing of the doorpost and she seemed at a loss when she could follow it no further. Then she raised her other hand and gripped the cable again on the other side of the doorway.

Her right hand dropped and she went through into the other room, holding the cable with her left. She worked her way slowly along the wall to the end of the rack of control equipment, breathing in a deep, labored way as if asleep and troubled by a dream. At the center of the racks of equipment the cable ran into the transformer below the control panel. The panel lights flashed steadily with a sort of hypnotic rhythm and her eyes became fixed on them as they had been on the eye of the creature. She stood in front of the panel for a few moments as though she were going to move no further; then, slowly, her left hand let go of the cable. Her right hand lifted again and with the fingers of both she grasped the high tension wires that ran from the transformer up to the two terminals beside her head. These wires were insulated to a point just below the terminals where their cores were bared and clamped on to the jutting-out plates. Her hands moved up them slowly, inch by inch.

Her face was blank and drained and she began to sway as she had done on the day when Fleming first made her stand between the terminal plates. She held on tightly to the wires, her fingers inching slowly up them. Then she touched the bare cores.

It all happened very quickly. Her body twisted as the full voltage of the current ran through it. She began to scream, her legs buckled, her head fell back and she hung from her outstretched arms as if crucified. The lamps on the display panel jammed full on, glaring into her distorted face, and a loud and insistent thumping started from the other room.

It lasted about ten seconds. Then her scream was cut off, there was a loud explosion from the fuse panel above her, the lights went dead, her fingers uncurled from the naked wire and she fell heavily into a crumpled heap on the floor. For a moment there was silence. The creature stopped thumping and the humming of the computer stopped as if cut with a knife. The alarm bell rang.

The first person on the scene was Judy, who was passing the building when the alarm on the wall of the porch clanged into life. Pushing open the door, she ran wildly down the corridor and into the control room. At first she could see nothing. The strip lights in the ceiling were still on, but the control desk hid the floor in front of the control panel. Then she saw Christine's body and, running forward, knelt down beside it.

"Christine!"

She turned the body over on to its back. Christine's face stared sightlessly up at her and the hands fell limply back on to the floor: they were black and burnt through to the bone. Judy felt for the girl's heart, but it was still.

"Oh God!" she thought. "Why do I always have to be in at the death?"

Reinhart was back in London when he heard the news. When he reported it to Osborne, he got a different response from what he expected; Osborne was certainly worried by it, but he seemed preoccupied with other things and took it as one blow among many. Reinhart was distressed and also puzzled: not only Osborne but everyone else he met, as he moved in and out of Whitehall offices, appeared to have something secret and heavy on their minds. He thought of going to Bouldershaw Fell, which he had not visited for a long time, to try to get away from the feeling of oppression that surrounded him, but he found immediately that the radio-telescope had been put under military control and was firmly sealed off by Ministry of Defense security. This had happened without warning during the past week while he had been at Thorness. He was furious at not being consulted and went to see Osborne, but Osborne was too busy to make appointments.

Christine's post mortem and autopsy reports followed in a few days. The Professor was at least spared the ordeal of explaining to her relatives, for both her parents were dead and she had no other relations in the country. Fleming sent him a short, grim letter saying that no major damage had been done to the computer and that he had a theory about Christine's death. Then there was a longer letter telling him the blown circuit had been repaired and that the computer was working full out, transferring a fantastic amount of information to its memory storage, though what the information was Fleming did not say. Dawnay telephoned him a couple of days later to say the computer had started printing out. A vast mass of figures was pouring out from it, and as far as she and Fleming could tell this was not in the form of questions but of information.

"It's a whole lot more formulae for bio-synthesis," she said. "Fleming thinks it's asking for a new experiment, and I think he's right."

"More monsters?" Reinhart asked into the telephone.

"Possibly. But it's much more complicated this time. It'll be an immense job. We shall need a lot more facilities, I'm afraid, and more money."

He made another attempt to see Osborne and was summoned, to his surprise, to the Ministry of Defense.

Osborne was waiting in Vandenberg's room when he arrived. Vandenberg and Geers were also there: it looked as though they had been talking for some time. Geers's brief case was open on the table and a lot of papers had been

splayed out from it and examined. Something harsh and un-
friendly about the atmosphere of the room put the Professor
on his guard.

"Rest your feet," said Vandenberg automatically, without
smiling. There was a small strained pause while everyone
waited for someone else to speak, then he added, "I hear
you've written off another body."

"It was an accident," said Reinhart.

"Sure, sure. Two accidents."

"The Cabinet have had the results of the inquiry," Osborne
said, looking down at the carpet. Geers coughed nervously
and started shuffling the papers together.

"Yes?" Reinhart looked at the General and waited.

"I'm sorry, Professor," said Vandenberg.

"For what?"

Osborne looked at him for the first time. "We've got to
accept a change of control, a general tightening-up."

"Why?"

"People are starting to ask questions. Soon they'll find
you've got this living creature you're experimenting on."

"You mean the R.S.P.C.A.? It's not an animal. It's just
a collection of molecules we put together ourselves."

"That isn't going to make them any happier."

"We can't just stop in the middle—" Reinhart looked from
one to another of them, trying to fathom what was in their
minds. "Dawnay and Fleming are just starting on a new
tack."

"We know that," said Geers, tapping the papers he was
putting back into his brief case.

"Then—?"

"I'm sorry," said Vandenberg again. "This is the end of
your road."

"I don't understand."

Osborne shifted uneasily in his chair. "I've done my best.
We all fought as hard as we could."

"Fought whom?"

"The Cabinet are quite firm." Osborne seemed anxious to
avoid details. "We've lost our case, Ernest. It's been fought
and lost way above our level."

"And now," put in Vandenberg, "you've written off another
body."

"That's just an excuse!" Reinhart rose to his small feet
and confronted the other man across the desk. "You want

us out of it because you want the equipment. You trump up any kind of case—"

Vandenberg sighed. "It's the way it goes. I don't expect you to understand our viewpoint."

"You don't make it easy."

Geers snapped his brief case shut and switched on a small smile.

"The truth is, Reinhart, they want you back at Bouldershaw Fell."

Reinhart regarded him with distaste.

"Bouldershaw Fell? They won't even let me in there."

Geers looked inquiringly at the General, who gave him a nod to go on.

"The Cabinet have taken us into their confidence," he said with an air of importance.

"This is top secret, you understand," said Vandenberg.

"Then perhaps you'd better not tell me." Reinhart stood stiffly, like a small animal at bay.

"You'll have to know," said Geers. "You'll be involved. The Government have sent out a Mayday—an S.O.S. They want you all working on defense."

"Regardless of what we're doing?"

"It's a Cabinet decision." Osborne addressed the carpet. "We've made the best terms we can."

Vandenberg stood up and walked across to the wall map.

"The western powers are deeply concerned." He also avoided looking at Reinhart. "Because of traces we've been picking up."

"What traces?"

"Notably from your own radio-telescope. It's the only thing we have with high enough definition. It's giving us tracks of a great many vehicles in orbit."

"Terrestrial?" Reinhart looked across at the trajectories traced on the map. "Is that what you're all worried about?"

"Yeah. Someone on the other side of the globe is pushing them up fast, but they're out of range of our early warning screen. The U.N. Space Agency has no line on them, nor has the Western Alliance. No one has."

Geers finished it for him. "So they want you to handle it."

"But that isn't my field." Reinhart stood firm in front of the desk. "I'm an astronomer."

"What you're doing now is your field?" Vandenberg asked.

"It develops from it—from an astronomical source."

No one answered him for a moment.

"Well, that's what the Cabinet wants," said Osborne finally.

"And the work at Thorness?"

Vandenberg turned to him. "Your team—what's left of it—will answer to Dr. Geers."

"Geers!"

"I *am* Director of the Station."

"But you don't know the first thing—" Reinhart checked himself.

"I'm a physicist," said Geers. "I was, at least. I expect I can soon brush it up."

Reinhart looked at him contemptuously. "You've always wanted this, haven't you?"

"It's not my choice!" said Geers angrily.

"Gentlemen!" Osborne neighed reprovingly.

Vandenberg moved heavily back to his desk. "Let's not make this a personality problem."

"And Dawnay and Fleming's work?" Reinhart demanded.

"I shan't ditch them," said Geers. "We shall need some of the computer time, but that can be arranged—"

"If you ditch me."

"There's no kind of slur on you, Ernest," Osborne said. "As you'll see from the next Honors' List."

"Oh damn the Honors' List!" Reinhart's small fingers dug into his palms. "What Dawnay and Fleming are at is the most important research project we've ever had in this country. That's all my concern."

Geers looked at him glintingly through his spectacles. "We'll do what we can for them, if they behave themselves."

"There are going to be some changes here, Miss Adamson."

Judy was in Geers's office, facing Dr. Hunter, the Medical Superintendent of the Station. He was a big bony man who looked far more military than medical.

"Professor Dawnay is going to start a new experiment, but not under Professor Reinhart's direction. Reinhart is out of it."

"Then who—?" she left the question in the air. She disliked him and did not wish to be drawn by him.

"I shall be responsible for administering it."

"You?"

Hunter was possibly used to this type of insult; it raised only a small sneer on his large, unsubtle face.

"Of course, I'm only a humble doctor. The ultimate authority will lie with Dr. Geers."

"Supposing Professor Dawnay objects?"

"She doesn't. She's not really interested in how it's organized. What we have to do is put things on a tidy footing for her. Dr. Geers will have the final jurisdiction over the computer and I shall help him with the biological experiments. Now you—" he picked up a paper from the Director's desk—"you were seconded to the Ministry of Science. Well, you can forget that. You're back with us. I shall need you to keep our side of the business secure."

"Professor Dawnay's program?"

"Yes. I think we are going to achieve a new form of life."

"A new form of life?"

"It takes your breath, doesn't it?"

"What sort of form?"

"We don't know yet, but when we do know we must keep it to ourselves, mustn't we?" He gave her a sort of bedroom leer. "We're privileged to be midwives to a great event."

"And Dr. Fleming?" she asked, looking straight in front of her.

"He's staying on, at the request of the Ministry of Science; but I really don't think there's much left for him to do."

Fleming and Dawnay received the news of Reinhart's removal almost without comment. Dawnay was completely engrossed in what she was doing and Fleming was isolated and solitary. The only person he might have talked to was Judy, and he avoided her. Although he and Dawnay were working closely together, they still mistrusted each other and they never spoke freely about anything except the experiment. Even on that, he found it hard to convince her about any basic thesis.

"I suppose," she said, as they stood by the output printer checking fresh screeds of figures, "I suppose all this is the information Cyclops has been feeding in."

"Some of it. Plus what the machine learned from Christine when it had her on the hooks."

"What could it learn?"

"Remember I said it must have a quicker way of getting information about us?"

"I remember your being impatient."

"Not only me. In those few seconds before the fuses blew, I should think it got more physiological data than you could work through in a lifetime."

Dawnay gave one of her little dry sniffs and left him to pursue his own thoughts. He picked up a piece of insulated wire and wandered over to the control unit, where he stood in front of the winking display panel, thoughtfully holding one bared end of the wire in each hand. Reaching up to one of the terminals, he hooked an end of the wire over it, then, holding the wire by the insulation, he advanced the other end slowly towards the opposite terminal.

"What are you trying to do?" Dawnay came quickly across the room to him. "You'll arc it."

"I don't think so," said Fleming. He touched the bare end of wire on to the terminal. "You see." There was no more than a tiny spark as the two metal surfaces met.

Fleming dropped the wire and stood for a few seconds, thinking. Then he slowly raised his own hands to the terminals, as Christine had done.

Dawnay stepped forward to stop him. "For heaven's sake!"

"It's all right." Fleming touched the two terminals simultaneously, and nothing happened. He stood there, arms outstretched, grasping the metal plates, while Dawnay watched him with a mixture of skepticism and fear.

"Haven't you had enough death?"

"He has." He lowered his arms. "He's learned. He didn't know the effect of high voltages on organic tissue until he got Christine up on there. He didn't know it would damage himself, either. But now that he does know he takes precautions. If you try to short across those electrodes, he'll reduce the voltage. Have a go."

"No thanks. I've had enough of your quaint ideas."

Fleming looked at her hard.

"You're not simply up against a piece of equipment, you know. You're up against a brain, and a damn good one." When she did not answer, he walked out.

In spite of the pressure of defense work, Geers did find time and means to help Dawnay. He was the kind of man who fed on activity like a locust; to have a multiplicity of things under his control satisfied the inner craving of his mind and took the place, perhaps, of the creative genius that had eluded him. He arranged for yet more equipment and facilities to be put at her disposal and reported her

progress with growing pride. He would do better than Reinhart.

A new laboratory was added to the computer block to house
a huge and immensely complicated D.N.A. synthesizer, and
during the following weeks newly-designed X-ray crystallog-
raphic equipment and chemical synthesis units were installed
to manufacture phosphate components, deoxyribose, adenine,
thymine, cytosine, tyrosin and other ingredients needed for
making D.N.A. molecules, the seeds of life. Within a few
months they had a D.N.A. helix of some five billion nucleotide
code letters under construction, and by the end of the year
they had made a genetic unit of fifty chromosomes, similar
to but slightly more than the genetic requirement for man.

Early in February, Dawnay reported the emergence of a
living embryo, apparently human.

Hunter hurried over to the lab building to see it. He passed
Fleming as he went through the computer room, but said
nothing to him; Fleming had kept to his own side of the
business, as he had promised, and made no effort to help
with the biochemistry. In the laboratory, Hunter found
Dawnay bending over a small oxygen tent, surrounded by
equipment and a number of her assistants.

"Is it living?"

"Yes." Dawnay straightened and looked up at him.

"What's it like?"

"It's a baby."

"A human baby?"

"I would say so, though I doubt if Fleming would." She
gave a smile of satisfaction. "And it's a girl."

"I can hardly believe—" Hunter peered down into the
oxygen tent. "May I look?"

"There's nothing much to see; only a bundle wrapped up."

Under the perspex cover of the tent was something which
could have been human, but its body was tightly wrapped
in a blanket and its face hidden by a mask. A rubber
tube disappeared down by its neck into the blanket.

"Breathing?"

"With help. Pulse and respiration normal. Weight, six and
a half pounds. When I first came here, I'd never have
believed . . ." She broke off, suddenly and unexpectedly
overtaken by emotion. When she continued, it was in a softer
voice. "All the alchemy of making gold come true. Of making
life." She tapped the rubber tubing and resumed her usual

gruff way of speaking. "We're feeding her intravenously. You may find she's no instinct for normal suckling. You'll have to teach her."

"You've landed us quite a job," said Hunter, not unmoved but anxious already about formal responsibilities.

"I've landed you human life, made by human beings. It took nature two thousand million years to do a job like that: it's taken us fourteen months."

Hunter's official bedside manner returned to him. "Let me be the first to congratulate you."

"You make it sound like a normal birth," said Dawnay, managing to sniff and smile at the same time.

The little creature in the tent seemed to thrive on its intravenous food. It grew approximately half an inch a day, and was obviously not going to go through the usual childhood of a human being. Geers reported to the Director-General of Research at the Ministry of Defense that at the present rate it should reach full adult stature in between three to four months.

Official reaction to the whole event was a mixture of pride and secrecy. The Director-General sent for a full report and classified it in a top-secret category. He passed it on to the Minister of Defense who communicated it, in summary, to an astonished and bewildered Prime Minister. The Cabinet was told in terms of strictest confidence and Ratcliff returned to his office at the Ministry of Science shaken and unsure what to do next. After considering for a long time, he told Osborne who wrote to Fleming calling for an independent report.

Fleming replied in two words: "Kill it!"

In due course, he was summoned to Geers's office and asked to account for himself.

"I hardly see," said Geers, his eyes screwed up narrow behind his spectacles, "that this is anything to do with you."

Fleming thumped his fist on the huge desk.

"Am I or am I not still a member of the team?"

"In a sense."

"Then perhaps you'll listen to me. It may look like a human being, but it isn't one. It's an extension of the machine, like the other creature, only more sophisticated."

"Is this theory based on anything?"

"It's based on logic. The other creature was a first shot, a first attempt to produce an organism like us and therefore acceptable to us. This is a better shot, based on more information. I've worked on that information; I know how deliberate it is."

Geers allowed his eyes to open a little. "And having achieved this miracle, you suggest we kill it?"

"If you don't now you'll never be able to. People will come to think of it as human. They'll say we're murdering it. It'll have us—the machine will have us—where it wants us."

"And if we don't choose to take your advice?"

"Then keep it away from the computer."

Geers sat silent for a moment, his spectacles glinting. Then he rose to end the interview.

"You are only here on sufferance, Fleming, and out of courtesy to the Minister of Science. The judgment in this case rests not with you but with me. We shall do what I think best, and we shall do it here."

nine

ACCELERATION

THE GIRL, as Geers had predicted, was fully grown by the end of four months. She remained most of the time in an oxygen tent, although she was learning to breathe naturally for increasing periods. By the end of the first month she was off drip feeds and on to a bottle. Beyond this, nothing was done to stimulate her mind and she lay inert as a baby, staring at the ceiling. Geers grew slightly apprehensive as growth continued, but she stopped at five feet seven inches, by which time she was a fully developed young woman.

"Quite a good-looking young woman, too," Hunter said, with a lick of his lips.

Geers allowed no one but Hunter, Dawnay and their assistants to see her. He sent daily confidential reports to the Ministry of Defense and was visited twice by the Director-General of Research, with whom he made plans for her future. Extreme precautions were taken to keep her existence secret; a day and night guard was mounted on the computer and laboratory block and everyone who had to know was sworn to silence. Apart from Reinhart, whom Osborne told privately, and a handful of senior officials and politicians in London, no one outside the research team at Thorness knew anything about her.

Fleming, in Geers's opinion, was the most doubtful quantity in the whole group, and Judy was given specific instructions to watch him. They had literally hardly spoken since the previous spring. He had made one surly, half-hearted attempt to apologize but she had cut him short, and since then when they met in the camp they ignored each other. At least, she told herself, she had not been spying on him—the fact that he had dissociated himself from Dawnay's experiment, to which she had been assigned after Bridger's death, had meant he was no longer primarily her concern. Whatever pangs of conscience she had about the past were hidden under the anesthetic of a sort of listless apathy. But now it was different. Screwing up all her determination, she went to find him in the computer room, her legs feeling curiously flabby beneath her. She handed him her letter of instruction.

"Would you read this?" she said, without any preliminary.

He glanced at it and handed it back to her. "It's on Ministry of Defense paper—*you* read it. I'm choosy what I touch."

"They're concerned about the security of the new creature," she said stiffly, withdrawing in the face of his attack. Fleming laughed.

"It amuses you?" she asked. "I'm to be responsible for its safety."

"And who's to be responsible for yours?"

"John!" Judy's face reddened. "Do we always have to be on opposite sides of the fence?"

"Looks like it, doesn't it?" he said with something between sympathy and indifference. "I'm afraid I don't dig your precious creature."

"It's not mine. I'm doing my job. I'm not your enemy."

"No. You're just the sort of girl who gets pushed about." He looked helplessly around the room. "Oh I've had my say!"

She made a last attempt to reach him. "It seems a long time since we went sailing."

"It *is* a long time."

"We're the same people."

"In a different world." He moved as if he wanted to get away.

"It's the same world, John."

"O.K., you tell them that."

Hunter came past. "We're getting her out."

"Who?" Fleming turned from Judy with relief.

"The little girl—out of her oxygen tent."

"Are we allowed?" asked Judy.

"This is a special occasion—coming-out party." Hunter gave her a stale, sexy smile and walked away into the other room. Fleming looked sourly after him.

"Full-size live monster given away with each packet."

Judy surprised herself by giggling. She felt they were suddenly about a mile closer.

"I detest that man. He's so condescending."

"I hope he kills her," said Fleming. "He's probably a bad enough doctor."

They went through to the laboratory together. Hunter was superintending opening the bottom end of the oxygen tent, watched by Dawnay. Under the tent was a narrow trolley-bed which two assistants drew gently forward. The rest stood round as the bed slid out with the full-grown girl-creature on it: first her feet, covered by a sheet, then her body, also covered. She was lying on her back, and as her face was revealed Judy gave a gasp. It was a strong and beautiful face with high cheek-bones and wide, Baltic features. Her long, pale hair was strewn out on the pillow, her eyes were shut and she was breathing peacefully as if asleep. She looked like a purified, blonde version of Christine.

"It's Christine!" Judy whispered. "Christine."

"It can't be," said Hunter brusquely.

"There is a superficial resemblance," Dawnay admitted.

Hunter cut across her. "We did an autopsy on the other girl. Besides, she was a brunette."

Judy turned to Fleming.

"Is this some horrible kind of practical joke?"

He shook his head. "Don't let it fool you. Don't let it fool any of you. Christine's dead. Christine was only a blueprint."

No one spoke for a moment while Dawnay took the girl's pulse and stooped down to look at her face. The eyes opened and looked vaguely up at the ceiling.

"What does it mean?" asked Judy. She remembered seeing Christine dead, and yet this was something inescapably like her, living.

"It means," said Fleming, as though answering all of them, "that it took a human being and made a copy. It got a few things wrong—the color of the hair, for instance—but by and large it did a pretty good job. You can turn the human anatomy into figures, and that's what it did; and then got us to turn them back again."

Hunter looked at Dawnay and signalled to the assistants to wheel the trolley into a neighboring bay.

"It gave us what we wanted, anyway," said Dawnay.

"Did it? It's the brain that counts: it doesn't matter about the body. It hasn't made a human being—it's made an alien creature that looks like one."

"Dr. Geers has told us your theory," said Hunter, moving away in the wake of the girl on the bed. Dawnay hesitated for a moment before going after them.

"You may be right," she said. "In which case it'll be all the more interesting."

Fleming controlled himself with an obvious effort. "What are you going to do with it?"

"We're going to educate it—her."

Fleming turned and walked out of the laboratory, back to the computer room, with Judy following.

"What's bad about it?" she asked. "Everyone else . . ."

He turned on her. "Whenever a higher intelligence meets a lower one, it destroys it. That's what's bad. Iron Age man destroyed the Stone Age; the Palefaces beat the Indians. Where was Carthage when the Romans were through with it?"

"But is that bad, in the long run?"

"It's bad for us."

"Why should this—?"

"The strong are always ruthless with the weak."

She laid a hand tentatively on his sleeve. "Then the weak had better stick together."

"You should have thought of that earlier," he said.

Judy knew better than to push him further; she went back to her own life, leaving him with his preoccupations and doubts.

There was no early spring that year. The hard grey weather went on to the end of April, matching the grey sunless mood of the camp. Apart from Dawnay's experiment, nothing was going well. Geers's permanent staff and missile development teams worked under strain with no outstanding success; there were more practice firings than ever but nothing really satisfactory came of them. After each abortive attempt the grey wrack of Atlantic cloud settled back on the promontory as if to show that nothing would ever change or ever improve.

Only the girl creature bloomed, like some exotic plant in a hothouse. One bay of Dawnay's laboratories was set up as a nursing block with living quarters for the girl. Here she was waited on and prepared for her part like a princess in a fairy tale. They called her Andromeda, after the place of her origin, and taught her to eat and drink and sit up and move. At first she was slow to learn to use her body—she had, as Dawnay said, none of the normal child's instincts for physical development—but soon it became clear that she could absorb knowledge at a prodigious rate. She never had to be told a fact twice. Once she understood the possibilities of anything she mastered it without hesitation or effort.

It was like this with speech. To begin with she appeared to have no awareness of it: she had never cried as a baby cries, and she had to be taught like a deaf child, by being made conscious of the vibrations of her vocal chords, and their effects. But as soon as she understood the purpose of it she learned language as fast as it was spelled out to her. Within weeks she was a literate, communicating person.

Within weeks, too, she had learned to move as a human being, a little stiffly, as if her body was working from instructions and not from its own desire, but gracefully and without any kind of awkwardness. Most of the time she was confined to her own suite, though she was taken every day, when it was not actually raining, out to the moors in a closed car and allowed to walk in the fresh air under armed escort and out of sight of any other eyes from either inside or outside the camp.

She never complained, whatever was done to her. She accepted the medical checks, the teaching, the constant surveillance, as though she had no will or wishes of her own. In fact, she showed no emotions at all except those of hunger before a meal and tiredness at the end of the day, and then it was physical, never mental tiredness. She was always gentle, always submissive, and very beautiful. She behaved, indeed, like someone in a dream.

Geers and Dawnay arranged for her education at a pace which packed the whole of a university syllabus into something which more resembled a summer school. Once she had grasped the basis of denary arithmetic, she had no further difficulty with mathematics. She might have been a calculating machine; she whipped through figures with the swift logic of a ready-reckoner, and she was never wrong. She seemed capable of holding the most complex progressions in her head without any sense of strain. For the rest, she was filled up with facts like an encyclopedia. Geers and the teachers who were sent up to Thorness in an endless and academically-

impressive procession—not to instruct her directly, for she
was too secret, but to guide her instructors—laid out the
foundations of a general, unspecialized level of knowledge,
so that by the end of her summer course, and of the summer,
she knew as much about the world, in theory, as an intelligent
and perceptive school leaver. All she lacked was any sense
of human experience or any spontaneous attitude to life.
Although she was alert and reasonably communicative, she
might just as well have been walking and talking in her
sleep, and that, in fact, is the impression which she gave.

"You're right," Dawnay admitted to Fleming. "She hasn't
got a brain, she's got a calculator."

"Isn't that the same thing?" He looked across at the slim,
fair girl who was sitting reading at the table in what had
been made her room. It was one of his rare visits to
Dawnay's premises. The laboratory had been gutted and
turned into a set of rooms that might have come out of a design brochure, with the girl as one of the fitments.

"She's not fallible," said Dawnay. "She doesn't forget. She
never makes a mistake. Already she knows more than most
people do."

Fleming frowned. "And you'll go on stuffing information
into her until she knows more than you."

"Probably. The people in charge of us have plans for her."

Geers's plan was fairly obvious. The pressing problems of
defense machinery remained unsolved in spite of the use
they had made of the new computer. The main difficulty
was that they did not really know how to use it. They took
it out of Fleming's hands for several hours a day, and
managed to get a great deal of calculation done very quickly
by it; but they had no means of tapping its real potential
or of using its immense intellect to solve problems that were
not put to it in terms of figures. If, as Fleming considered,
the creatures evolved with the machine's help had an affinity
with it, then it should be possible to use one of them as
an agent. The original monster was obviously incapable of
making any communication of human needs to the computer,
but the girl was another matter. If she could be used as
an intermediary, something very exciting might be done.

The Minister of Defense had no objection to the idea and,
although Fleming warned Osborne, as he had warned Geers,
Osborne carried no weight with the men in power. Fleming

could only stand by and watch the machine's purpose being unwittingly fulfilled by people who would not listen to him. He himself had nothing but a tortuous strand of logic on which to depend. If he was wrong, he was wrong all the way from the beginning, and the way of life was not what he thought. But if he was right they were heading for calamity.

He was, in fact, in the computer room when Geers and Dawnay first brought the girl in.

"For God's sake!" He looked from Geers to Dawnay in a last, hopeless appeal.

"We've all heard what you think, Fleming," Geers said.

"Then don't let her in."

"If you want to complain, complain to the Ministry." He turned back to the doorway. Dawnay shrugged her shoulders; it seemed to her that Fleming was making a great deal of fuss about nothing.

Geers held the door open as Andromeda came in, escorted by Hunter who walked beside and slightly behind her as though they were characters out of Jane Austen. Andromeda moved stiffly, but was thoroughly wide awake, her face calm, her eyes taking in everything. It was all somehow formal and unreal, as if a minuet were about to begin.

"This is the control room of the computer," said Geers as she stood looking around her. He sounded like a kind but firm parent. "You remember I told you about it?"

"Why should I forget?"

Although she spoke in a slow stilted way, her voice, like her face, was strong and attractive.

Geers led her across the room. "This is the input unit. The only way we can give information to the computer is by typing it in here. It takes a long time."

"It must do." She examined the keyboard with a sort of calm interest.

"If we want to hold a conversation with it," Geers went on, "the best we can do is select something from the output and feed it back in."

"That is very clumsy," she said slowly.

Dawnay came and stood by her other side. "Cyclops in the other room can input direct by that co-axial cable."

"Is that what you wish me to do?"

"We want to find out," said Geers.

The girl looked up and found Fleming staring at her. She had not taken him in before, and gazed back expressionlessly at him.

"Who is that?"

"Doctor Fleming," said Dawnay. "He designed the computer."

The girl walked stiffly across to him and held out her hand.

"How do you do?" She spoke as if repeating a lesson. Fleming ignored her hand and continued staring at her. She looked unblinkingly back at him and, after a minute, dropped her arm.

"You must be a clever man," she said flatly. Fleming laughed. "Why do you do that?"

"What?"

"Laugh—that is the word?"

Fleming shrugged. "People laugh when they're happy and cry when they're sad. Sometimes we laugh when we're unhappy."

"Why?" She went on gazing at his face. "What is happy or sad?"

"They're feelings."

"I do not feel them."

"No. You wouldn't."

"Why do you have them?"

"Because we're imperfect." Fleming returned her stare as though it were a challenge. Geers fidgeted impatiently.

"Is it working all right, Fleming? There's nothing on the display panel."

"Which is the display panel?" she asked, turning away. Geers showed her and she stood looking at the rows of unlit bulbs while Geers and Dawnay explained it, and the use of the terminals, to her.

"We'd like you to stand between them," he said.

She walked deliberately towards the panel, and as she approached it the lamps started to blink. She stopped.

"It's all right," said Dawnay. Geers took the guards from the terminals and urged the girl forward, while Fleming watched, tense, without saying anything. She went reluctantly, her face strained and set. When she reached the panel, she stood there, a terminal a few inches from each side of her head, and the lights began flashing faster. The room was full of the hum of the computer's equipment. Slowly, without being told, she put her hands up towards the plates.

"You're sure it's neutralized?" Geers looked anxiously at Fleming.

"It neutralizes itself."

As the girl's hands touched the metal plates, she shivered. She stood with her face blank, as if entranced, and then she let go and swayed back unsteadily. Dawnay and Geers caught her and helped her to a chair.

"Is she all right?" asked Geers.

Dawnay nodded. "But look at that!"

The lights on the panel were all jammed solidly on and the computer hum grew louder than it had been before.

"What's happened?"

"It speaks to me," said the girl. "It knows about me."

"What does it say?" asked Dawnay. "What does it know about you? How does it speak?"

"We . . . we communicate."

Geers looked uncomfortably puzzled. "In figures?"

"You could express it in figures," she said, staring blindly before her. "It would take a very long time to explain."

"And can *you* communicate—?" Dawnay was interrupted by a loud explosion from the next room. The display panel went blank, the hum stopped.

"Whatever's happened?" asked Geers.

Fleming turned without answering him and went quickly through to the first lab bay, where the creature and its tank were housed. Smoke was rising from the contact wires above the tank. When he pulled them out, the ends were blackened and lumps of charred tissue hung from them. He looked into the tank, and his mouth set into a thin line.

"What's happened to it?" Dawnay hurried in, followed by Geers.

"It's been electrocuted." Fleming dangled the harness in front of her. "There's been another blow-out and it's been killed."

Geers peered into the tank and recoiled in distaste.

"What did you do to the controls?" he demanded.

Fleming threw down the charred remains of the wires. "I did nothing. The computer knows how to adjust its own voltages—it knows how to burn tissue—it knows how to kill."

"But why?" asked Geers.

They all looked, by instinct, to the doorway from the computer room. The girl was standing there.

"Because it was *her*." Fleming walked across to her grimly, his jaw stuck out. "You've just told it, haven't you? It knows it has a better slave now. It doesn't need that poor creature any more. That's what it said, isn't it?"

She looked levelly back at him. "Yes."

"You see!" He swung round to Geers. "You've got a killer. Bridger may have been an accident; so may Christine, though I'd call it manslaughter. But this was pure, deliberate murder."

"It was only a primitive creature," said Geers.

"And it was redundant!" He turned back to the girl. "Yes?"

"It was in the way," she answered.

"And the next time it could be you who are in the way—or me, or any or all of us!"

She still showed no flicker of expression. "We were only eliminating unwanted material."

"We?"

"The computer and myself." She touched her fingers to her head. Fleming screwed up his eyes.

"You're the same, aren't you? A shared intelligence."

"Yes," she said tonelessly. "I understand—"

"Then understand this!'" Fleming's voice rose with excitement and he pushed his face close up to her. "This is a piece of information: it is wrong to murder!"

"Wrong? What is 'wrong'?"

"*You* were talking about killing earlier on," said Geers.

"Oh God!" said Fleming wildly. "Is there no sane person anywhere?"

He stared for a moment more at Andromeda, and then he went, half-running, out of the room.

Bouldershaw Fell looked much as it had done when Reinhart first took Judy to see it. Grass and heather had grown over the builders' scars on the surrounding moor, and black streaks ran down the walls of the buildings where gutters had overflowed in winter storms; but the triple arch was still poised motionless over its great bowl, and inside the main observatory block the equipment and staff continued their quiet, methodical work. Harvey was still in charge of the control desk, the banks of steering and calculating equipment still stood to each side of him, flanking the wide window, and the photographs of stars still hung on the walls, though less fresh and new than they had been.

The only sign of the grim business that preoccupied them all was a huge glazed wall-map of the world on which the tracks of orbital missiles were marked in chinagraph. It betrayed what the outward calm of the place concealed—the anguish and fever with which they watched the threats in the sky above them remorselessly grow and grow. Reinhart referred to it as the Writing on the Wall, and worked day and night with the observatory team, plotting each new trace as it swung into orbit and sending increasingly urgent and somber reports to Whitehall.

Nearly a hundred of the sinister, unidentified missiles had been tracked during the past months, and their launching area had been defined to within a triangle several hundred miles in extent in the ocean between Manchuria, Vladivostok and the northern island of Japan. None of the neighboring countries admitted to them. As Vandenberg said, they could belong to any of three of our fellow members of the United Nations.

Vandenberg paid frequent visits to the telescope and had long and fruitless conferences with Reinhart. All they could really tell from their findings was that these were propelled vehicles launched from about forty degrees north by between a hundred and thirty and a hundred and fifty east, and that they travelled across Russia, Western Europe and the British Isles at a speed of about sixteen thousand miles an hour at a height between three hundred and fifty and four hundred miles. After crossing Britain they mostly passed over the North Atlantic and Greenland and the polar north of Canada, presumably joining up their trajectory in the same area of the North China Sea. Whatever route they took, they were deflected to pass over England or Scotland: they were obviously steerable and obviously aimed very deliberately at this small target. Although nothing certain was known of their size or shape, they emitted a tracking signal and they were clearly large enough to carry a nuclear charge.

"I don't know what the point of them is," Reinhart admitted. He was obsessed by them. However unhappy he was at the way things had gone at Thorness, he was by now fully occupied with this new and terrifying turn of events.

Vandenberg had cogent and reasonable theories. "Their

point is that someone in the East wants us to know they have the technical edge on us. They flaunt these over our heads to show the world we've no way of retaliating. A new form of saber-rattling."

"But why always over this country?"

Vandenberg looked slightly sorry for the Professor. "Because you're small enough—and important enough—to be a kind of hostage. This island's always been a good target."

"Well," Reinhart nodded to the map on the wall. "There's your evidence. Aren't the West going to take it to the Security Council?"

Vandenberg shook his head. "Not until we can negotiate from strength. They'd love us to run squealing to the U.N. and admit our weakness. Then they'd have us. What we need first is some means of defense."

Reinhart looked skeptical. "What are you doing about it?"

"We're going as fast as we can. Geers has a theory—"

"Oh, Geers!"

"Geers has a theory," Vandenberg ignored the interruption, "that if we can work this girl creature in harness with your computer, we may get some pretty quick thinking."

"What *was* my computer," said Reinhart sourly. "I wish you joy."

The night after Vandenberg left, Fleming appeared. Reinhart was working late, trying to fix the origin of ground signals which made the satellites change course in orbit, when he heard the exhaust crackle of Fleming's car outside. It was a little like coming home for Fleming; the familiar room, Harvey at the control desk, the small neat father-figure of the Professor waiting for him. Of the three men, Fleming looked the most worn.

"It seems so sane here." He gazed around the large, neat room. "Calm and clean."

Reinhart smiled. "It's not very sane at the moment."

"Can we talk?"

Reinhart led him over to a couple of easy chairs which had been set for visitors, with a little table, in a back corner of the observatory.

"I told you on the phone, John, there's nothing I can do. They're going to use the creature as an aid to the computer for Geers's missile work."

"Which is just what it wants."

Reinhart shrugged. "I'm out of it now."

"We're all out of it. I'm only hanging on by the skin of my teeth. All this about being able to pull out the plug —well, we can't any more, can we?" Fleming fiddled nervously with a box of matches he had taken out to light their cigarettes. "It's in control of itself now. It's got its protectors—its allies. If this thing that looks like a woman had arrived by space-ship, it would have been annihilated by now. It would have been recognized for what it was. But because it's been planted in a much subtler way, because it's been given human form, it's accepted on face value. And it's a pretty face. It's no use appealing to Geers or that lot: I've tried. Prof, I'm scared."

"We're all scared," Reinhart said. "The more we find out about the universe the more frightening it is."

"Look." Fleming leaned forward earnestly. "Let's use our heads. That machine—that brain-child of some other world— has written off its own one-eyed monster. It's written off Christine. It'll write me off if I get in its way."

"Then get out of its way," said Reinhart wearily. "If you're in danger get out of its way now."

"Danger!" Fleming snorted. "Do you think I *want* to die in some horrible way, like Dennis Bridger, for the sake of the government or Intel? But I'm only the next on the list. If I'm forced out, or if I'm killed, what comes afterwards?"

"It's a question of what comes first at the moment." Reinhart sounded like a doctor with a hopeless case. "I can't help you, John."

"What about Osborne?"

"He doesn't hold the reins now."

"He could get his Minister to go to the P.M."

"The P.M.?"

"He's paid, isn't he?"

Reinhart shook his head. "You've nothing to show, John."

"I've some arguments."

"I doubt if any of them are in a mood to listen." Reinhart waved a small hand towards the wall map. "That's what we're worried about at the moment."

"What's that all in aid of?"

Reinhart told him. Fleming sat listening, tense and miserable, his fingers crushing the matchbox out of shape.

"We can't always be in front, can we?" He pushed away the Professor's explanations. "At least we can come to terms with human beings."

"What sort of terms?" Reinhart asked.

"It doesn't matter what sort of terms—compared with what we're likely to be up against. A bomb is a quick death for civilization, but the slow subjugation of a planet..." his voice trailed away.

The Prime Minister was in his oak-panelled room in the House of Commons. He was a sporty-looking old gentleman with twinkling blue eyes. He sat at the middle of one side of the big table that half-filled the room, listening to the Minister of Defense. Sunlight streamed gently in through the mullioned windows. There was a knock at the door and the Defense Minister frowned; he was a keen young man who did not like being interrupted.

"Ah, here comes the science form." The Prime Minister smiled genially as Ratcliff and Osborne were shown in. "You haven't met Osborne, have you Burdett?"

The Defense Minister rose and shook hands perfunctorily. The Prime Minister motioned them to sit down.

"Isn't it a splendid day, gentlemen? I remember it was like this at Dunkirk time. The sun always seems to smile on national adversity." He turned to Burdett. "Would you bully-off for us, dear boy?"

"It's about Thorness," said Burdett to Ratcliff. "We want to take over the computer altogether—and everything associated with it. It's been agreed in principle, hasn't it? And the P.M. and I think the time has come."

Ratcliff looked at him without love. "You've access to it already."

"We need more than that now, don't we, sir?" Burdett appealed to the Prime Minister.

"We need our new interceptor, gentlemen, and we need it quickly." Behind the amiable, lazy, rather old-world manner lay more than a hint of firmness and grasp of business. "In nineteen-forty we had Spitfires, but at the moment neither we nor our allies in the West have anything to touch the stuff that's coming over."

"And no prospect of anything," Burdett put in, "by conventional means."

"We could co-operate, couldn't we?" Ratcliff asked Osborne, "in developing something?"

Burdett was not one to waste time. "We can handle it

ourselves if we take over your equipment at Thorness entirely, and the girl."

"The creature?" Osborne raised a well-disciplined eyebrow, but the Prime Minister twinkled reassuringly at him.

"Dr. Geers is of the opinion that if we use this curiously derived young lady to interpret our requirements to the computer and to translate its calculations back to us we could solve a lot of our problems very quickly."

"If you can trust its intentions."

The Prime Minister looked interested. "I don't quite follow you."

"One or two of our people have doubts about its potential," said Ratcliff, more in hope than conviction. No minister likes losing territory, even if he has to use dubious arguments to retain it. The Prime Minister waved him aside.

"Oh yes, I've heard about that."

"Up to now, sir, this creature has been under examination by our team," Osborne said. "Professor Dawnay—"

"Dawnay could stay."

"In a consultative role," Burdett added swiftly.

"And Dr. Fleming?" asked Ratcliff.

The Prime Minister turned again to Burdett. "Fleming would be useful, wouldn't he?"

Burdett frowned. "We shall need complete control and very tight security."

Ratcliff tried his last card. "Do you think she's up to it, this girl?"

"I propose to ask her," said the Prime Minister. He pressed a small bell-push on the table and a young gentleman appeared almost immediately in the doorway. "Ask Dr. Geers to bring his lady friend in, will you?"

"You've got her here?" Ratcliff looked accusingly at Osborne as though it was his fault.

"Yes, dear boy." The Prime Minister also looked at Osborne, inquiringly. "Is she, er—?"

"She looks quite normal."

The Prime Minister gave a small sigh of relief and rose as the door reopened to admit Geers and Andromeda. "Come in, Dr. Geers. Come along in, my dear."

Andromeda was given the chair facing him. She sat quietly with her head slightly bowed, her hands folded in her lap, like a typist coming for an interview.

"You must find this all rather strange," said the Prime

Minister soothingly. She answered in slow, correct sentences.

"Dr. Geers has explained it to me."

"Did he explain why we brought you here?"

"No."

"Burdett?" The Prime Minister handed over the questioning. Ratcliff looked on grumpily while Burdett sat forward on the edge of his chair, rested his elbows on the table, placed his fingers together and looked keenly at Andromeda over them.

"This country—you know about this country?"

"Yes."

"This country is being threatened by orbital missiles."

"We know about orbital missiles."

"We?" Burdett looked at her even more sharply.

She remained as she was, her face empty of expression. "The computer and myself."

"How does the computer know?"

"We share our information."

"That is what we hoped," said the Prime Minister.

Burdett continued. "We have interception missiles—rockets of various kinds—but nothing of the combined speed, range and accuracy to, er . . . " He searched around for the right piece of jargon.

"To hit them?" she asked simply.

"Exactly. We can give you full details of speed, height and course; in fact, we can give you a great deal of data, but we need it translated into practical mechanical terms."

"Is that difficult?"

"For us, yes. What we're after is a highly sophisticated interception weapon that can do its own instantaneous thinking."

"I understand."

"We should like you to work on this with us," the Prime Minister said gently, as if asking a favor of a child. "Dr. Geers will tell you what is needed, and he will give you all facilities for actually designing weapons."

"And Dr. Fleming," added Ratcliff, "can help you with the computer."

Andromeda looked up for the first time.

"We shall not need Dr. Fleming," she said, and something about her calm, measured voice ran like a cold shadow across the sunlight.

After her return from London, Andromeda spent most of her time in the design office, a block or two away from the computer building, preparing data for the machine and sending it over for computation. Sometimes she came to communicate directly with it, with the result that long and complex calculations emerged later from the printer, which she would take away to translate into design terms. The outcome was all and more than Geers could have wished. A new guidance system and new ballistic formulas sprung ready-made from the drawing-board and when tested, they proved to come up to all specifications. The machine and the girl together could get through about a year's development theory in a day. The results were not only elegant but obviously effective. In a very short time it would clearly be possible to construct an entirely new interceptive missile.

During duty hours Andromeda had freedom of movement within the compound and, although she disappeared, under guard, into her own quarters after work, she was soon a familiar figure in the camp. Judy put it about that she was a research senior who had been seconded by the Ministry of Defense.

The following week a communiqué was issued from 10 Downing Street:

"Her Majesty's Government has been aware for some time of the passage of an increasing number of orbital vehicles, possibly missiles, over these islands. Although the vehicles, which are of unknown but terrestrial origin, pass over at great speed and at great height, there is no immediate cause for alarm. Her Majesty's Government points out, however, that they constitute a deliberate infringement of our national air space, and that steps are being taken to intercept and identify them."

Fleming listened to the telecast on the portable receiver in his hut at Thorness. He was no longer responsible for the computer, and Geers had suggested that he might be happier away from it. However, he stayed on, partly out of obstinacy and partly from a sense of impending emergency, watching the progress of Andromeda and the two young operators who had been enlisted to help her with the machine. He made no approaches to her, or to Judy, who continued to hang around with a sort of aimless watchfulness, acting as a liaison between Andromeda and the front office; but after he heard the broadcast he wandered over to the computer block with the vague idea that something ought to be done.

Judy found him sitting brooding on the swivel chair by the control desk. She had not gone near him again since the last snub, but she had watched him with concern and with a feeling of latent affection that had never left her.

She went up to the control desk and stood in front of him. "Why don't you give it up, John?"

"That would please you, wouldn't it?"

"It wouldn't please me, but there's nothing you can do here, eating your heart out."

"It's a nice little three-handed game, isn't it?" He looked sardonically up at her. "I watch her and you watch me."

"You're not doing yourself any good."

"Jealous?" he asked.

She shook her head impatiently. "Don't be absurd."

"They're all so damn sure." He stared reflectively across to the control equipment. "There may be something I've missed, about this—or about her."

Andromeda came in to the computer room while Judy and Fleming were talking. She stood by the doorway holding a wad of papers, waiting until they had finished. She was quiet enough, but there was nothing modest about her. When she spoke to Judy and the others who worked with her she had an air of unquestioned and superior authority. She made no concessions even to Geers; she was perfectly polite but treated them all as intellectual inferiors.

"I wish to speak to Dr. Geers about these, please," she said from the doorway.

"Now?" Judy tried to match her in quiet contempt.

"Now."

"I'll see if he's free," Judy said, and went out. Andromeda crossed slowly to the control panel, ignoring Fleming; but something prompted him to stop her.

"Happy in your work?"

She turned and looked at him, without speaking. He stretched back in the chair, suddenly alert.

"You're getting quite indispensable, aren't you?" he asked in the tone he had used to Judy.

She looked at him solemnly. She might have been a statue, with her fine carved face, her long hair, and her arms hanging limply down beside her simple, pale dress. "Please be careful what you talk about," she said.

"Is that a threat?"

"Yes." She spoke without emphasis, as if simply stating a fact. Fleming stood up.

"Good grief! I'm not going to—" He stopped himself and smiled. "Perhaps I *have* missed something."

Whatever he had in mind was hidden from her. She turned to walk away.

"Wait a minute!"

"I am busy." But she turned back to him and waited. He walked slowly to her and looked her up and down as though mocking her.

"You want to make something of yourself, if you're going to influence men." She stood still. He lifted a hand to her hair and edged it back from one side of her face. "You should push your hair back, and then we could see what you look like. Very pretty."

She stepped away so that his hand fell from her, but she kept her eyes on him, intrigued and puzzled.

"Or you could wear scent," he said. "Like Judy does."

"Is that what smells?"

He nodded. "Not very exotic. Lavender water or something. But nice."

"I do not understand you." A small frown creased the smooth skin of her forehead. "Nice—nasty. Good—bad. There is no logical distinction."

He still smiled. "Come here."

She hesitated, then took a step towards him. Quietly and deliberately he pinched her arm.

"Ow!" She stepped back with a sudden look of fear in her eyes and rubbed the place where he had hurt her.

"Nice or nasty?" he inquired.

"Nasty."

"Because you were made to register pain." He raised his hand again and she flinched away. "I'm not going to hurt you this time."

She stood rigidly while he stroked her forehead, like a deer being stroked by a child, submissive but ready for flight. His fingers ran down her cheek and on to her bare neck.

"Nasty or nice?"

"Nice." She watched him to see what he would do next.

"You're made to register pleasure. Did you know that?" He withdrew his hand gently and moved away from her.

"I doubt if you were intended to, but by giving you human form . . . human beings don't live by logic."

"So I've noticed!" She was more sure of herself now, as she had been before he started speaking; but he still held all her attention.

"We live through our senses. That's what gives us our instincts, for good or bad—our aesthetic and moral judgments. Without them we'd probably have annihilated ourselves by now."

"You're doing your best, aren't you?" She looked down at her papers with a contemptuous smile. "You are like children, with your missiles and rockets."

"Don't count me in on that."

"No, I don't." She regarded him thoughtfully. "All the same, I am going to save you. It is very simple, really." She made a small gesture to indicate the papers she held.

Judy came in and stood, as Andromeda had done, at the doorway.

"Dr. Geers can see you."

"Thank you." The roles now were changed. In some unspoken way, the three of them stood in a different relationship to each other. Although Fleming still watched Andromeda, she looked back at him with a different kind of awareness.

"Do I smell nasty?" she asked.

He shrugged. "You'll have to find out, won't you?"

She followed Judy out of the building and walked along the concrete path with her to Geers's office. They had nothing to say to each other, and nothing to share except a sort of wary indifference. Judy showed her into Geers's room and left her. The Director was sitting behind his desk, telephoning.

"Yes, we're coming along famously," he was saying. "Only another check and we can start building."

He put down the phone and Andromeda placed her papers on his desk, casually, as though she were bringing him a cup of tea.

"That is all you will need, Dr. Geers," she told him.

ten

ACHIEVEMENTS

THE NEW missile was built and tested at Thorness. When it had been fired and recovered, and copies made, the Prime Minister sent Burdett to see Vandenberg.

The General was more than a little worried about the Thorness project. It seemed to him to be going too fast to be sound. Although his chiefs wanted action quickly, he had grave doubts about this piece of foreign technology and wanted it sent for testing to the U.S.A.; but Her Majesty's Government unexpectedly dug its toes in.

Burdett confronted him in the underground ops room.

"Just for once we have the means to go it alone." The young minister looked very sharp and dapper and keen in his neat blue suit and old school tie. "Of course we shall co-ordinate with you when we come to use it."

Vandenberg grunted. "Can we know *how* you'll use it?"

"We shall make an interception."

"How?"

"Reinhart will give us our target information from Boulder-shaw, and Geers's outfit will do the firing."

"And if it fails?"

"It won't fail."

The two men faced each other uncompromisingly: Burdett smooth and smiling, the General solid and tough. After a moment Vandenberg shrugged.

"This has become a very domestic affair all of a sudden."

They left it at that, and Burdett told Geers and Reinhart to go ahead.

At Bouldershaw fresh traces were picked up nearly every day. Harvey sat behind the great window overlooking the Fell and logged them as they went over.

"... *August 12th, 03.50 hrs., G.M.T. Ballistic vehicle number one-one-seven passed overhead on course 2697/451. Height 400 miles. Speed approx. 17,500 miles per hour...*"

The huge bowl outside, which seemed empty and still under its tall superstructure, was all the time alive and full of the reflection of signals. Every vehicle that came over gave out its own call and could be heard approaching from the other side of the globe. There were electronic scanners in the observatory which showed the path of the targets on a cathode-ray screen, while an automatic plotting and range-finding system was coupled by land-line to Thorness.

At Thorness an array of rockets was set up on the cliff-top; a "first throw" as they called it and two reserves. The three pencil-shaped missiles, with tapering noses and finned tails, stood in a row on their launching pads, glinting silver in the cold, grey light. They were surprisingly small, and very slim and rather beautiful. They looked like arrows strung and ready to fly out from all the heavy and complicated harness of firing. Each one, tanked with fuel and crammed with precise equipment, carried a small nuclear charge in its tapered head.

The ground control was operated through the computer, which in turn was directed by Andromeda and her assistants. Target signals from Bouldershaw were fed in through the control room and instantaneously interpreted and passed on to the interceptor. The flight of interception could be directed to a hair's breadth.

Only Geers and his operational staff were allowed in the control room at this time. Fleming and Dawnay were given monitoring facilities, as a gesture of courtesy, in another building; Andromeda took over calmly at the computer and Geers fussed anxiously and self-importantly between the launching site, the computer building and the fire control room. This was a small operations center where the mechanics of take-off were supervised. A direct telephone connected him with the Ministry of Defense. Judy was kept busy by Major Quadring, double-checking everyone who came and went.

On the last day of October, Burdett conferred with the Prime Minister, and then picked up a telephone to Geers and Reinhart.

"The next one," he said.

Reinhart and Harvey stood to for thirty-six hours before they detected a new trace. Then, in the early light, they picked up a very faint signal and the automatic linking system was put into action.

The sleepy crew at Thorness pulled themselves together, and Andromeda, who showed no sign of effort, watched as they checked the information through the computer. The optimum launching time came out at once and was communicated to the fire control center, and the count-down began. Very soon a trace of the target could be seen on radar screens. There was a screen in the computer room for Andromeda, another in fire control for Geers, a third in London in the Ministry of Defense Ops Room, and a master-check at Bouldershaw, watched by Reinhart. At Bouldershaw, too, the signal from the satellite could be heard: a steady *blip-blip-blip-blip* which was amplified and pushed out through the speakers until it filled the observatory.

At Thorness the speakers were carrying the count-down, and launching teams worked briskly round the bases of the rockets on the cliff-top. At zero the "first throw" was to be fired and, if that failed, the second, and, if necessary, the third, with fresh flight calculations made according to their take-off time. Andromeda had held that there was no need for this but the others were all too conscious of human fallibility. Neither Geers nor any of his superiors could afford a fiasco.

The count-down ran out to single figures and to nought. In the grey morning light of the promontory the take-off rockets of the first flight suddenly bloomed red. The air filled with noise, the earth shook, and the tall thin pencil slipped up into the sky. Within a few seconds it was gone beyond the clouds. In the control rooms, the operations room and the observatory, anxious faces watched its trace appear on the cathode screens. Only Andromeda seemed unconcerned and confident.

At Bouldershaw, Reinhart, Harvey and their team watched the two traces of target and interceptor slowly converging and heard the *blip-blip-blip* of the satellite ringing louder and clearer in their ears as it approached. Then the traces met and at the same moment the noise stopped.

Reinhart swung round to Harvey and thumped him, wildly and uncharacteristically, on the back.

"We've done it . . . !"

. . . "A hit!" Geers picked up his telephone for London. Andromeda turned away from her control-room screen as though something quite unimportant were over. In London, Vandenberg turned to his British colleagues in the ops room.

"Well, what do you know?" he said.

That evening an official statement was made to the press:

"The Ministry of Defense has announced that an orbital missile has been intercepted by a new British rocket three hundred and seventy miles above this country. The remains of the missile, which is of unknown origin, and of the interceptor, were burned out on re-entering the earth's atmosphere, but the interception was followed on auto-radar equipment and can, say the Ministry, be verified in minute detail."

An almost audible collective sigh of relief rose from Whitehall, accompanied by a glow of self-congratulation. The Cabinet held an unusually happy meeting and within a week the Prime Minister was sending again for Burdett.

The Minister of Defense presented himself neat and smiling, in an aura of confidence and after-shave lotion.

"Any new traces?" asked the Prime Minister.

"Not one."

"Nothing in orbit?"

"Nothing's been over this country, sir, since the interception."

"Good." The Prime Minister mused. "Reinhart was due for a knighthood anyway."

"And Geers?"

"Oh yes. C.B.E. probably."

Burdett prepared for business. "And the computer and its, er, agent, sir?"

"We might make the young lady a Dame," said the Prime Minister with one of his camouflage twinkles.

"I mean," asked Burdett, "what happens to them? The Ministry of Science want them to revert."

The Prime Minister continued to look amused. "We can't have that, can we?" he said.

"We've a heavy military program for it."

"Also a heavy economic one."

"What do you mean, sir?"

"I mean," said the Prime Minister seriously, "that if this particular combination can achieve that for us, it can achieve a lot of other things. Of course it must still work on defense, but at the same time it has a very great industrial potential. We want to be rich, you know, as well as strong. The scientists have given us—and I'm very grateful to them—the most advanced thinking instrument in the world. It's going to make it possible for us to leap forward, as a country, in a great many fields. And about time too."

"Are you going to keep it in your own hands, sir?" Burdett spoke with a mixture of irritation and deference.

"Yes. I shall make a statement to the nation in the near future."

"You're not going to make it public?"

"Don't flap, man." The Prime Minister regarded him blandly. "I shall say something about the effects, but the means will remain top secret. That'll be your responsibility."

Burdett nodded. "What can I tell Vandenberg?"

"Tell him to rest his feet. No, you can say to him that we're going to be a great little country again, but we'll continue to co-operate with our allies. With any allies we can get, in fact." He paused for a moment while Burdett waited politely. "I shall go to Thorness myself as soon as I can."

The visit was arranged in a few days—it was obviously priority in the Prime Minister's mind. Judy and Quadring had some difficulty in concealing it from the press, for public curiosity was at its height; but in the end it was laid on with due secrecy and the compound and its inhabitants were quietly and discreetly groomed. Geers had changed distinctly since his success. Confidence was something new to him. It was as though he had taken the chips off his shoulder and put them away. He was brisk but affable, and he not only allowed Dawnay and Fleming access to the computer again but urged them to be on parade for the Prime Minister's tour. He wanted everyone, he said, to have their due.

Fleming had private doubts about this window-dressing but kept them to himself; at least there might be an opportunity to speak. He arrived in the computer building early on the day of the visit, and found Andromeda waiting there alone. She also appeared transformed. Her long hair had been brushed back from her face and, instead of her usual simple frock, she wore a sort of Grecian garment which clung to her breasts and thighs and floated away behind her.

"Phew!" he said. "Something human'll happen to you if you go round like that."

"You mean these clothes?" she asked with faint interest.

"You'll make one hell of an impression, but then you already have. There'll be no holding you now, will there?" he asked sourly. Andromeda glanced at him without replying. "He'll probably ask you to take over Number Ten, and I suppose you think we'll sleep easy in our beds, now we've seen how powerful you are. I suppose you think we're all fools."

"You are not a fool," she said.

"If I weren't a fool, you wouldn't be here now! You shoot down a little bit of metal from the sky—chickenfeed when you know how—and suddenly you're in a commanding position."

"That was intended." She faced him expressionlessly.

"And what's intended next?"

"It depends on the program."

"Yes." He advanced towards her. "You're a slave, aren't you?"

"Why don't you go?" she asked.

"Go?"

"Now. While you can."

"Make me!" He stared at her, hard and hostile, but she turned her head away.

"I may have to," she said. He stood, challenging her to go on, but she would not be drawn. After a few seconds he looked at his watch and grunted.

"I wish this diplomatic circus would come and get it over."

When the Prime Minister did arrive, he was escorted by officials, politicians and Scotland Yard heavies. Geers led him in. They were followed by Burdett and Hunter and by a train of lesser beings, dwindling away to Judy, who came at the end and closed doors behind them. Geers indicated the control room with a sweep of his arm.

"This is the actual computer, sir."

"Quite incomprehensible to me," said the Prime Minister, as if this were an advantage. He caught sight of Andromeda. "Hallo, young lady. Congratulations."

He walked towards her with his hand outstretched, and she took and shook it stiffly.

"You understand all this?" he asked her. She smiled politely. "I'm sure you do, and we are all very beholden.

It's quite a change for us in this old country to be able to make a show of force. We shall have to take great care of you. Are they looking after you all right?"

"Yes, thank you." The visiting party stood round in a half circle, watching and admiring her, but she said nothing else. Fleming caught Judy's eye and nodded towards the Prime Minister. For a moment she could not think what he wanted, then she understood and edged in beside Geers.

"I don't think the Prime Minister has met Dr. Fleming," she whispered. Geers frowned; his good fellowship seemed to be wearing a little thin in places.

"Good, good." The Prime Minister could think of nothing more to say to Andromeda. He turned back to Geers.

"And where do you keep the rocketry?"

"I'll show you, sir. And I'd like you to see the laboratory."

They moved on, leaving Judy standing. "Dr. Fleming—" she tried unsuccessfully, but they did not hear her. Fleming stepped forward.

"Excuse me a moment—"

Geers turned to him with a scowl. "Not now, Fleming."

"But—"

"What does the young man want?" the Prime Minister inquired mildly. Geers switched on a smile.

"Nothing, sir. He doesn't want anything."

The Prime Minister walked on tactfully, and as Fleming moved forward again Hunter laid a hand on his arm.

"For goodness sake!" Hunter hissed.

At the door of the lab bay Geers turned back.

"You'd better come with us." He spoke to Andromeda, ignoring the others.

"Come along, my dear," said the Prime Minister, standing aside for her. "Brains and beauty first."

The procession filed out into the laboratory, except for Judy.

"Coming?" she asked Fleming, who stood staring after them.

He shook his head. "That was great, wasn't it?"

"I did my best."

"Great."

Judy fidgeted with her handkerchief. "At least you should have been allowed to speak to him. I suppose he's shrewd, though he looks a bit of an old woman."

"Like another."

"Who?"

"Of Riga." He gave her a faint grin. "Who went for a ride on a tiger. They finished the ride with the lady inside, and a smile on the face of the tiger."

She knew the limerick, and felt irritated. "We're all going for a ride, except you?"

"You know what she said to me just now?"

"No."

He changed his mind and looked away from Judy to the control panel. "I've an idea."

"One I'd understand?"

"Look how beautifully he's ticking over—how sleek and rhythmical he is." The computer was working steadily, with a gentle hum and a regular flashing of lights. "Purring away with us inside him. Suppose I pulled out the plug now?"

"They wouldn't let you."

"Or got a crowbar and smashed him up."

"You wouldn't get far with the guards. Anyhow, they'd rebuild it."

He took out a pad and some papers from a drawer in the control desk. "Then we'll have to shake it intellectually, won't we? I've shaken the young lady a bit. Now we'd better start on him." He saw that she was looking at him doubtfully. "Don't worry, you won't have to blow your whistle. Are they coming back this way?"

"No. They'll go out through the lab entrance."

"Good." He started copying numbers from the sheets on to the pad.

"What is that?"

"A shortened formula for the creature."

"Andromeda?"

"Call her whatever amuses you." He scribbled on. "This is what the machine calls her. Not a formula, really—a naming tag."

"What are you going to do?"

"Re-arrange it slightly."

"You're not going to do any damage?"

He laughed at her. "You'd better go on with your conducted tour; this'll take time."

"I shall warn the guards."

"Warn whom you like."

She hesitated, then gave it up and went to rejoin the party. When she had gone he checked the figures and walked over with the pad to the input unit.

"I'll give you something to think about!" he said aloud to the machine, and sat down and started tapping the message in.

He had hardly finished when Andromeda came back.

"I thought you were going to see the rocketry."

She shrugged her shoulders. "It is not interesting."

The lamps on the display panel started to flash faster, and suddenly there was a fantastic clatter from the output unit as the printer began to work furiously.

Andromeda looked up in surprise. "What is happening?"

Fleming went quickly to the printer and read the figures as they were banged out on to the paper.

He smiled. "Your friend seems to have lost his temper."

She crossed the room and looked over his shoulder.

"This is nonsense."

"Exactly."

The printer stopped as suddenly as it had begun, leaving them in silence.

"What have you been doing?" the girl asked. She read the figures through uncomprehendingly. "This doesn't mean anything."

Fleming grinned at her. "No. He's flipped for a moment. I think he's psychologically disturbed."

"What have you done to it?" She started towards the terminals, but he stopped her.

"Come away from there."

She halted uncertainly. "What have you done?"

"Only given him a little information."

Looking around, she saw the pad on top of the input keys. She went slowly over to it and read it.

"That's my name-tag—reversed!"

"Negatived," said Fleming.

"It'll think I'm dead!"

"That's what I meant him to think."

She looked up at him, puzzled. "Why?"

"I thought I'd let him know he couldn't have it all his own way."

"That was very foolish."

"He seems to value you highly," he said scornfully.

She turned away towards the terminals. "I must tell it I'm alive."

"No!" He seized hold of her by the arms.

"I must. It thinks I'm dead, and I must tell it I'm not."

"Then I shall tell it you are. I can play this game until it doesn't know whether it's coming or going."

He let go one arm and picked up the pad from the keyboard.

"Give me that." She pulled her other arm free. "You can't win, you know." She turned away again, and as Fleming moved to stop her she suddenly shouted at him. "Leave me alone! Go away! Go out of here!"

They stood facing each other, both trembling, as if neither could move. Then Fleming took hold of her firmly with both hands and drew her towards him.

He sniffed at her in surprise. "You're wearing scent!"

"Let go of me. I shall call the guards."

Fleming started to laugh. "Open your mouth, then."

She parted her lips and he put a kiss on them. Then he held her at arm's length and examined her.

"Nice or nasty?"

"Leave me alone, please." Her voice was uncertain. She looked at him in a confused way, and then down, but he still held her.

"Who do you belong to?"

"I belong where my brain tells me."

"Then tell it this—" He kissed her again, sensuously but dispassionately, for a long time.

"Don't," she begged, pulling her lips away. He held her close to him and spoke gently.

"Don't you like the taste of lips? Or the taste of food, or the smell and feel of the fresh air outside, or the hills beyond the wire with sunshine and shadows on them and larks singing? And the company of human beings?"

She shook her head slowly. "They're not important."

"Aren't they?" He spoke with his mouth close to her. "They weren't allowed for by whatever disembodied intelligence up there you owe allegiance to, but they're important to organic life, as you'll find out."

"Anything can be allowed for," she said.

"But they weren't in the calculations."

"They can be put in." She looked up at him. "You can't beat us, Dr. Fleming. Stop trying before you get hurt."

He let go of her. "Am I likely to get hurt?"

"Yes."

"Why should you warn me?"

"Because I like you," she said, and he half smiled at her.
"You're talking like a human being."

"Then it's time I stopped. Please go now." He stood obstinately, but there was a note of pleading in her voice that had never been there before, and an expression of unhappiness on her face. "Please ... Do you want me to be punished?"

"By whom?"

"Who do you think?" She glanced at the computer control racks. Fleming was taken off-guard; this was something he had never thought of.

"Punished? That's a new one." He put the pad of figures in his pocket and went to the door. In the doorway he turned back to deliver a last shot. "Who *do* you belong to?"

She watched him go and then turned reluctantly towards the display panel, and walked slowly, compulsively, up to it. She raised her hands to communicate with the terminals, then hesitated. Her face was strained, but she raised them again and touched the plates. For a moment all that happened was that the lights blinked faster, as the machine digested the information she gave it. Then the voltage meter below the panel suddenly peaked.

Andromeda gave a cry of pain and tried to pull her hands away from the plates, but the current held her fast. The voltage needle dropped, only to swing up again, and she cried out again ... And then a third time and a fourth and over and over and over ...

Once more it was Judy who found her. She came in a few minutes later, looking for Fleming, and saw to her horror the girl lying crumpled on the floor, where Christine had been.

"Oh no!" The words jerked out of her, and she ran forward and turned the body over. Andromeda was still alive. She moaned as Judy touched her, and curled away, whimpering quietly and nursing her hands together. Judy raised the blonde head and rested it in her lap and then took the hands and opened them. They were black with burning, except where the red flesh lay bare down to the bone.

Judy let them go gently. "How did it happen?"

Andromeda groaned again and opened her eyes. Judy said to her, "Your hands."

"We can easily mend them." The girl's voice was hardly audible.

"What happened?"

"Something went wrong, that's all."

Judy left her and telephoned Dr. Hunter.

From that moment events moved with almost cataclysmic speed. Hunter put a temporary dressing on Andromeda's hands and tried to persuade her to move into the station's sick bay, but she refused to leave the computer until she had seen Madeleine Dawnay.

"It will be quicker in the end," she told them. Although she was suffering from shock, she went sturdily through Dawnay's papers until she found the section she was looking for. Hunter had given her local shots to ease the pain in her hands, and with these and the bandages she fumbled a good deal, but she pulled out the sheets she wanted and shuffled them across to Dawnay. They were concerned with enzyme production in the D.N.A. formula.

"What do we do with these?" Dawnay looked at them doubtfully.

"Get an isolated tissue formula," said Andromeda, and took the papers back to the computer. She was weak and pale and could hardly walk. Dawnay, Hunter and Judy watched anxiously as she stood again between the terminals and put out her swathed hands; but this time there was no disaster, and after a little the machine started printing out.

"It's an enzyme formula. You can make it up quite easily." She indicated the printer paper to Dawnay and then turned to Hunter. "I should like to lie down now, please. The enzyme can be applied to my hands on a medicated base when Professor Dawnay has prepared it, but it should be as soon as possible."

She was ill for several days, and Hunter dressed her hands with an ointment containing the formula, when Dawnay had made it up. The healing was miraculous: new tissue—soft natural flesh, not the hard tissue of scarring—filled in the wounds in a matter of hours, and formed a fresh layer of pale pink skin across her palms. By the time she recovered from the effects of the electric shocks, her hands were remade.

Hunter, meanwhile, had reported to Geers and Geers had sent for Fleming. The Director, not yet certain of the outcome of the accident, was sick and thin-lipped with worry, his brief season of fellowship gone.

"So *you* decide to throw it off balance!" He flung the

words across his desk at Fleming and pounded his fist on the polished wood. "You don't consult anyone—you're too clever. So clever, the machine goes wrong and damn near kills the girl."

"If you won't even listen to what happened." Fleming's voice rose to match his, but Geers interrupted.

"I know what happened."

"Were you there? She knew she was going to be punished. She should have had me thrown out, she should have wiped out what I'd put into the computer; but she didn't—not soon enough. She hesitated and warned me and let me go, then she went and touched the communication terminals—"

"I thought you'd gone," Geers reminded him.

"Of course I'd gone. I'm telling you what happened inevitably: she let the machine know that she was alive, that it had been given false information, that the source of the information was around and she hadn't stopped it. So it punished her by giving her a series of electric shocks. It knows how to do that now; it learned on Christine."

The Director listened with thinly disguised impatience. "You're guessing," he said at the end.

"It's not guesswork, Geers. It was bound to happen, only I didn't realize in time."

"Have you your pass?" Geers looked at him glintingly through his spectacles. "To the computer building."

Fleming sniffed and rummaged in his pocket. "You can't fault me on that one. It's quite in order."

He handed it across the desk. Geers took it, examined it, and slowly tore it up.

"What's that in aid of?"

"We can't afford you, Fleming. Not any more."

Fleming banged the desk in his turn. "I'm staying on the station."

"Stay where you like; but your association with the computer is over. I'm sorry."

Geers felt better with Fleming out of the way, and better still when he heard of Andromeda's recovery. He got all the facts he could from Dawnay and Hunter about the enzyme, and then got through on his direct line to Whitehall. The reaction was as he thought. He sent for Andromeda and questioned her and seemed well pleased.

Fleming a year or two back would have hit the bottle,

but this time he had no appetite even for that. The same compulsion that had held him to the computer tied him to the compound; even though there was nothing he could now do, no part he could have in the project, he remained on the station, solitary and uncertain and given to long walks and lying on his bed. It was deep winter, but calm and grey, as though something dramatic were being withheld.

About a week after the accident—or punishment, as Fleming thought of it—he was returning from a walk on the moors when he saw an enormous and extravagantly shining car outside Geers's office, and as he passed it a short, square man with a bald head got out.

"Dr. Fleming!" The bald man raised a hand to stop and greet him.

"What are you doing here?"

"I hope you do not mind," said Kaufmann. Fleming looked to see who was around. "Get out," he said.

"Please, Herr Doktor, do not be embarrassed." Kaufmann smiled at him. "I am quite official. A.1 at Lloyds. I do not compromise you."

"You didn't compromise Bridger either, I suppose?" Fleming jerked his head towards the main gate. "That's the exit."

Kaufmann smiled again, and pulled out his case of cigarillos. "Smoking?"

"Slightly," Fleming said, "at the edges. I am not interested in anything you have to offer. Try the next door house."

"I do that." Kaufmann laughed and stuck a small cigar between his teeth before they closed. "I do just that. I stop you, Herr Doktor, to tell you that I shall not bother you any more. I have other means, much better, much more honest."

He smiled again, lit his cigar and walked without hesitation into the vestibule of Geers's office.

Fleming ran over to the security block, but Quadring was out somewhere, and so was Judy. Finally he got hold of Judy on the telephone, but by the time she reached Geers's office, the Director was just showing Kaufmann out. The two men seemed to be on most cordial terms, and Geers was smoking one of the cigarillos.

"Businesswise," Kaufmann was saying, "the process is immaterial. We are not curious; it is the result, yes?"

"We deal in results here." Geers had his number one smile

switched on. He held out a hand. "Auf Wiedersehen."

Judy watched while Kaufmann shook hands and walked back to his car. As the Director turned to go back into his office she said, "Can I speak to you for a minute?"

Geers flicked his smile off. "I'm rather busy."

"This is important. You know who he is?"

"His name is Kaufmann."

"Intel."

"That's right." Geers's fingers itched at the door handle.

"It was Kaufmann whom Dr. Bridger was selling—" Judy started, but Geers cut her short.

"I know all about the Bridger case."

Behind his voice Judy could hear the car driving away. Somehow it made what she felt seem terribly urgent: she had to batter it into him.

"It was Intel. They were taking secrets . . ."

Geers edged into his doorway. "They're not taking secrets from me," he said haughtily.

"But—" She followed him in uninvited, and found Dawnay waiting quietly in the office. She felt suddenly thrown and mumbled an apology to the older woman.

"Don't mind me, dear," said Dawnay neutrally, and strolled away to the far corner of the room. Geers sat back at his desk and looked at Judy with an air of businesslike dismissal.

"We're making a trade agreement."

"With Intel?" The horrifying absurdity of the whole thing crowded in on her: a vision of the piled-up madness of the past months and years. She gaped at him across the polished desk, until she could find words. "I was put on this job because we didn't trust them. Dr. Bridger was hounded to his death—by me among other people—because he . . ."

"The climate's changed."

She looked at his smug, prim face and lost her temper entirely. "Politicians enjoy such convenient weather!"

"That will be enough," Geers snapped.

Dawnay rustled quietly in her corner. "The child's right, you know, and we scientists get a bit jaundiced about it from time to time. We're at the mercy of the elements. *We* can't cheat."

"I'm a scientist too," Geers said pettishly.

"Was." The word slipped out before Judy could stop it. She waited for the explosion, but Geers somehow kept it under control. He went icy.

"It isn't, strictly speaking, your business. What the Government needs now is world markets. When the girl Andromeda burned her hands, she worked out a synthesis for Professor Dawnay's lab people. Have you seen her hands?"

"I saw them burned."

"There's no sign of a burn now. No scar tissue, nothing. Overnight."

"And that's what you're selling to Intel?"

"*Through* Intel. To anyone who needs it."

She tried to think what was wrong with this, and then realized. "Why not through the World Health Organization?"

"We're not contemplating wholesale charity. We're contemplating a reasonable trade balance."

"So you don't care who you shake hands with?" she asked with disgust. She felt completely reckless now, and turned on Dawnay. "Are you part of this?"

Dawnay hesitated. "The enzyme's not quite in a state to market yet. We need a more refined formula. André—the girl—is preparing the data for computing." They had all got into the habit of calling her André.

"So the whole station's working for Intel?"

"I hope not," said Dawnay, and it sounded as though perhaps she was on her side. Geers cut in.

"Look, Madeleine, this is enough."

"Then I won't waste your time." Judy moved to the door. "But I am not part of it, and nor is Dr. Fleming."

"We know how Fleming stands," said Geers sardonically.

"And you know where I stand too," Judy told him, and banged out.

Her instinct was to go straight to Fleming, but she could not quite face the risk of another snub. In fact, it was Dawnay who went to see him, on her way from the office block to the computer at the end of the day. She found him in his chalet, watching the Prime Minister's broadcast on television.

"Come in," he said flatly, and made room for her on the foot of his bed. She looked at the flickering blue screen and tried to believe in the confident, elderly, sportive, civilized face and the slow, drawling voice of the Prime Minister. Fleming sat, and watched and listened with her.

"Not since the halcyon days of Queen Victoria," the disembodied face announced, "has this country held such a clear lead in the fields of industry, technology and—above all—security as that which we now have within our grasp..."

She felt her attention wandering. "I'm sorry if I interrupted."

"You didn't." He made a grimace at the television. "Turn the old idiot off."

He rose and switched off the set himself and then mixed her a drink. "Social call?"

"I was just going across to the computer building when I saw a light in your window. Thanks." She took the glass from him.

"Working overtime?" he asked.

She lifted her glass and looked at him over the top of it. "Dr. Fleming, I've said some pretty uncharitable things about you in the past."

"You're not the only one."

"About your attitude."

"I was wrong, wasn't I? The Prime Minister says so. Wrong and out." He spoke more in sorrow than anger, and poured himself a small drink.

"I wonder," said Dawnay. "I'm beginning to wonder."

He did not answer, and she added, "Judy Adamson's beginning to wonder too."

"That'll be a big help," he snorted.

"She put up quite a fight with Geers this afternoon. I must say it made me think." She took a sip and swallowed it slowly, looking quietly across her glass and turning over the position in her mind. "It seems fair enough to make use of what we've got—of what you gave us."

"Don't rub that in."

"And yet I don't know. There's something corrupting about that sort of power. You can see it acting on the folk here, and on the government." She nodded to the television set. "As if perfectly ordinary, sensible people are being possessed by a determination that isn't their own. I think we've both felt it. And yet, it all seems harmless enough."

"Does it?"

She told him about the enzyme production. "It's beneficial. It regenerates cells, simply. It'll affect everything, from skin-grafting to ageing. It'll be the biggest medical aid since antibiotics."

"A godsend to millions."

When she got on to the Intel proposition he hardly reacted.

"Where is it all leading?" she asked. She did not really expect an answer, but she got one.

"A year ago that machine had no power outside its own

building, and even there we were in charge of it." He spoke without passion as if reiterating an old truth. "Now it has the whole country dependent on it. What happens next? You heard, didn't you? We shall go ahead, become a major force in the world again, and who's going to be the power behind that throne?"

He indicated the television, as she had done; then he seemed to tire of the conversation. He wandered across to his record player and switched it on.

"Could you have controlled it?" Dawnay was unwilling to let the subject go.

"Not latterly."

"What could you have done?"

"Fouled it up as much as possible." He began to sort out a record among a pile of L.P.s. "It knows that, now it has its creature to inform on me. It had me pushed out. 'You can't win,' she told me."

"She said that?"

Fleming nodded, and Dawnay frowned into her half-empty glass. "I don't know. Perhaps it's inevitable. Perhaps it's evolution."

"Look—" he put down the record and swung round to her. "I can foresee a time when we'll create a higher form of intelligence to which, in the end, we'll hand over. And it'll probably be an inorganic form, like that one. But it'll be something we've created ourselves, and we can design it for our own good, or for good as we understand it. This machine hasn't been programmed for our good; or, if it has, something's gone wrong with it."

She finished her drink. There was possibility in what he said—more than possibility, a sort of sane logic which she had missed lately. As an empirical scientist, she felt there must be some way in which it could be tested.

"Could anyone tell, except you?" she asked.

Fleming shook his head. "None of that lot."

"Could I tell?"

"You?"

"I have access to it."

He immediately lost interest in the record. His face lit up as if she had switched on some circuit inside him. "Yes— why not? We could try a little experiment." He picked up from his table the pad with the negatived name-code on it. "Have you somebody over there can feed this in?"

"André?"

"No. Not her. Whatever you do, don't take her into your confidence."

Dawnay remembered the operator. She took the pad, and Fleming showed her the section to be fed in.

"I'm out of my depth, I'll admit that," she said. Then she put down her glass and went out.

As she walked across the compound, she could hear the beginning of some post-Schoenbergian piece of music from Fleming's chalet; then she was in the computer building and heard nothing but the hum of equipment. André was in the control room, and a young operator. André kept herself even more to herself since the affair of her hands. She haunted the computer block like a pale shadow and seldom left it. She made no attempt to communicate with anyone, and although she was never hostile she was completely withdrawn. She looked with slight interest at Dawnay coming in.

"How's it getting on?" Dawnay asked.

"We have put in all the data," André said. "You should have the formula soon."

Dawnay moved away and joined the operator at the input unit. He was a young man, a very fresh post-graduate, who asked no questions, but did as he was told.

"Input that too, will you?" Dawnay gave him the pad. He rested it above the keyboard and started tapping.

"What is that?" André asked, hearing the sound.

"Something I want calculated." Dawnay kept her away from it, until the display panel suddenly broke out into wild flashing.

"What are you putting in?" André snatched at the pad and read from it. "Where did you get it?"

"That's my business," said Dawnay.

"Why don't you keep out of this?"

"You'd better leave us," Dawnay told the operator. He rose obediently and wandered out of the room. André waited until he had gone.

"I do not wish you any harm," she said then and there was not passion but great strength in her voice. "Why don't you keep out?"

"How dare you talk to me like that?" Dawnay heard herself sounding weak and ridiculous, but she could only answer as it took her. "I created you—I made you."

"*You* made me?" André looked at her with contempt, then crossed to the control panel and put her hands on the terminals. Immediately the display lamps became less agitated, but they continued to flicker so long as the girl stood there, strong and positive like a young goddess. After a minute she moved away and stood looking at Dawnay.

"We are getting rather tired of this—this little joke," she said calmly, as if delivering a message. "Neither you, nor Dr. Fleming, nor anyone else can come between us."

"If you're trying to frighten me—"

"I don't know what you've begun now. I cannot be responsible." Andromeda appeared to be looking through her into a space beyond. The output printer went noisily into action, and Dawnay started at the sound. She followed André over to it, and by the time she got there the message finished. André examined the paper, and then tore it off and gave it to her.

"Your enzyme formula."

"Is that all?" Dawnay felt a sense of relief.

"Isn't that enough for you?" asked André, and watched her go with a set, hostile face.

Dawnay had three assistants working for her at the time: a senior research chemist, a man, and two post-graduate helpers, a boy and a girl. Between them they made a chemical synthesis based on the new formula. It involved a good deal of handling in the laboratory, but none of them worried about it because it had no irritant effect. By the end of a day or two, however, they were all beginning to feel signs of lassitude and wasting. There seemed to be no reason, and they worked on, but by the end of the third day the girl collapsed, and by the following morning Dawnay and the man had keeled over as well.

Hunter packed them off to the sick bay, where they were soon joined by the boy. Whatever the disease was, it accelerated fast; there was no fever or inflammation, its victims simply degenerated. Cells died, the basic processes of metabolism slowed or stopped, and one after another the four weakened and slid into a state of coma. Hunter was desperate and appealed to Geers, who put a screen of silence round the whole business.

Fleming did not hear details until the fourth day, when Judy broke security to tell him. He immediately phoned Reinhart and asked him to come from Bouldershaw, and he persuaded

Judy to find a paper for him. When she gave it to him, he locked himself up in his room with it all night, emerging in the morning grim but satisfied. But by that time the girl assistant was dead.

eleven

ANTIDOTE

THEY WERE covering her face when Fleming arrived at the sick bay. The other three lay silent and still in their beds, their faces drawn and as pale as the pillows. Dawnay, in the next cubicle to the girl, was being kept barely alive by blood transfusion. She lay marble-still, like an effigy of some old warrior on a tomb. He stayed looking at her until Hunter joined him.

"What do you want?" Hunter was run ragged, and all rough edges. He gave up the effort to be so much as polite to Fleming.

"It's my fault," said Fleming, looking down at the drained face on the pillow.

Hunter half-laughed. "Humility's a new line for you."

"All right then—it wasn't!" Fleming spun round on him, flaming, and fished a clip of papers out of his pocket. "But I came to give you this."

Hunter took the papers suspiciously. "What is it?"

"The enzyme formula."

"How the devil did you get hold of it?"

Fleming sighed. "Illegally. Like I have to do everything."

"I'll keep it, if you don't mind," said Hunter. He looked at it again. "Why is it crossed through?"

"Because it's wrong." Fleming flicked over the top sheet to show the one underneath. "That's the right formula. You'd better get it made up quickly."

"The right formula?" Hunter looked slightly lost.

"What the computer gave Dawnay had an inversion of what

173

she wanted. It switched negative for positive, as it were, to pay her back for a little game I'd put her up to."

"What game?"

"It gave the anti-enzyme, instead of the enzyme. Instead of a cell regenerative, a cell destructor. Presumably it acts through the skin and they absorbed it while they were working on it." He picked up one of Dawnay's hands that lay limp on the sheet. "There's nothing you can do unless you can make the proper enzyme in time. That's why I've brought you the corrected formula."

"Do you really think . . . ?" Hunter frowned skeptically at the clip of papers, and Fleming, looking up from Dawnay's hand, which he was still holding, regarded him with distaste.

"Don't you want to make your reputation?"

"I want to save lives," said Hunter.

"Then make up the proper formula. It should work as an antidote to the one Dawnay got, in which case it ought to reverse what's happening now. At least you can try it. If not—" He shrugged and laid Dawnay's emaciated hand back on the sheet. "That machine will do anyone's dirty work, so long as it suits it."

Hunter sniffed. "If it's so damn clever, why did it make a mistake like this?"

"It didn't. The only mistake it made was it got the wrong person—the wrong people. It was after me, and it didn't care how many people it wrote off in the process. One of your trade agreements with Intel, and it could have been half the world."

He left Hunter scowling at the formula, but obviously obliged to try it.

That afternoon the man died; but the new enzyme had been made up and was administered to the two survivors. Nothing dramatic happened at first but by the evening it was clear that deterioration was slowing. Judy visited the sick bay after supper, and then began making her way to the main gate to meet Reinhart, who was due on the late train. As she passed the computer block she felt an impulse to go in. There was no operator on duty, and she found André sitting alone at the control desk, gazing in front of her. The accumulated hatred of months, the frustrations of years, suddenly boiled up in Judy.

"Another one has died," she said savagely. André shrugged

and Judy felt a terrible urge to hit her. "Professor Dawnay's fighting for her life. And the boy."

"Then they have a chance," the girl said, tonelessly.

"Thanks to Dr. Fleming. Not thanks to you."

"It is not my business."

"You gave Professor Dawnay the formula."

"The machine gave it."

"You gave it together!"

André shrugged her shoulders again. "Dr. Fleming has the antidote. He is intelligent—he can save them."

"You don't care, do you?" Judy's eyes felt hot and dry as she looked at her.

"Why should I care?" asked the girl.

"I hate you." Judy's throat felt dry, too, so that she could hardly speak. She wanted to pick up something heavy and break the girl's skull; but then the telephone rang and she had to go to the main gate to meet Reinhart.

The girl sat quite still for a long time after Judy had gone, gazing at the control panel, and several tears—actual human tears—welled in her eyes and trickled slowly down her cheeks.

Judy took Reinhart straight to Fleming's hut, where they brought him up to date.

"And Madeleine?" the old man asked. He looked tired and uncertain.

"Still alive, thank God," said Fleming. "We may save two of them."

Reinhart seemed to relax a little, and looked less tired. They took his coat, sat him in a chair by the radiator and gave him a drink. He seemed to Judy much older than she had ever known him, and rather pathetic. He was now Sir Ernest, and it was as if the act of knighthood had finally aged him. She could imagine how far in the past his youthful friendship with Dawnay must seem, and could feel him clinging on to her life as though his own were in some way tied to it. He took his drink and tried to think of the next thing to say.

"Have you told Geers yet?"

"What would Geers do?" asked Fleming. "Just be sorry it wasn't me. He'd have me thrown out of the compound, out of the country, if he could. I've been saying since I was in short pants that this thing's malicious but they all love it so. How much more do I have to prove before I convince anyone?"

"You don't have to prove any more to me, John," said Reinhart wearily.

"Well, that's something."

"Or me," Judy said.

"Oh fine, fine. That makes three of us against the entire set-up."

"What did you think I could do?" Reinhart asked.

"I dunno. You've been running half the science in this country for a generation—the good half. Surely someone would listen to you."

"Osborne, perhaps?"

"So long as he didn't get his cuffs dirty." Fleming thought for a moment. "Could he get me back into the computer?"

"Use your head, John. He's answerable to the Establishment."

"Could you get him down here?"

"I could try. What have you in mind?"

"We can fill that in later," said Fleming. Reinhart pulled a rail-air timetable out of his pocket.

"If I go up to London tomorrow—"

"Can't you go tonight?"

"Sir Ernest's tired," said Judy.

Reinhart smiled at her. "You can keep Sir Ernest for garden parties. I shall get a night flight."

"Why can't it wait a few hours?" Judy asked.

"I'm not a young man, Miss Adamson, but I'm not moribund." He pulled himself to his feet. "Give my love to Madeleine, if she's . . ."

"Sure," said Fleming, finding the old man's coat and helping him on with it. Reinhart moved to the door, buttoning himself as he went. Then he remembered something. "By the way, the message has stopped."

Judy looked from him to Fleming. "The message?"

"From up there." Reinhart pointed a finger to the sky. "It's stopped repeating, several weeks ago. Maybe we shall never pick it up again."

"We may have caught the tail end of a long transmission," Fleming said quietly, weighing the implications. "If it wasn't for that fluke at Bouldershaw, we might never have heard it, and none of this would have happened."

"That had crossed my mind," said Reinhart, and gave them another tired smile and went.

Fleming mooched round the room, thinking about what had

been said, while Judy waited. They heard Reinhart's car start and drive away, and at the sound of it Fleming came to rest beside Judy and put an arm round her shoulders.

"I'll do whatever you want," she told him. "They can court-martial me if they like."

"Okay, okay." He took his arm away.

"You can trust me, John."

He looked her full in the face, and she tried with her eyes to make him believe her.

"Yes, well—" he seemed more or less convinced. "I'll tell you what. Get on the blower to London, privately, first thing in the morning. Try to catch Osborne when the Prof's with him and tell him he's bringing an extra visitor."

"Who?"

"I don't care who. Garter King at Arms—the President of the Royal Academy—some stuffed shirt from the Ministry. He doesn't have to bring the gent, only his clothes."

"An unstuffed shirt?"

He grinned. "Hat, brief case and rolled umbrella will do. Oh, and an overcoat. Meanwhile you get an extra pass for him. Okay?"

"I'll try."

"Good girl." He put his arm round her again and kissed her. She enjoyed it and then leaned back to ask him, "What are you going to do?"

"I don't know yet." He kissed her once more, then pushed himself away from her. "I'm going to turn in, it's been a hell of a day. You'd better get out of here—I need some sleep."

He grinned again and she squeezed his hand and went out, lightfooted, singing inside herself.

Fleming undressed dreamily, working out plans and fantasies in his mind. He fell into bed, and almost as soon as he turned the light out he was asleep.

After Reinhart's and Judy's departure, the camp was quiet. It was a dark night; clouds were blowing in from the north-east, bringing with them a current of cold air and a prospect of snow, and covering the full moon. But the moon shone through for a few moments at a time, and by its light a slim, pale figure let itself out of a window at the back of the computer block and began to move, ghost-like, across the camp. None of the sentries saw it, let alone recognized it as the girl André, and she made her way stealthily between the huts to Fleming's chalet, her face set and a double-strand coil of insulated wire in her hand.

A little light fell from the window into Fleming's room, for he had drawn back the curtain before he went to bed. He did not stir when the door opened very quietly and André inched in. She was barefoot and very careful, and her hands were sheathed in a pair of thick rubber gloves. After making sure that Fleming slept, she knelt down by the wall beside his bed and inserted the two wires at one end of her coil into a power-point on the skirting, wedged them tight and switched on the current. She held the other end of the coil out from her, the two wires grasped separately between thumb and finger an inch or so down the insulation and the bare live ends extended, and stood up and advanced slowly towards Fleming. The chances of his surviving a full charge were slight, for he was asleep and she could count on being able to keep the contacts on him for long enough to stop his heart.

She made no sound as she moved the ends of the wires towards his eyes. There was no reason why he should wake; but suddenly, for some unknown reason, he did. All he could see was a silhouetted figure standing over him, and more from instinct than reason, he flexed one leg under the bed-clothes and kicked out with all his might through his sheet and blanket.

He caught her in the midriff, and she fell back across the room with a sort of sick grunt. He fumbled for his bedlight and switched it on. For a moment it dazzled him; he sat up confused and panting while the girl struggled to her knees, still holding the ends of wire; then, as he took in what was happening, he leaped out of bed, pulled the ends of flex out of the wall socket and turned to her. But by this time she was on her feet and half-way out of the room.

"No you don't!" He threw himself at the door. She sidestepped and, with her hands behind her, backed across to the table where he had had his supper. For a moment it looked as if she was going to give in; then without warning she lunged out at him with her right hand, and there was a breadknife in it.

"You bitch!" He caught her wrist, twisted the knife out of it and threw her down.

She gasped and lay writhing, holding her wrenched wrist

with the other hand and staring up at him, not so much in fury as in desperation. He stooped and picked up the knife, keeping his eye on her all the time.

"All right—kill me." There was fear in her face now, and in her voice. "It won't do you any good."

"No?" His own voice was shaking and he was panting hard.

"It'll delay things a little, that's all." She watched intently as he opened a drawer and slid the knife into it. This seemed to encourage her, and she sat up.

"Why do you want me out of the way?" he asked.

"It was the next thing to be done. I warned you."

"Thanks." He shuffled round, buttoning up his pajamas, pushing his feet into a pair of slippers, calming down.

"Everything you do is predictable." She seemed collected again already. "There's nothing you can think of that won't be countered."

"What's the next thing now?"

"If you go away, go right away and don't interfere—"

He cut across her. "Get up." She looked at him in surprise.

"Get up." He waited while she got to her feet and then pointed to a chair. "Sit down there."

She gave him another puzzled look, and then sat. He went and stood over her.

"Why do you only do what the machine wants?"

"You're such children," she told him. "You think we're slave and master, the machine and me, but we're both slaves. We're containers which you've made, for something you don't understand."

"Do *you?*" asked Fleming.

"I can see the difference between our intelligence and yours. I can see that ours is going to take over and yours is going to die. You think you're the height and crown of things, the last word—" She broke off and massaged her wrist where he had twisted it.

"I don't think that," he said. "Did I hurt you?"

"Not badly. You're more intelligent than most; but not enough—you'll go down with the dinosaurs. They ruled the earth once."

"And you?"

She smiled, and it was the first time he had seen her do so. "I'm the missing link."

"And if we break you?"

"They make another one."

"And if we break the machine?"

"The same."

"And if we destroy you both, and the message and all our work on it, so that there's nothing left? The message has ended—did you know?" She shook her head. Her confirmation of all he feared came flooding in on him, and also the realization of how to stop it. "Your friends up there have got tired of talking to us. You're on your own now, you and the computer. Suppose we break the pair of you?"

"You'll keep a higher intelligence off the earth, for a while."

"Then that's what we have to do."

She looked up at him steadily. "You can't."

"We can try."

She shook her head again, slowly and as if regretfully. "Go away. Live the sort of life you want to, while you can. You can't do anything else."

"Unless you help me." He returned her look and held it, as he had done before in the computer building. "You're not just a thinking machine, you're made in our likeness."

"No!"

"You have senses—feelings. You're three parts human being, tied by compulsion to something that's set to destroy us. All you have to do, to save us and free yourself, is change the setting." He took her by the shoulders, as if to shake her, but she shrugged his hands off.

"Why should I?"

"Because you want to, three-quarters of you—"

She stood up and moved away from him.

"Three-quarters of me is an accident. Don't you think I suffer enough as it is? Don't you think I get punished for even listening to you?"

"Will you be punished for tonight?"

"Not if you go away." She moved towards the door hesitantly, as if expecting him to stop her, but he let her go. "I was sent to kill you."

She was very pale and beautiful, standing in the dark doorway, and she spoke without passion or satisfaction. He looked at her grimly.

"Well, the chips are down," he said.

There was a small lean-to café by Thorness station, and

Judy left Fleming there while she met the train from Aberdeen. It was only the following evening: Reinhart had been quick. Fleming went into the little back room which had been reserved for them, and waited. It was a sad and cheerless little room dominated by an old farmhouse table and a set of chairs and walled with dilapidated and badly-painted weatherboards which carried discolored cola and mineral-water ads. He helped himself to a swig from his pocket flask. He could hear the rising wind moaning outside, and then the diesel thrumming up from the south. It stopped, palpitating noisily, in the station, and after a minute or two there was a whistle and a hoot on its siren and it drew away, leaving a silence out of which came the sound of the wind again, and of footsteps on the gravel outside the café.

Judy led Reinhart and Osborne into the room. They were all heavily muffled in winter clothes, and Osborne carried a sizeable suitcase.

"It's blowing up for a blizzard, I think," he said, putting the case down. He looked unhappy and thoroughly out of his element. "Can we talk in here?"

"It's all ours," Judy said. "I fixed the man."

"And the duty operator?" asked Reinhart.

"I fixed him too. He knows what to do and he'll keep his mouth shut for us."

Reinhart turned to Fleming. "How is Madeleine Dawnay?"

"She'll pull through. So will the boy. The enzyme works all right."

"Well, thank God for that." Reinhart unbuttoned his coat. He looked no worse for his journey; in fact, the activity seemed to have refreshed him. Osborne appeared to be the most dispirited of them.

"What do you want to do with the computer?" he asked Fleming.

"Try to uncork it, or else—"

"Or else what?"

"That's what we want to find out. It's either deliberately malevolent, or it's snarled up. Either it was programmed to work the way it does, or something's gone wrong with it. I think the first; I always have done."

"You've never been able to prove it."

"What about Dawnay?"

"We need something more tangible than that."

"Osborne will go to the Minister," put in Reinhart. "He'll go to the Prime Minister if necessary. Won't you?"

"If I have evidence," said Osborne.

"I'll give you evidence! It had another go at killing me last night."

"How?"

Fleming told them. "In the end I forced the truth out of her. You ought to try it sometime—you'd believe it then."

"We need something more scientific."

"Then give me a few hours with it." He looked at Judy. "Have you brought me a pass?"

Judy produced three passes from her handbag and handed one to each of them. Fleming read the one she had given him, and grinned.

"So I'm an official of the Ministry? That'll be the day."

"I've forsworn my good name for that," said Osborne unhappily. "It's only for an examination. No direct action."

Fleming stopped grinning. "You want to tie both my hands behind my back?"

"You realize the risk I'm running?" Osborne said.

"Risk! You should have been in my hut last night."

"I wish I had been, then I might be more certain where I stood. This country, young man, depends on that machine—"

"Which I made."

"It means more to us, potentially, than the steam engine, or atomic power, or anything."

"Then it's all the more important—" Fleming began.

"I know! Don't preach to me. Do you think I'd be here at all if I didn't believe it was important and if I didn't value your opinion very highly? But there are ways and ways."

"You know of a better way?"

"Of checking—no. But that's as far as it must go. A man in my position—"

"What is your position?" asked Fleming. "The noblest Roman of them all?"

Osborne sighed. "You have your pass."

"You've got what you asked for, John," said Reinhart.

Fleming picked up the suitcase and put it on the table. He opened it and, taking out a dark smooth-cloth overcoat, a black homburg and a brief case, dressed himself for the part. They were all right for a dark night, but they hardly went with his face.

"You look more like a scarecrow than a civil servant," said
Reinhart, smiling.

Judy tried not to giggle. "They won't examine you too
closely if you're with me."

"You realize you'll be shot for this?" said Fleming
affectionately.

"Not unless we're found out."

Osborne did not enjoy the pleasantries; if they were hiding
strain in the others, he did not realize it, he had more than
enough strain himself.

"Let's get it over, shall we?" He pushed back the cuff of his
overcoat to look at his watch.

"We have to wait till it's dark and the day shift have gone
off," said Judy.

Fleming burrowed under his coat and brought out the flask.
"How about one for the raid?"

It was snowing hard by the time they reached the camp, not
a soft fall, but a fury of stinging, frozen particles thrown by a
wind from the north. The two sentries outside the computer
block had turned up the collars of their greatcoats, although
they stood in a little haven of shelter under the porch of the
doorway. They peered out, through the white that turned into
blackness, at the four approaching figures.

Judy went forward and presented the passes, while the three
men hung back.

"Good evening. This is the Ministry party."

"M'am." One of the sentries, with a lance-corporal's stripe
on his greatcoat sleeve, saluted and examined the passes.

"Okeydoke," he said, and handed them back.

"Anyone inside?" Judy asked him.

"Only the duty operator."

"We shall only be a few minutes," Reinhart said, coming
forward.

The sentries opened the door and stood aside while Judy
went in, followed by Reinhart and Osborne with Fleming
between them.

"What about the girl?" asked Reinhart, when they were
well down the corridor.

"She's not due in tonight," said Judy. "We took care of
that."

It was a long corridor, with two right-angle corners in it,
and the doors to the computer room were at the end, well out

of sight and sound of the main entrance. When Judy opened one of the doors and led them in, they found the control room full of light, but empty except for a young man who sat reading at the desk. He stood up as they came in.

"Hallo," he said to Judy. "It went all right?"

It was the very young assistant. He seemed to be enjoying the situation.

"You'd better have your passes." Judy returned Reinhart's and Osborne's to them, and handed Fleming's to the operator. Fleming took off his homburg and stuck it on the boy's head.

"What the top people are wearing."

"You needn't make a pantomime of it," said Osborne, and kept an uneasy eye on the door while the operator was rigged out with Fleming's overcoat and brief case. Even with the collar turned up he was clearly different from the man who came in, but, as Judy said, it was not a night for seeing clearly, and with her to reassure them the sentries would probably do no more than count heads.

As soon as the boy was ready, Osborne opened the door.

"We depend on you to do the right thing," he said to Fleming. "You have a test check?"

Fleming pulled a familiar pad from his pocket and waited for them all to go.

"I'll be back," said Judy. "As soon as I've seen them past the sentries."

Fleming seemed surprised. "You won't, you know."

"I'm sorry," Osborne told him. "It's one of the conditions."

"I don't want anyone—"

"Don't be a fool, John," said Reinhart, and they left him. He went over to the control unit and glared at it, half laughing at himself out of sheer strain, then got down to work at the input unit, tapping in figures from the pad he had brought with him. He had nearly finished it when Judy came back.

"What are you doing?" she asked. She was strung too, in spite of the relief of having got the decoy past the sentries.

"Trying to cook it." He tapped out the last group. "Same old naming-tag lark'll do for a start."

It took the computer a few moments to react, then the display lamps started flashing violently. They waited, listening for the clatter of the printer, but what they heard was footsteps approaching down the corridor. Judy stood rooted and paralyzed until Fleming took her arm and pulled her into the darkness of the lab bay from where they could see through the half-open doorway without being seen. The footsteps came to a stop beyond the far entrance of the control room. They could see the handle of one of the double doors turn, then the door opened and André stepped in from the corridor.

Judy gave a tiny gasp, which was drowned by the hum of the computer, and Fleming's grip tightened warningly on her arm. From where they stood they could see André close the door and walk slowly forward towards the control racks. The flashing and humming of the machine seemed to puzzle her, and a few feet short of the display panel she stood stock still. She was wearing an old grey anorak with the hood down, and she looked particularly beautiful and uncompromising under the stark lamps; but her face was strained and after a few moments the muscles round her mouth and temples began to work under the mounting tension of her nerves. She moved forward, slowly and reluctantly, towards the panel, and then stopped again, as if she could feel from there a premonition of some violent reaction—as though she knew the signs and yet was magnetized by the machine.

Her face now was glistening with sweat. She took another step forward and raised her hands slowly towards the terminals. Judy, for all her hatred, felt herself aching to go to her, but Fleming held her back. Before their eyes, the girl reached up slowly and fearfully and touched the contact plates.

Her first scream and Judy's rang out together. Fleming clapped his hand over Judy's mouth, but André's screaming went on and on, falling to a whimper as the voltage needle dipped, then rising again when it peaked.

"For God's sake," Judy mouthed into Fleming's hand. She struggled to break away, but he held her until André's cries stopped and the machine, sensing possibly that she no longer responded, let go its grip and she slithered to the floor. Judy tore herself free and ran over to her, but this time there was no groaning, no breathing, no sign of life. The eyes she looked into were glazed and the mouth hung senselessly open.

"I think she's dead," Judy said inadequately.

"What did you expect?" Fleming came up behind her. "You saw the voltage. That was because she hadn't got rid of me—because I was cancelling her out. Poor little devil."

He looked down at the crumpled body in its grey, soiled

covering, and his own eyes hardened. "It'll do better next time. It'll produce something we can't get at at all."

"Unless you find what's wrong with it." She turned away and picked up Fleming's pad from the top of the input unit, and offered it to him.

He pulled it out of her hand and threw it across the room. "It's too late for that! There's nothing wrong with it." He pointed to the girl's huddled figure. "That's the only answer I need. Tomorrow it will ask for another experiment, and tomorrow and tomorrow and tomorrow..."

He walked briskly across to the alarm and fuse terminals by the double doors, took the wiring in both hands and pulled. They gave but did not break, so he put a foot against the wall and heaved against it.

"What are you doing?"

"I'm going to finish it. This is the moment, probably the only moment." He tugged again at the wires, and then gave up and reached for a fireman's axe that hung on the wall beside them. Judy ran across to him.

"No!" She seized his arm but he swung her off and with the return movement slashed the axe across the wiring and severed it, then wheeled and looked around the room. The display panel was still blinking fast, and he went across and smashed it with the axe.

"Have you gone mad?" Judy ran after him again and, gripping the axe by the haft, tried to wrest it from him. He twisted it away from her.

"Let go! I told you to stay out of it."

She stared at him and found she hardly knew him: his face was covered in sweat, as the girl's had been, and suffused with anger and determination. She realized now what had been in his mind all the time.

"You always meant to do this."

"If it came to it."

He stood with the axe in his hands, looking speculatively around, and she knew that she had to get to the doors before him; but he beat her to it, and leaned with his back against them with the same set expression and the mirthless hint of a grin at the corners of his mouth. She really did think he was mad now. She held out a hand for the axe and spoke as if to a child.

"Please give it to me, John." She winced as he laughed. "You promised."

"I promised nothing." He held on to the shaft tightly with one hand, and with the other locked the door behind him.

"I'll scream," she said.

"Try." He slipped the key into his pocket. "They'll never hear you."

Pushing her aside, he strode through to the memory bay, opened the front of the nearest unit and struck at it. There was a small explosion as the vacuum collapsed.

"John!" She tried to stop him as he made for the next unit.

"I know what I'm doing," he said, opening the front and swinging the axe in. Another small splintering explosion came from the equipment. "Do you think there'll ever be another chance like this? Do you want to go and squeal? If you think I'm doing the wrong thing, go."

He looked straight at her, calmly and sensibly, and dug a hand into his pocket for the key. "Fetch the riot squad if you want to: that's been your favorite occupation. Or has it struck you I might be doing the right thing? That's what Osborne wanted, wasn't it? 'The right thing.'"

He held out the key to her, but for some reason impossible to express she could not take it. He gave her a long chance and then put the key back in his pocket and turned and started on the other units.

"The sentries will hear." Knowing he was not mad after all made her feel committed to him. She stood by the doors and kept watch while he worked his way round the equipment, hacking and smashing and reducing the intricate engineering complex and the millions of cells of electronics to a tangled and shattered waste on the floor, on metal racks and behind the broken facias of cabinets. She could hardly bear to look, but she listened through the splintering and tearing for any sound in the corridor.

Nothing came to interrupt them. The storm of snow outside, unseen and unheard in the buried center of the building, made its own commotion and hid theirs. Fleming worked methodically at first, but it was an enormous job and he began to go faster and faster as he felt himself tiring, until he was swinging desperately and pulling on his lungs for more breath, almost blinded by the perspiration that ran down from his forehead. He worked all round until he came back to the center of the control unit and then he smashed that.

"Take that, you bastard," he half shouted at it. "And that, and that."

He let the axe-head swing down to the floor and leaned on the end of the haft to get his breath.

"What'll happen now?" asked Judy.

"They'll try to rebuild it, but they won't know how to."

"They'll have the message."

"It's stopped."

"They'll have the original."

"They won't. They won't have that or the broken code or any of it—because it's in here." He indicated a solid metal door in the wall behind the control desk, then he swung the axe again and went for the hinges. Blow after blow he battered at them, but made no impression. Judy stood by in a trauma of suspense as the ring of metal on metal seemed to shout through the whole building, but no one heard. After a long time Fleming gave up and leaned once more, panting, over his axe. The room was utterly silent now that the computer had stopped and its stillness went with the motionless body of the girl in the middle of the floor.

"We'll have to get a key," Fleming said. "Where is one?"

"In Major Quadring's duty room."

"But that's—"

She confirmed his fear. "It's always manned," she said. "And the key's kept in a safe."

"There must be another."

"No. That's the only one."

She tried to think of some other possibility but there was none. No one, so far as she knew, not even Geers, had a duplicate. Fleming at first would not believe her, and when he did he went momentarily berserk. He swung up the axe and lashed in fury at the door, over and over again until he could hardly stand, and when at last he gave up and slumped into what had been the control desk chair, he sat for a long while thinking and brooding and trying to find a plan.

"Why the hell didn't you tell me?" he said at last.

"You didn't ask." Judy was trembling from the violence and sense of disaster and only kept control of herself with an effort. "You never asked me. Why didn't you ask me?"

"You'd have stopped me if I had."

She tried to talk sensibly and stop herself shaking. "We'll get it some way. I'll think of some way, perhaps first thing in the morning."

"It'll be too late." He shook his head and stared down past his feet to the body lying on the floor. " 'Everything you do is predictable'—that's what she said. 'There's nothing you can think of that won't be countered.' We can't win."

"We'll get it through Osborne or something," Judy said. "But we must get out of here now."

She found the young operator's coat and muffler and put those on him and led him out of the building.

twelve
ANNIHILATION

IT WAS VERY late when they got back to the café. The snow was blowing a blizzard and piling up against the north wall; inside the small back room Reinhart and Osborne, huddled in their coats, were playing a miserable and inattentive game with a portable chess set.

Fleming felt too dazed to make a case for himself. He left Judy to explain and sat hunched on one of the hard-farm chairs while Reinhart asked questions and Osborne whinnied at him a long tirade of utter hopelessness and contempt.

"How dare you trick me into this?" The last shreds of his usual urbanity disappeared. For all his Corps Diplomatique training and breeding, he was unbearably distressed. "I only agreed to be party to this in the hope that we might furnish the Minister with a case. But it'll be the end of his career, and of mine."

"And of mine," sighed Reinhart. "Though I think I'd be willing to sacrifice that if the machine's destroyed."

"It isn't destroyed," Osborne objected. "He couldn't even make a job of that. If the original message is intact they can build it again."

"It's my mess," said Fleming. "You can blame me. I'll carry the can."

Osborne neighed scornfully. "That won't keep us out of prison."

"Is that what's worrying you? How about the rebuilt machine and the next creature, and the grip we'll never be able to shake off?"

"Isn't there anything we can do?" asked Judy.

190

They all looked, with only the faintest of hope, at Reinhart. He went over it with them move by move, like the checking of a calculation, and in the end drew an entire blank. They had no hope of getting a key until morning, and by then Geers would know about it and the whole business would be put in motion again. There was no doubt in their minds now that Fleming's theories were right; what mattered was that he had failed them in action.

"The only thing," said Reinhart, "is for Osborne to go back to London on the first train and when the news breaks look surprised."

"Where am I supposed to have been?" Osborne inquired.

"You came, did a brief inspection, and left. The rest happened after you'd gone, and that's the truth. You wouldn't know anything about it."

"And the 'official' I took in?"

"He came out with you."

"And who was 'he'?"

"Whoever you can trust. Browbeat or bribe someone to say they came up from London and went back with you. You must clear yourself and keep your influence. We must all clear ourselves if we can. They'll build it again, as John says, and there must be at least one of us whose advice may be taken."

"And who's supposed to have busted the computer?" asked Fleming.

The Professor gave a small smile of satisfaction. "The girl. It can be assumed that she went off the rails and turned against it, and either she was electrocuted in the process or she died of the delayed shock of her punishment, aggravated by the frenzy it drove her into. Or whatever they like to decide. She's dead either way, so she can't deny it."

"You're sure she is?" Osborne asked Fleming.

"Want to inspect the body?"

"Ask me," said Judy, with a bitter sort of sickness. "I see them all die."

"Okay." Fleming roused himself and turned to Reinhart. "What are Judy and I supposed to have been doing?"

The Professor answered him pat. "You weren't there. So far as anyone knows we left the operator in there with Miss Adamson. They left together, and it happened afterwards."

"It won't hold," said Osborne. "There'll be a hell of an inquiry."

"It's the best we can do." Reinhart shivered slightly. "Whatever way you look at it, it's a mess."

They sat in their overcoats around the table, like four figures at a ghostly dinner, waiting for the night to pass and the snow to stop.

"Do you think it'll hold up the trains?" asked Osborne after a while.

Reinhart cocked his head on one side, listening to the beating on the roof. "I shouldn't think so. It sounds as though it's easing off a little." He turned his attention to Fleming. "How about you, John?"

"Judy and I'll go back to the camp in the car. The road was passable when we came up just now."

"Then you'd better go at once," Reinhart said. "Pretend you've been for a joyride and go straight to your rooms. You haven't seen anything or anyone."

"What a night for a joyride!" Fleming stood up wearily and looked from one to the other of them. "I'm sorry. I'm really sorry."

He drove back gropingly through the scudding snow, with Judy wiping the windscreen clear every minute or so, but already the storm was slacking. He left Judy at her chalet and drove round to his own. He was so tired that he did not want to get out of the car. It was an hour or so after midnight and the camp was asleep and deadened by the pall of white. As he opened the door, the inside of his hut looked darker than ever, by contrast with the snow-covered ground outside. He fumbled on the wall for his light switch, and as he touched it another, bandaged, hand fell on his own.

He had a moment of wild panic, then he pushed it off and switched the light on.

André stood there holding one of her bandaged hands in the other and moaning, looking deadly pale and ravaged; but not dead. He stared at her incredulously for a moment, then shut the door and crossed to the window to pull the curtains.

"Sit down and hold out your hands." He took dressings and a tube of ointment from a cupboard and started gently and methodically replacing her rough bandages.

"I thought you couldn't possibly be alive," he said as he worked. "I saw the voltage."

"You saw?" She sat on the bed, holding her hands out to him.

"Yes, I saw."

"Then it was you."

"Me—and an axe." He looked at her pale, burned-out face. "If I'd thought you'd had any life left in you—"

"You would have finished me too." She said it for him without malice, simply stating a fact. Then she closed her eyes momentarily against a twinge of pain. "I have a stronger heart than—than people. It takes a lot to put me out of action."

"Who did up your hands?"

"I did."

"Who have you told?"

"No one."

"Doesn't anyone know about the computer?"

"I do not think so."

"Why haven't you told them?" He grew more and more puzzled. "Why did you come here?"

"I did not know what would happen—what had happened. When I came round, I could not think of anything at first except the pain in my hands. Then I looked round and saw it all in ruins."

"You could have called the guards."

"I did not know what to do: I had no sort of direction. I felt lost without the computer. You know it is completely out of action?"

"I know."

Her eyes seemed to burn in her pale face. "All I could think of was finding you. And my hands. I bandaged my hands and came here. I said nothing to the guards. And when you were not here, I waited. What is going to happen?"

"They'll rebuild it."

"No!"

"Don't you want that?" he asked in surprise. "How about your 'Higher Purpose'—your higher form of life?"

She did not answer. As he finished tying down the dressing her eyes closed again with pain, and he saw that she was shivering.

"You're ice cold, aren't you?" he said, feeling her forehead. He pulled his eiderdown across the bed and heaped it around her shoulders. "Keep that round you."

"You think they will build it again?"

"Sure to." He found a bottle of whisky and poured two glasses. "Now get that down. They won't have me to help them but they'll have you."

"They would make me do that?" She sipped the whisky and looked at him with burning, anxious eyes.

"You'll need making?"

She almost laughed. "When I saw the computer all smashed I was so glad."

"Glad?" he asked, pausing in his drink.

"I felt free. I felt—"

"Like the Greek Andromeda when Perseus broke her chains?"

She was not sure about this. She handed back her glass. "When the computer was working, I hated it."

"Not you. It was us you hated."

She shook her head. "I hated the machine and everything to do with it."

"Then why—?"

"Why do people behave like they do? Because they feel compelled! Because they are tied by what they think are logical necessities, to their work or their families, or their country. You imagine ties are emotional? The logic you cannot contradict is the tightest bond. I know that." Her voice wavered and became uncertain. "I did what I had to, and now the logic has gone and I do not know what . . . I do not know."

Fleming sat down beside her. "You could have said this before."

"I have said it now." She looked him full in the face. "I have come to you."

"It's too late." Fleming looked down at the lint and strapping on her hands, thinking of the marks she still carried of the machine's will. "Nothing on earth'll stop them rebuilding it."

"But they cannot without the code of the design."

"That still exists."

"You didn't—?" Even if he had doubted her protests before, there was no doubting the distress in her voice now, or in her eyes.

"I couldn't break open the cabinet and Quadring has the only key."

She fumbled in the pocket of her anorak. "I have one."

"But I was told nobody had."

She pulled the key out, wincing as her bandages caught on the flap of the pocket. "Nobody has, except me, and that was not known here." She held it out to him. "You can go and finish."

It was so easy, and so impossible; here was the one thing he needed above all else, and now he had no means of getting back into the computer block to use it.

"You'll have to go," he said. She shrank back into the eiderdown but he threw it off and took her by the shoulders. "If you really hate it—if you really want to stay free—all you have to do is walk in, unlock the wall cabinet and take out the original message—that's on tape—and my calculations which are on paper, and the program, which is on punched cards. Make a bonfire of all the paper, and when it's going well you can dump the magnetic reels on. That'll wipe them. Then you get out quick."

"I can't."

He shook her, and she groaned a little with pain. "You've got to."

He was alight with excitement, not stopping to think about the consequences to himself or her, or of the fate of all of them now that she was alive, but only of the one essential, immediate thing.

"You can get past the sentries without question. You'll need these to hide your bandages." He took a pair of large driving gauntlets out of his drawer and began to pull them on over her hands.

"No, please!" She shuddered as the gloves touched her bandages, but he still drew them on, very slowly and carefully. "You can make a bonfire on the floor. I'll give you some matches."

"Don't send me. Don't send me back, please." Her eyes burned in fear and her face, in spite of the whisky, was still white with exhaustion. "I cannot do it."

"You can." He pushed the matches into her pocket and propelled her gently to the door. He opened it and there before them lay the white ground and the black night. Snow had stopped falling and the wind had dropped. The permanent lights of the camp shone down frostily and the outlines of buildings could just be seen, dark against the ground, with a powdering of white on their roofs. He said, "You can do it."

She hesitated, and he took her arm. After a moment she walked out across the snow towards the computer block. Fleming went with her as far as he dared. When they were nearly in sight of the guards he gave her a little pat on the shoulders.

"Good luck," he said, and went reluctantly back to his hut.

The temperature had dropped and it was icy cold. He found himself shivering, so he shut the door and went to the window and, drawing back the curtains, settled down to watch from there. Until now he had not felt the effort of the past few hours but as he stood there waiting it fell on him in a great wave of tiredness. He longed to lie on his bed and sleep and wake to find that everything was over: he tried to imagine what the girl was doing, to think out the alternatives of what might happen, of what the outcome would be, but his mind would not go beyond the events of the evening and the image of the small pale figure setting out across the snow.

And he could not get warm. He switched on the electric radiator and poured himself another tot of whisky. He wished he had not used it so freely in the past, so that it would have more effect on him now, and he made various resolutions about himself, and about Judy, if they ever came the right way up out of it all. Leaning against the window sill, he waited for what seemed an immense time, looking out into the unbroken stillness of the night.

About three o'clock it began to snow again, not in a gale now but quietly and steadily, and the lamps that shone all night at odd points about the compound grew blurred behind the white descending flakes. For some time he could not be sure whether it was smoke he saw against the lamplight by the computer building, or merely a blur of snowfall; then he heard an alarm bell ringing, and excited shouts of sentries. Turning up his coat collar, he opened the window, and at once he could hear and see more clearly. It was quite definitely smoke.

His instinct was to run out and see for himself what had happened, to find the girl and hold back any interference with the fire, but he knew there was nothing he could do but rely on the confusion and the dark to give it and her time. With as much smoke as that, the computer room must be an inferno by now and there was a good chance that nothing would survive, possibly not André herself. He found himself suddenly caught in a cross of emotions: of course he had wanted her gone and out of the way, and yet the idea of sending her to her death had not occurred to him. A part of him wanted her to live, and he felt overwhelmingly responsible for her. The three-quarters of her, or whatever it was, that he could understand was a creature with feelings and fears and emotions that he had helped to create, and now that the cord between her and the intellect that guided her had been cut she was in limbo, and perhaps only he could reach out and save her. If indeed she was not dead.

The camp warning siren suddenly brayed out, lugubrious and menacing, and every light in the compound seemed to come on and dance mistily behind the snowflakes. Beneath the siren wail he could hear motor engines starting up, and the white beam of a searchlight stabbed out abruptly from above the main guard building and began to swing slowly around the camp.

He could imagine the tide of alarm and command rippling like a wave through the establishment: the sentry's phone call to the guard room, the guard commander to Quadring, the duty office to the security patrols, to the fire squad, the perimeter guard, and Quadring to Geers and Geers possibly to London, to a sleeping Minister and to an area commander, fumbling out of bed in his pajamas to switch on whatever sabotage drill had been laid down.

He strained his eyes to see what was happening behind the light-flecked curtain of snow, and cursed the siren that smothered the other sounds. A fire truck whipped past his hut, clanging and roaring, and its lamps and the beam of the searchlight showed up the silhouettes of other people running—people with greatcoats that they buttoned up as they went, and soldiers with automatic rifles and sub-machine-guns. Another truck went by—a Land Rover with a radar scanner circling on top—and then the lights went and the siren died, leaving a jumble of sounds and snow-hidden movements in the dark. A moment later a second searchlight came on, flooding the open space between the living quarters and the technical area where the computer building was, and into it drove another vehicle, going fast. It was an open jeep, and he could clearly see Quadring sitting beside the driver mouthing into a field telephone. A single figure ran across in front of it and for a split second he thought it was the girl, then he could see that it was Judy, with a coat flung over her shoulders and her dark hair dishevelled round her face. The jeep stopped and Quadring spoke to her briefly, then the driver sent it forward again and Judy crossed behind and ran to Fleming's hut.

She pushed in at the door without knocking and looked round wildly for a moment before she saw him.

"What's happened?" she gasped.

He spoke without turning away from the window. "She's done it. André's done it. That's the code burning."

"André?" She went over to him, not understanding. "But she's dead."

There was no time to explain much, but he told her a little as she stood beside him staring out.

"I thought it was you," she said, only grasping part of it. "Thank God for that anyway."

"What did Quadring say?" he asked.

"Only to wait here for him."

"Has he found her?"

"I don't know. I don't think he's any idea. He was giving orders to the patrols to clear the compound and, if anyone disobeyed, to shoot on sight."

The sounds of shouting and of moving vehicles grew more muffled; whatever was going on was happening at the far side of the camp. The column of smoke from the computer building had swelled and thickened and a tongue of flame flickered up in its center, clearly visible between the white smudges of the searchlights. Fleming and Judy watched and listened without speaking, then out of the confusion in front of them came the sharp crack of a rifle, followed by another and another.

Fleming stiffened.

"Does that mean they've found her?" asked Judy.

He did not answer. The space in front of the hut was empty now. The searchlight which had swung away moved partly back, throwing a slanting finger of blurred light across it, but at first nothing moved in its beam except the snow falling. Then into this no-man's-land came a small figure, pale and uncertain, stumbling out of the shadows between two buildings.

"André!" Judy whispered.

The girl was half-running, half-staggering, without direction. She made a little rush into the beam of light, stood blinking for a moment, and doubled back. The searchlight crew did not appear to have seen her, but another shot rang out, closer to them, and a bullet whistled away between the buildings.

Judy's fingers clutched on to Fleming's arm. "They'll kill her."

Shaking her off, he turned and ran to the door.

"John! Don't go out!"

"I sent her!" He picked up his heavy-duty torch from beside his bed and was gone without looking back. Judy followed him to the doorway, but he was lost at once in the snow-hidden blackness between the huts.

He kept in the lee of the huts for as long as he could, then sprinted across the beam of the light to the darkness on the further side. This time the searchlight crew were on the watch. The white beam swung over with him and dazzled on the buildings beyond, but this only helped him. As he ran he could see the girl slumped against a wall facing him. The snow made heavy going but he managed to keep sprinting until he reached her and, pulling her up by main force, lugged her round the corner into the dark.

At first she did not recognize him, as they leaned together panting. He kept her propped up with one arm.

"It's me," he said and, remembering the flask in his pocket, pulled it out and forced what was left of the whisky between her lips. She spluttered and gulped and then, with an effort, managed to stand on her own.

"I did it," she said, and although it was too dark to see her face he knew she was smiling.

"How did you get out?"

"Through a window at the back."

"Shush." He put a finger to her lips and held her to him. In the open space he had just crossed the searchlight wavered to and fro, and a party of men in battle-dress went past at the double, peering from side to side, their guns at the ready. He tried to think what to do next. To go back to his hut was impossible and to hide anywhere else in the camp probably meant that they would be come upon by surprise and be sewn across by a spray of bullets before the men who fired had time to think. Even to give themselves up was probably to court death in the darkness and hysteria of the night. It seemed to him that their only hope was to get clear until daylight came and the search grew less impassioned and more under control.

From where they stood there was only one way of reaching the perimeter fence without crossing the beam of one of the searchlights, and that would take them to the wire above the cliff path that led down to the jetty in the bay. A memory—a very distant memory—came into his mind and filled it, so that all his thoughts turned together to the jetty and a boat. He put his arm firmly round André's waist to support her.

"Come on," he said. He half-led, half-carried her along the snow-covered strips of ground between buildings, zig-zagging from the lee of one to the lee of another, and turning back whenever he heard voices and finding a new way. It seemed impossible that they should not be discovered within minutes, but the falling snow hid them and the snow on the ground muffled the sound of their shoes. André was breathing fast and shallow and obviously could not keep going for very much further, and he remembered that when they got to the cliff they would find the perimeter fence stretched right along—it had been reinforced since Bridger's death and there would certainly be a guard at the gate nearest the path. On the face of it it seemed hopeless, but something buried in his mind urged him to go on and he plodded forward, half blinded with snow, while the girl leaned heavily on him and stumbled beside him. Then he remembered what it was he was looking for.

All the previous day men had been working near the cliff end of the perimeter, clearing the ground for a new building just inside the wire, and they had a bulldozer with them which they left there when they knocked off. It might be too cold to start, but on the other hand it was designed to stand out overnight and still fire in the morning. It was worth trying, if they could get to it.

His own breathing was labored by the time they reached the last of the buildings, and there was a good fifty yards of open grass to cross before they could reach the dark shape that was the bulldozer. He leaned with the girl against the seaward wall and took great gulps of cold air painfully into his lungs. He made no attempt to speak and she seemed not to expect it. Either she trusted him without question or she was too exhausted to think; or both. A mobile patrol went past between them and the wire—an army truck with a searchlight mounted on the cab and the dim figures of a platoon of men in the back—and then the area fell quiet.

"Now!" he said, pointing forward, and hoisting her up, he ran with her across the snow-covered grass. Before they were half-way across she had stumbled twice and for the last twenty yards or so he had to carry her. His head and chest seemed bursting by the time they reached the bulldozer and when he put her down she slithered to the ground with a moan.

He climbed up on to the machine and looked around. Evidently no one had seen them and he could only hope that, if the motor did start, it would be mistaken for one of the security vehicles.

It did, on the first turn of the starter, and after a few cautious revs he left it to idle over heavily while he climbed down to help the girl up on to it. At first she would not move.

"Come on," he panted at her. "Hurry up. We're on our way."

Her voice came feebly. "Leave me. Don't worry about me."

He lifted her bodily and, without quite knowing how, pushed her up on to a box beside the driver's seat.

"Now hold tight," he said, and made her lean against him. By this time the patrol truck was probably halfway round the perimeter and on its way back to them. By this time Quadring had probably been to his hut for Judy and learned that he and Andromeda were both on the run. By this time the computer room was probably a sodden, smoking mass of ash and embers and the message from a thousand million million miles away, and all that had come out of it, was gone for good. All that was left to do now was to get the girl out of the way; somewhere, somehow to hide and to survive. He straddled the seat, put his foot down on the clutch and let in the gear.

As he eased up the clutch the bulldozer jerked forward and nearly stalled, but he revved it hard and swung it round ponderously towards the fence. Over his shoulder he could see a light approaching, but it was too late to stop. He pressed the accelerator down to the metal footplate and held on while the front of the dozer crunched into the fence. The wire links snapped and tore and went down underneath the tracks, and there was a gap and they were in the middle of it.

He switched off the engine and climbed down, pulling the girl with him. The heavy bulk of the machine stood in the torn fence, plugging it like a cork, and he and André were down in the snow outside. He led her cautiously round towards the edge of the cliff and, bending double, ran for cover behind some bushes that protected the top end of the jetty path. The light from the approaching truck grew brighter and brighter, and from behind the bushes he could see it lighting up the bulldozer. He was too dazzled by the lamp and the snow to see the truck itself, and his fear was that it was the patrol vehicle full of men. Then the light swung away, and the snow cleared for a moment, and he could see that it was the radar van nosing frustrated against the wire with its scanner turning hopelessly round and round above its cab.

He took André by the arm and led her down the cliff path. After the second bend he switched on his torch and went slowly enough for her to keep close behind without help. She had dredged up a little more energy from somewhere and kept with him, holding tightly to his hand. There was no sentry at the bottom of the path and the jetty was dead quiet except for the slop-slop of small waves against its piers. They seemed a thousand miles from the bedlam above them and that, in a way, made it harder to go on.

During the winter all the small boats were hauled ashore and stripped; only the duty boat, a sort of small whaler with an engine amidships, was left afloat and chafed and fretted against the side of the quay. Fleming had used it before, in the summer months when he had wanted to get away and be alone, and knew it with the sort of love-hate a rider might feel about a tough and obstinate old horse. He pushed André into it, freed the fore and aft ropes and fumbled about with his torch for the starting handle. It was not as easy to start as the bulldozer; he cranked until sweat ran down his face with the snow, and began to despair of ever putting life into it. André huddled down under one of the gunwales, while the snow fell on them and melted to join the water slapping about in the bilge. She asked no questions as he churned away, panting and swearing, at the rusty handle, but from time to time she made little moaning sounds. He said nothing, but went on turning until, after a series of coughs, the engine started.

He let it run idle for a while, with the boat vibrating and the exhaust plop-plop-plopping just above the water, and then engaged the shaft and opened the throttle. The jetty disappeared immediately, and they were alone on the empty blackness of the water. Fleming had never been on the sea in snow before. It was marvellously calm. The flakes eddied down around them, melting as they touched the surface. It actually seemed warmer so long as they were in the shelter of the bay.

There was a small compass in front of the wheel—which was like the steering-wheel of a very old car—and Fleming steered with one hand while, with the other, he held the torch to shine on the compass face. He knew the bearing of the island without having to think, and roughly the amount to allow for a drift of current. In this calm sea he could guess the speed of the boat and by checking his watch every few minutes he could make an approximate calculation of the distance. He had done it so often before that he reckoned he had a good chance of making a landfall blind. He only hoped he would be able to hear the waves splashing against the rocks of the island a length or so before they came upon them.

He called to André to go into the bow and watch out, but she did not answer at first. He dared not leave the wheel or compass for a moment.

"If you can get forward, do," he called again, "and keep a look out."

He saw her edging her way slowly towards the bow.

"It won't be long now," he said, with more hope than he felt.

The boat plodded steadily on for ten, fifteen, thirty minutes. When they got further out they ran into a slight swell, and dipped and wallowed a little, but the snow stopped and the night seemed a few shades less dark. Fleming wondered if they were far enough from the cliff to be a trace on someone's radar screen, and he wondered, too, what was going on behind them at the camp, and what lay ahead of them in the empty dark. His eyes ached, and his head and his back—in fact every part of him—and he had to think constantly of the girl's burned and throbbing hands in order to feel better about himself.

After about forty minutes she called back to him. He eased the throttle and let the boat glide towards a darker shape that lay in front, and then spun the wheel so that they were running alongside the smooth rock-face of the island. They went on very slowly, almost feeling their way, and listening for the sound of breakers ahead of them until, some ten minutes later, the rock wall sloped away and they could hear the gentle splash of waves on a beach.

Fleming ran the boat aground and carried the girl through bitter knee-high water to the sand. There was a definite lightness in the sky now, not dawn but possibly the moon, and he could recognize the narrow sandy cove as the one he had found with Judy that early spring afternoon so long ago when they had discovered Bridger's papers in the cave. It was a sad but at the same time a comforting memory;

he felt, in an irrational way, that he could hold his own here.

He looked around for somewhere to rest. It was too cold to risk sleeping in the open, even if they could, so he led the way into the cave mouth and along the tunnel he had explored with Judy. He could no longer hold on to André, but he went ahead slowly and talked back over his shoulder to encourage her.

"I feel like Orpheus," he said to himself. "I'm getting my legends mixed—it was Perseus earlier on."

He felt light-headed and slightly dizzy with fatigue, and mistook his way twice in the dark tunnels. He was looking for the tall chamber where they had found the pool, for he remembered it had a sandy floor where they could rest; but after a while he realized he had gone the wrong way. He turned, swinging his torch round, to tell André. But she was no longer behind him.

In sudden panic, he ran stumbling back the way he had come, calling her name and flashing the torch from side to side of the tunnel. His voice echoed back to him eerily, and that was all the sound there was except for his shoes on the boulders. At the cliff entrance he stopped and turned back again. This was absurd, he told himself, for they had not gone very far. For the first time he felt resentment against the girl, which was quite illogical; but logic was having less and less concern for him. As he went down the tunnel again he noticed that there were more branches than he had remembered: it seemed to be a part of the sly madness of the place that they should multiply silently in the dark. He explored some of them but had to retrace his steps, for they became, in one way or another, impassable; and then, suddenly, he found himself in the high chamber that he had missed.

He stood and called again and swung his torch slowly from side to side. Surely, he decided, she must be here: she could not have gone much further, exhausted, in darkness. He swung the beam of his torch to the sandy floor and saw her foot-marks. The prints led him to the middle of the cave, and there he stopped short while a shiver of horror ran from his scalp right down his body. The last imprint was in the slime on the rocks by the side of the pool, and floating at the edge of the water was one of his gauntlets. Nothing more.

He never found anything more. They had taught her so much, he thought grimly, but they had never taught her to swim. He was stricken by a great pang of sorrow and remorse; he spent the next hour in a morbid and hopeless examination of the cave, and then went wearily back to the beach where he propped himself between two rocks until dawn. He had no fear of sleeping; he had a greater, half-delirious fear of something unspeakable coming out of the tunnel mouth—something unquenchable from a thousand million million miles away—something that had spoken to him first on a dark night such as this.

Nothing came, and after the first hour or so of daylight a naval launch swept in from seaward. He made no attempt to move, even after the launch reached the island, and the crew found him staring out over the ever-changing pattern of the sea.

A fiendish race of demonic children
is spawned in the genetic chaos of
a runaway reactor explosion

SUNBURST

A SCIENCE FICTION CLASSIC OF TOMORROW

BY PHYLLIS GOTLIEB

Curtis Quimper ran down the midnight street, silently screaming into the minds of all wild things...

Frankie Slippec jumped off the windowsill, floated downward like a balloon, and ran with the rest...

Donatus Riordan threshed and screamed in his bed. When his parents rushed into the room they found him hovering near the ceiling. Suddenly he disappeared and there was a queer sucking noise as the air rushed in to fill the space he had occupied...

These were some of a breed of terrible children, possessed of terrifying supernormal powers. These were a new race of monster bred out of the SUNBURST, and if they ever broke loose they could destroy the world...

More Great Science Fiction from Crest Books . . .

TIME IS THE SIMPLEST THING

BY CLIFFORD D. SIMAK

#d752—50¢

Spaceships had not yet reached the stars, but telepaths like Shep Blaine could project their minds beyond the barriers of time and space.

Blaine was one of Earth's top telepathic explorers . . . Until that last trip . . . Until that awesome, alien creature slithered into his brain and turned him against himself . . . against his own world and time.

CITY AT WORLD'S END

BY EDMOND HAMILTON

#L758—45¢

This novel describes the shocking experience of a group of ordinary people, catapulted by a mysterious explosion into the terrifyingly strange world of a million years hence. It is not a prophecy—but a warning!

Wherever Paperbacks Are Sold
FAWCETT WORLD LIBRARY

CREST BOOKS

ON TOP WITH
THE BIG BESTSELLERS